SEND MORE
IDIOTS

T0078291

Also by Tony Perez-Giese

Pac Heights

SEND MORE
IDIOTS

A Novel

TONY PEREZ–GIESE

ARCHWAY
PUBLISHING

Cover design by Jade Kraus
Cover photo by Anthony "Rocky Horror" Flores & Bianca Cervantes
Author photo by Walter Abeson

Archway Publishing books may be ordered
through booksellers or by contacting:

Archway Publishing
1663 Liberty Drive
Bloomington, IN 47403
www.archwaypublishing.com
1-(888)-242-5904

ISBN: 978-1-4808-1349-6 (sc)
ISBN: 978-1-4808-1350-2 (e)

Library of Congress Control Number: 2014920858

Printed in the United States of America.

Archway Publishing rev. date: 12/19/14

For Mom, Dad and CPG.

Cartel Massacre Rocks Juarez

JUAREZ, Mexico, November 14, 2012 AP—

Sixteen suspected drug traffickers were shot to death in a Juarez safe house Tuesday morning, marking a clear escalation in the war between rival cartels for control of the border between the United States and Mexico.

Police discovered the bodies after receiving an anonymous tip. The bodies were bound hand and foot, and all of them had been killed by single gunshots to the head. A note taped to the wall inside the safe house is reported to have read, **"Send more idiots like these so we can kill them."**

"There's clearly an ongoing turf war in Juarez right now," said DEA spokesman Mike McClesky. "Shake-ups in the cartel hierarchy have created a free-for-all environment." Authorities estimate that nearly $5 billion of narcotics illegally cross the border between Juarez and El Paso each year, making it one of the one of the most lucrative entry points for cocaine, heroin and marijuana. Juarez has been ravaged by violence between rival *narcotraficante* gangs this year, with over 3,000 drug-related murders reported by Mexican police. Authorities point to the death of former Sinaloa kingpin Arturo Beltrán Leyva as the beginning of the recent surge in violence as rival gangs fight to fill the vacuum created by his death. Beltrán Leyva died in 2009 during a 90-minute firefight with Mexican Naval Special Forces sent to apprehend him.

CHAPTER ONE

The Mexican punched me so hard that I said my mother's name, which is interesting, because I don't like my mother.

"¿*Quién es Elizabeth?*" the hitter asked, looking over his shoulder at the men who had formed a semi-circle around me in the parking lot.

Amazingly, I didn't go down with the first shot. Even though I stood half a foot taller than the Mexican, it had been a long time since I'd been pasted like that. Square on the jaw, uppercut. I managed to keep my legs under me, even though I dropped the digital camera.

I'd been working in Mexico for three years, so my Spanish was pretty good—good enough so that I could make out the tall man in the aviator sunglasses telling the guy to hit me again. I was so stunned from the first punch that I didn't even try to get my hands up.

Next thing I knew, I was looking at the dirt from the dirt's point of view. I saw several pairs of ostrich-skin cowboy boots closing in around me, and, through the boots, I spotted the little kid at the edge of the parking lot. He was the same urchin who'd been watching me since I'd pulled into the building site ten minutes earlier. The kid wore a washed-out Boston Celtics T-shirt and shorts that had dark stains down the front, like he'd been wiping his hands on them for a week solid. The odd thing

1

was that the boy, who couldn't have been more than eight years old, was holding a brand-new BlackBerry.

The guys grabbed me by the ankles and dragged me across the lot. Just before I went down into that hole of unconsciousness, I saw the little kid wave goodbye. He wasn't smiling.

———

I came to on the floor of a vehicle with someone's boot on my neck, my cheek mashed into an empty bag of pork rinds. My hands had been duct-taped behind my back and my legs similarly bound. The Mexicans jabbered above me as the car jounced along the potholed street. A lasso of pain cinched tighter around my head with each bump.

"You're losing your right, Lalo," one of the guys said in Spanish. "That *pinche güey* didn't even take a step back after that first punch. He called you 'Elizabeth.'"

"He's been eating too much of that American ass," another voice said.

"Fuck you guys. I had to reach up to hit him."

"Doesn't matter. Used to be you got a guy like that, he went down. From now on we use baseball bats, like the boss said."

"Any of you want to step out of the car and try me?" the one called Lalo challenged. "I've still got the hands of stone."

"More like *la boca de panocha*."

"Your mother would know."

"Your sister!"

"Pull over!"

"You bitches shut up," the driver said, "or I'll shoot both of you."

That ended that.

The realization that I was in serious trouble came through loud and clear despite the throbbing of my skull. As I struggled to pull breath with the boot on my neck and my hands taped behind my back, I knew it would probably get worse. Anyone who lives in El Paso knows about folks getting kidnapped, jacked up and killed. More than thirty people—and I'm talking *Americans*—had gone missing along the border recently. It was worse for the Mexicans. Over 3,000 murders. In one year. Death had gotten to be such a regular thing that you stopped paying attention to the articles in the newspaper; a 55-gallon oil drum along the highway with a decomposed body inside; hands sticking out of the sand dunes, the bodies purposely not buried all the way; corpses discovered gussied up with yellow ribbons wrapped around their necks. That is, if they still had heads. The *narcos* do most of it, but there's lots of chatter about it being the Mexican Army or *federales* on the cartel payrolls. Some of the Mexicans I worked with were convinced that DEA or CIA were pulling triggers. Or it was the *chupacabra*, that mythical blood-sucking goat stalking the darkness on its hind legs. But most people had stopped trying to figure out who— or what—was behind it. There were too many bodies to keep track of.

I could tell we were on a dirt road from the bounc-ing of the vehicle, but that didn't tell me much. Only a third of the streets in Juarez are paved, despite the fact that something like a billion dollars' worth of drugs are shipped through there on a monthly basis. Only a small portion of that loot stays in the pockets of your American dimebag dealers, so you'd think the Mexicans could afford a bit of asphalt with the surplus. The car hit another pothole and I felt the floorboards hard against my ribs.

"Listen," I said in Spanish, "you got the wrong guy."

The man sitting over me ground his boot harder into my neck.

"I've got money," I said.

Another passenger laughed. "I bet you do."

"Please—"

"No talking!" The man above me stomped my lower back.

I started thinking back to what I might've done to deserve this. I'd only been in Juarez for half an hour, so I couldn't have pissed anyone off that badly. I'd come to the construction site to do a simple broker's evaluation, legwork for a stateside agent who wanted pictures of the facility. I'd e-mail the digital photos to him when I got back to the office, and he'd pay me a thousand dollars. Standard pre-lunch activity.

I thought about my Tahoe, although I could guess that it was already on the way to the chop shop. If I managed to get myself out of this mess, I'd have to hoof it back across the bridge. I didn't know if I even had my passport in my pocket any longer, and I wondered about how long the lines were going to be at Customs. I'll admit it was a strange thought process, considering these guys were probably going to kill me.

"I'm a real estate—"

"What did I just say?" the guy above me asked.

"This is—"

Something cracked the back of my skull, and the black rushed in from all sides.

CHAPTER TWO

I had a glimmer of hope that when I came out of the pit of unconsciousness I would be back in El Paso with a hangover. Instead, I was duct-taped to a wooden chair inside a stifling room. Once I realized where I was, the pounding in my skull started to keep time with my pulse, which was going *bam-bam-bam*. The room was lit by a desk lamp in one corner, where two guys were reading magazines and smoking cigarettes. Wisps of bluish smoke trailed through the dim light. The floors were concrete and the walls corrugated steel. A warehouse. Not much to go on. Juarez is filled with warehouses. My nose started running, and I sniffed as quietly as possible. One of the guys heard me and looked over. He nudged the fellow sitting next to him.

In Spanish he said, "I guess we better get him." He walked past the circle of light, and I heard him knock on a door. The door cracked open and a wedge of pus-colored illumination slid across the concrete floor.

"He's awake," the Mexican said. He closed the door and went back to his periodical.

I tried to slow my heart down, but the bindings around my hands and feet were so tight. I couldn't stop thinking about pliers, hacksaws, ball-peen hammers and ice picks. I tried to rock the chair, but it was bolted down. I looked at the mooring and saw the dark stains on the concrete, and that got my heart bumping so hard that it felt like it was climbing up my throat.

A figure emerged from the office, and I heard his hard-soled footsteps come across the room. He stopped right at the edge of the light so I could only see his pressed blue jeans in the rays cast from the lamp. He regarded me for a minute or so.

I opened my mouth to speak, but my tongue was huge and dry. I worked my jaw, but there was no saliva. When I finally spoke, my voice came out a rasp. "There's been a mistake."

"I won't argue with that," the man said in perfect English. He circled behind me, still careful to stay out of the light. I craned my neck to follow him, but he stopped right on my six. I heard him shaking something. The two Mexicans hadn't looked up from their magazines.

"It would be in our best interests to get this over with as quickly as possible," the guy behind me said.

I tried to speak again, but my tongue stuck to the roof of my mouth.

"Esteban," the man behind me said. "*Agua.*"

The tall guy with the aviators let out a big sigh before he came over with a bottle of water and poured it at my mouth. Most of it splashed down the front of my shirt, but I got enough to get my voice working again.

"I work for Bowden-Everitt," I croaked. "I'm a real estate agent. I was doing a broker's evaluation. I must've gotten the wrong building. You're an American, right? Help me out of this."

"Broker's evaluation?"

"I take pictures and send them to another agent so he can show the client. Saves him the trip."

"And you got lost?"

"I don't know. I thought I was in the right place. Next thing I know, a bunch of guys roll up and start beating the shit out of me."

"Unfortunate." The man hummed to himself for a moment. "Mistaken identity, huh?"

"Right," I said.

"Well, I guess we screwed up. Sorry about that."

My heart slowed down so that it wasn't bashing my ribs anymore. "I should have got better directions."

"I suppose that takes care of that." The man behind me clapped his hands. "Hey!" he called to the guys with the magazines. "He's a real estate agent. You fucked up and nabbed the wrong guy."

"*¿Mande?*" the one who'd brought me water asked.

"*El dice que hay un error.*" The man repeated. *"Dice que tus puta madres—*" The Mexicans put their magazines down.

"No!" I called out in Spanish. "That's not what I said. I said there was a mistake. *My* mistake. It's not your fault at all!"

"*Dice que ustedes son maricones que chupan* big dicks *cada noche.*"

The Mexicans stood over me while the man behind me continued talking. The shorter Mexican, the guy who'd first hit me back in the parking lot, started rolling his shoulders. He wore a Tweety Bird T-shirt tucked into his jeans, and his belt buckle was the size of a dessert plate. *Lalo* was written across the buckle in raised letters. I noticed the shirt because a lot of the young *narcos* have an affinity for Tweety Bird; Tweety Bird never gets caught by the cat.

"You calling us faggots?" Lalo asked.

"All I said was—"

He shot a short cross to my jaw, which snapped my teeth shut on my tongue. My head whipped back on my neck and I tasted a rush of salt.

"Hey," the taller Mexican said admiringly. "That's more like the old Lalo punch."

"See how I caught him right when his mouth was open?"

My chin fell onto my chest. I watched the blood drip onto the floor between my legs.

"You better not have knocked him out," the guy behind me said. "I've got places to be, *güey*"

Güey is Mexican slang for "dude" and is pronounced "way." I heard what sounded like rubber bands snapping, but I couldn't recall the Mexican word for "rubber."

"I'm here," I said, trying to be helpful.

The man behind me reached around and yanked my head up. I could smell the faint baby powder on his surgical gloves. He sprayed an aerosol up my nose. Bolts of fire shot through my sinuses, and I started jerking my head so violently that drops of blood splattered the boxer's Tweety Bird shirt. They all stepped back as I continued to shake gore, trying to get the burning out of my head. When I finally caught my breath, I screamed for all I was worth. A torrent of blood, mucus and tears streamed down my face.

"Cisneros!" the interrogator behind me shouted.

Through my sobs, I managed to ask who Cisneros was.

"I'm not going to say this again. Start talking some sense or I'll shoot this Mace right into your eyeball!" He cuffed me on the back of the head. A cell phone rang, and I heard his footsteps move away. He went into the office and closed the door.

Lalo looked down at his soiled tee shirt and scowled. He peeled it off and threw it on the floor.

"He ruined it, *güey*" his partner said.

"That was my favorite shirt," Lalo said to me. "My lucky shirt."

"*Lo siento,*" I said.

"Damn right you're sorry."

Lalo threw punches as he advanced on me. A few straight jabs whizzed past my ear and then a hook brushed the tip of my nose. His fists were coming so fast that I saw only blurs.

"C'mon," Lalo continued, still speaking Spanish so fast that I could barely keep up. "Tell us about the shipment. Was it Cisneros or those other whores who paid you? You tell me and Esteban about it and we'll make it easy for you." Lalo whipped a flurry of uppercuts. "Believe me, *güey*, this fucking *pendejo* will take you apart piece by piece if you don't tell us. Me and Esteban, we're the nice guys. But this other one—¡*ay, madre de Dios*!"

"He's right, *güey*," Esteban said, kicking an empty Modelo beer can. He shucked his short motorcycle jacket, the kind with the armor plates that racers wear. "This guy has no religion, no mercy. I saw him cut off a man's balls."

Lalo had worked up a sheen of sweat shadowboxing. He continued to duck and weave in front of me.

"Where is El Animal?" Esteban asked almost gently.

"Is he still here in Juarez? Be a friend and tell us. How much money did he pay you?"

I was straight-out weeping at this point. "On my mother's soul," I managed between sobs. "I have no idea who you're talking about." Again, in an out-of-body way, I found it interesting that the deeper into the shit I got, the more I invoked my mother's name. I don't think she would've approved.

"I work for Bowden-Everitt. I'll pay you anything, just for the love of God—"

Lalo landed a straight jab above my heart. The blow sounded like a watermelon dropped onto concrete, and my whole torso felt as if it had caved in. I worked my jaw, trying to bite off a piece of air to breathe. It took a minute before I could get my lungs working again.

Footsteps came back from the darkness.

"The jab looks a little soft these days, Lalo," the interrogator said from behind me. "Listen up," he continued. "Your boss and I want this guy alive. So don't kill the bastard, all right?"

"Okay, *güey*," Esteban said. "*Ándale, pues.*"

The man peeled off his surgical gloves and flipped them into my lap. He put his hand on my shoulder in an almost fatherly way. "I'll be back," he said.

Lalo and Esteban watched him leave. As soon as the door slammed shut, they both spat on the floor.

"I hate that guy," Lalo said. "Word gets out that the boss is talking to him and we're all dead."

"Treats us like we're peasants," Esteban added.

"Lost my punch? I'd like to get him in the ring for a round. Half a round. I'd mess him up so bad his dog wouldn't even recognize him." Lalo cracked his knuckles. "Any beer stashed in this place?"

Esteban gave the Modelo can another good boot. "I'll check the office. I think the boss has a fridge in there."

"Hey, hey!" Lalo said. "I don't want to be drinking the boss's beer."

"I'll just go and check."

Lalo pulled up a folding chair and took a seat. My chin was planted on my chest, and a steady drain of blood, snot and tears ran off my face. I couldn't feel my teeth. Lalo rested his forearms on the back of the chair and stared at me.

"You speak Spanish pretty good," he said.

I tried to raise my head. "I don't know what that guy is talking about," I gasped. "You hit like a goddamn mule kick."

Lalo smiled.

Esteban came back with two red-and-gold cans of Tecate. "See," Lalo said as he accepted his beer, "even this guy says I still have the punch. I hope these aren't the last beers in there."

"Plenty of beer in there," Esteban said, cracking his can. "It would be great if the boss set you up for some fights that you didn't have to throw—"

Lalo looked up sharply.

"I mean, if he'd set you up for good fights—competitive fights—you could work your way back up. You know what I'm saying."

"*Puta madre, güey.*"

"Hey," Esteban said, going over to the little table in the corner of the room and picking up his magazine.

"Look at these bikes. The boss said he was giving me the money. I mean, the guy said the boss was... Here." He opened the magazine and showed Lalo. "Suzuki 1100s. Best sport bikes in the world. The boss said—"

"The boss says a lot of things these days."

"He's serious this time, *güey*. He's got to spend his money on something, right? Besides, the boss loves racing."

"Just like he loves boxing," Lalo muttered.

"Marisella likes racing," Esteban said.

"What the hell does she know? She's sixteen years old. You better hope she still likes racing tomorrow, or you're not going to get any Suzukis."

"Suzukis suck," I said.

"What?" Esteban asked, looking about as shocked as if his can of beer had spoken up.

"Who's asking you?" Lalo pushed up from the chair.

Esteban dropped the magazine. "Who the hell is this guy?"

"It's a fact that Suzukis suck," I said, my swollen brain scrambling to come up with some words to reverse myself out of this situation. "If you want good bikes, you should get your boss to buy Yamahas."

"I can't believe this," Lalo said.

Esteban pulled a black automatic from under his shirt. "I don't care what the *pinche yanqui* said. This bastard is finished. We'll say he got loose and tried to escape."

Esteban pointed the pistol at my face, and as I looked into the muzzle, I flashed back to something Max Bowden, my boss, had once said about doing business in Mexico: Never tell a Mexican he doesn't know what he's talking about.

CHAPTER THREE

My boss—Old Boy Bowden, we called him—called my folks personally to tell them I'd gone missing. I could see him leaned way back in that burgundy leather swivel chair, his hand-tooled cowboy boots up on the desk, the phone in the crook of his shoulder, Lyndon B. Goddamn Johnson reincarnated. The situation was so grave that he dialed the phone personally instead of having his secretary, Carol, do it for him. Carol had been ringing my cell constantly for the previous three days. We had honchos from Caterpillar coming down from Illinois looking to lease factory space the week I got snatched. Since I was handling the Bowden-Everitt end of the deal, the old boy was curious as to where I had gone off to. After three days of voice mail, they sent an intern to my apartment and found the place trashed.

Mom refused to believe it for the first two minutes, and then she dropped the phone and sprinted off to her medicine cabinet. Dad took it like he usually did: He sat on the sofa and stared out the big picture window in the living room. For as long as I can remember, that's what he did when he didn't have any fast answers. It was like he expected a sign to appear among the rhododendrons. Dad was kind of like my brother Jon that way. He never reacted the way you wanted him to.

Later that day, my folks got a detective with the El

Paso Police Department on the phone. The cop didn't offer much encouragement, and told them they shouldn't bother coming to Texas. They had surveillance tape from the international bridge that showed me crossing that morning on my way to the Juarez office, but that was all. I wasn't the first Yank to get lost on the other side of the border that year, and the cops had become resigned to the drill. Once the meds had kicked in and she could maintain an even strain, Mom called the consulate in Juarez. Although they were much more simpatico than the detective, they told her pretty much the same thing. Then my folks called their attorney, who in turn spent an hour on hold with the Drug Enforcement Administration. Same story. Even if you go missing in a place like Seattle, the cops pretty much throw up their hands. But down on the border, they didn't even waste the effort of dismay. In order to garner any attention as a missing person—in El Paso or El Segundo—you've got to be a cute little kid or a hot blonde bride in a slow news cycle. In the end, all I got was a snippet in the Metro section of the El Paso *Times*. "Real Estate Agent Missing."

My parents' attorney finally hired a private investigator who specialized in missing persons in Mexico. He promised to canvass Juarez, get in touch with his myriad contacts. All for the reasonable price of $250 a day—plus expenses. He earned his first dollar by advising my folks to contact their accountant to determine how much cash they could scare up in the event a ransom demand materialized. That probably freaked my parents out more than the fact that I might be dead.

And after that, there was nothing else to do about it

but wait for a phone call or for my body to turn up. The cops didn't have to admit the latter was the more likely possibility, since Juarez had been getting a significant amount of stateside press already that year. Articles about the Mexican government being overrun by *narcos* had appeared everywhere from *Forbes* to *Playboy*, citing the horrific body counts (an average weekend saw over thirty people killed) and the complete inability of the authorities to do anything about it. Optimism was hard to come by with all those corpses piling up.

Considering the situation, my brother Jon wasn't the last person I expected to show up in El Paso five days after old boy Bowden made the call to my parents, but he was pretty far down the list. All this family apathy in the face of my disappearance might seem strange, but you've never met my family.

—　—

The last time I'd seen my parents or my older brother, Jon, was Christmas. About the only thing I looked forward to during my obligatory holiday sojourns home was my brother's wife, Cheryl. Jon's old lady was so fine she gave you a stomachache just looking at her. So did my mom's rack of lamb. Dinner that night was marked by our silverware clinking against the china and my dad using his "Rabbit" bottle opener to de-cork wine faster than we could drink it. My brother, as usual, wasn't imbibing, so I had to do most of the work. Mom made her rote inquires about when my brother and Cheryl were going to have kids and if I was ever going to get married, and that pretty much exhausted the conversation. Mom had given up on me ever becoming a useful member of the family when I'd told her I wasn't going to follow Jon and Dad to the University of Colorado. The subsequent four years at a liberal arts college in California, followed by my decision to get into real estate as opposed to law had marked me as such a lost cause that even my move to the hinterlands of El Paso hadn't warranted a motherly expression of disappointment.

Thinking I was doing my father a favor, I kept draining my wine glass so he'd have an excuse to pop another bottle.

When everyone threw in their napkins after fifteen minutes, Cheryl and I immediately volunteered to wash the dishes. I don't particularly like pulling kitchen patrol, but I'd found that offering to clean up not only made me look helpful, it also was a great excuse to ditch out on the annual post-dinner Scrabble tournament. Plus, I'd learned from previous holiday experience that Cheryl took certain things very seriously, washing dishes being one of them. She rinsed and I loaded.

Cheryl was wearing a pair of snug True Religion jeans and a v-neck cashmere sweater. I guess she'd eaten too much lamb, because she had the top button of her pants undone, and I could see the lace fringe of her white panties. A strand of blonde hair kept falling into her eyes, and she brushed it back with her forearm to keep it out of her face. She got this furrow between her eyes when she concentrated, and that, combined with the panty line and cleavage I could spot when she dipped into the sink, had me trying to figure out a place to stow my hard-on.

"I'm trying to imagine you and Jon having sex," I said, apropos of nothing.

Cheryl stopped mixing suds for a moment and pushed that strand of hair back again. "What makes you think of that?"

I sloshed another dose of Merlot into a Santa mug. "I'm just thinking about how beautiful you are, and then I look at Jon and can't seem to reconcile the two of you in the sack."

Cheryl peeled off the yellow dish gloves and leaned against the counter. That furrow was between her eyes again, and I really wanted to reach out and grab a piece of her.

"That's a strange thing to bring up," she said after a moment.

"I'm not insinuating that he's ugly. It's just that I can't see you two—"

"Fucking," she said.

That word out of her mouth made me pause. "Yeah. That. Jon's always seemed kind of sexless to me."

"Where, may I ask, is this coming from?"

"Holiday Tourette's?"

Cheryl smiled.

"Really, it's a legit question. What brings someone like you and a guy like him together?"

"He's six feet tall, great body, makes half a mil a year, and that seems 'sexless' to you? I'm not sure your criteria are very up to date." She reached for my drink and took a sip. She made a face. "We take care of each other."

I had to admit that much seemed true. The most conversation I'd gotten out of Jon during the trip was when he'd let me test drive their new 500slc Benz. He was into the sunroof controls. Cheryl's four-carat pink-diamond wedding ring was glittering on the sill above the sink, and their house in Cherry Creek had a separate garage for the lawnmower.

"There's got to be more to it than that," I said.

Cheryl let out a little burp. "Such as?"

"A lot of things cross my mind," I said. "It just seems like you two aren't very... what's the word? Happy?"

Cheryl found a jug of Cascade under the sink and poured a measure into the dishwasher.

"Happy," she repeated, turning the washer on. "How would you know anything about it?"

"I mean, Jon is just so…blah. I for one don't think he appreciates you."

"Just because he's like that with *you* doesn't mean he's like that with *me*," Cheryl pointed out. "Besides, not everyone has to run around yelling about their *feelings* all the time."

"When we were growing up, I used to beat the hell out of him."

"So?"

"So, he's my older brother. It's supposed to be the other way around."

Cheryl patted me on the cheek "Awww. You just wanted a little attention."

"Doesn't that seem a bit odd to you?"

"It seems odd that you'd want someone to punch you. You know that marriage isn't all about sex, right?"

I fake-gaped at the suggestion and Cheryl laughed. She had a really nice laugh. Think about someone clinking a sterling-silver Tiffany knife against as Baccarat wine goblet. The girl had style for miles.

"Have you ever heard the line about behind every good-looking woman is a guy who's sick of sleeping with her?"

Now it was my turn to laugh.

Since we were both enjoying the other's humor so much, it seemed to be a good moment to ask Cheryl if I could kiss her. She looked me straight in the eye, and for a second, I could see her considering it. It amazes me how many outcomes our brains can flip through in just a couple of moments.

Cheryl finally bit her lower lip and shook her head.

"I'm already fucking one of the partners at his office," she said. "Making out with his little brother at this point would be overkill."

She took the mug from me, drained it in one swallow and dropped it to the floor. The mug shattered, and the circular base made a *wok-wok-wok* sound as it wobbled on the tile.

"Are you kids okay?" Mom called from the living room.

"Don't worry, Liz," Cheryl said. "It wasn't the china." She buttoned her jeans and gave me a good look at that perfect ass as she left the kitchen.

➤ ◄

I was so delighted with the news of Cheryl's infidelity that I moved my flight back a day and told Jon that I wanted to go skiing. It had proved difficult to keep the information under wraps, but I thought I'd spring it on my brother when we were on the ski lift. That way, he couldn't walk out on me before I could see his reaction.

"Jack Swanson," Jon said. "That figures."

Jack Swanson was the partner. Heavy flakes spun past us as we ascended the lift, and there was a layer of fog that concealed the skiers below us on the slope.

"Your wife's screwing your boss, and that's all you can say?"

Jon tapped his ski pole against the lift support as we glided by.

"It makes you look ridiculous," I continued.

Jon smiled faintly.

I looked at him in his blue ski parka with his goggles pushed up onto his forehead as he reached out with his pole to tap another passing support. It wasn't the first time I'd seen my father's face reflected in Jon's, but this was the first instance that I'd seen the same thing *under* the skin—the way the muscles gathered at the corner of his mouth, turning it up ever so slightly into a near grin. It wasn't so much a look of resignation as it was one of bemusement. I'm not trying to say that my dad and Jon were pessimists, but they always handled bad news with such a lack of reaction that it seemed like it had been what they'd expected all along. I suppose this was quite handy when sitting at the negotiating table trying to hack out a settlement, but in day-to-day life, it made me want to pound on their backs as if they were choking.

"There's got to be something inside you that feels this," I said.

"What do you want me to do?" he asked.

"Get pissed. Tell me I'm a liar. Anything."

"You don't understand Cheryl," he said.

"That's great, but—"

He cut me short. "But what?"

I shrugged.

"Is this why you wanted to come skiing?" he asked.

He didn't need to hear my reply.

We rode the next three minutes in silence, my brother continuing to tap his pole against every passing support, making dull pinging sounds. The visibility was so low that we must've been stuck right in the middle of a cloud. Fifty yards from the top of the lift, Jon nodded his head at nothing in particular before suddenly dropping his poles and pushing off the edge of the chairlift. He vanished into the fog as if he'd been sucked into a whirlpool.

"Did you see that?" the woman on the lift behind me said. "He jumped!"

I didn't hear him hit the ground.

I slid off the lift and headed straight to where I thought he'd crash-landed. Visibility was better on the ground, and I spotted Jon's blue parka right away. He'd fallen into an area cordoned off with orange netting, and was struggling to get his skis out of the waist-deep snow that had accumulated around the base of the support.

"What the hell was that all about?" I asked. Jon didn't appear to be hurt. Looking up, I could see that he'd only fallen fifteen feet.

"My binding came loose," he said. He tossed his skis and poles over the netting. The cloud around us started to crack open.

"So you decided to hop off the lift and fix it?"

"It broke when I hit the ground," Jon said, as if that explained everything.

A kid on the lift above us yelled, "Yard sale!"

Jon clambered over the fencing.

"Are you trying to kill yourself?" I asked.

Jon sat down and unbuckled his boots. One lens of his goggles had popped out of the frame.

"I was hoping to break my leg," he said matter-of-factly. He looked at the snowdrift he'd landed in and shook his head.

"You're serious?"

He went to work on his goggles. "Haven't you ever wished for that?" he asked without looking up.

I clicked out of my skis and sat down next to him. I couldn't think of anything to say.

"You never get that?" he asked.

I shook my head.

Jon snapped his boots back into the bindings. "Stupid, because I've done this run so many times that I knew it wasn't going to be a long fall." He looked over at me. "Seriously, you never get that?"

"Suicidal?"

He thought about that for a moment. "No, that's not it. I was just hoping...for something...*external* to happen."

"Aside from your wife nailing your boss?"

Jon got that bemused look on his face again. "I think that definitely qualifies as internal." He got up on his skis and looked himself over. "Not even a bruise." He pushed off with his poles and slid silently down the mountain.

CHAPTER FOUR

My landlord was the efficient type, so just a week after I got shanghaied by the Mexicans, he'd cleared out my apartment and put a "For Lease" shingle in the courtyard. My belongings had been stashed in a self-storage unit, and I figured he'd give it another week before he went ahead and auctioned everything, claiming the proceeds were needed to pay off back rent, damage deposit, etc. There wasn't much left, anyway. After they'd finished with me, the goons had come over and looted the place. They took my suits, the little bit of jewelry I had, and, of course, my Yamaha XR-11 street bike. They tossed the place like it was a run-of-the-mill robbery, but even the cops knew the ransacking was connected with my disappearance.

When the taxi dropped my brother off at the Monte Vista Apartments, the complex manager was in his trademark baggy gray sweats painting the fence by the swimming pool. He saw Jon cupping his eyes against the living room window to peer inside. The super's gray hair was tufted up in the back, and you could see the half moon of his pale gut peeking out from the bottom of his sweatshirt. After determining Jon's identity and expressing his regrets, he went into his office to retrieve the key (and the bill) for the self-storage unit. He also gave Jon directions to a nearby La Quinta.

"I didn't move anything until the cops went over the place," the landlord said. "They really trashed it."

"The cops?" Jon asked, setting his garment bag on the cement.

"No, no—the spics. They hit the day after your brother got…after he disappeared. Broke the lock on the door."

"You live here? In the complex?"

The manager set his feet apart slightly. "Yeah."

"You didn't see or hear anything?"

"I'm on the other side of the place," he said. "I don't hear much of anything. Besides, I'm not responsible for—"

"Damage or loss of tenant property. I'm sure it's stated clearly in the lease agreement."

"Hey, what do you expect? I went over this with the cops seven times. There wasn't nothing out of the ordinary. 'Cept maybe the fact your brother was down here to start with. Where you guys from, anyway?"

"Denver."

"Well, buddy, I don't mean to seem, um…"

"Callous?"

"Yeah. But shit like this happens all the time down here. Look over there." He pointed south. The brown landscape sloped down a mile, past squat neighborhoods, convenience stores and the I-10 until it hit the dirty trickle of the Rio Grande. Even from the parking lot, my brother could see that the riverbanks had been cemented, making the Big River look more like a huge drainage ditch. The thirty-story, red-and-white striped ASARCO smokestacks stood a few feet inside the U.S. line like huge, filthy candy canes missing their hooks. Beyond that, the recently installed border security fence protected the U.S. side of the frontier: 30-foot high nets of high-grade steel that looked like they'd been relocated from the T-Rex enclosure of *Jurassic Park*. The landscape on the Mexican side rose from the river into a barrio hodgepodge of adobe dissected by dirt roads and, beyond those shanty towns, sloped up to the barren foothills. From the parking lot of the apartment complex, you could see *La Bibla Es La Verdad Leela* marked in huge whitewashed letters on the side of the mountain looming over Juarez. Several green-and-white Border Patrol SUVs trolled the fence. Others were parked on higher outcroppings like birds of prey. "You see that?" the super asked.

"You mean Mexico?"

"Even with all that *migra* sitting right there, El Paso is crawling with illegals. They're like goddamn cockroaches. There's nothing we can do about it but put double locks on our doors. We catch them taking our stuff, and what happens? The cops send them right back over that ditch so they can come back the next night and steal whatever they missed the first time. And if they get your stuff across the river, forget about it, buddy. It's gone forever."

"I've heard that about people, too."

"Hey," the landlord said, "I'm sorry about your brother. Really. Hell, maybe it's like the cops said. Maybe he just decided to break for Acapulco and didn't tell any-one. I don't want to sound—"

"Callous."

"Yeah. But you're wasting your time. The spics are killing themselves like a video game over there."

"If it's so dangerous, why don't you move?"

The landlord set his feet shoulder width apart. "We may have to deal with the beaners coming across for our TVs and nobody knowing how to speak English no more, but at least they don't shoot each other on our side," he said. "Besides, I was born here. Just like the other fifteen white guys in El Paso."

The thumping of helicopter blades began to echo through the valley. With the increasingly louder reverberations bouncing off the jagged mountains on both sides of the border, it wasn't until the Border Patrol Huey banked around a bend in the river—contour-flying the frontier at 200 feet—that they could tell where the sound was coming from. The chopper slipped around the ASARCO towers and clattered off toward downtown El Paso.

"They're gonna blow those smokestacks up," the landlord said, as if the illegal immigrants had something to do with that, too.

The apartment manager scratched his gut and regarded Jon, who continued watching the Huey navigate the river. It was late afternoon, and El Paso was about to get its nightly reprieve from the dirt-brown moonscape that surrounded it every day. There were fifteen or twenty minutes at sunset when the sky washed over the two cities with watercolor reds and oranges and purples that could almost make you forget where you were. White-vapor jet contrails crisscrossed the sky so vividly against the colorful backdrop that you could make a good guess where each flight was bound—Phoenix, Los Angeles, Denver, Houston, Mexico City. In those few minutes every evening, even the traffic noise quieted down, like everyone had pulled over to the shoulder to appreciate the ethereal light.

"What *are* you doing down here?" the super asked.

Jon paused for a moment, distracted by the sky. "Looking for my brother," he said finally.

The manager shook his head as he walked away. "I'll call you a cab."

Jon stood in the parking lot until the sun finally dropped behind the Juarez mountains and the brilliant colors slipped away like a quilt pulled off the edge of a bed.

———

At night, it's hard to differentiate between El Paso and Juarez, as there's just the faintest break in the lights made by the river. But if you look hard enough, you can see that the quality of the light is different on the Mexican side; the Juarez bulbs give off a jaundiced glow, as if the electricity over there were more polluted than the American source. Sometimes late at night, you can even hear the difference: The howling dogs sound hungrier on the Juarez side, the music drifting out of the cantinas is more accordion-heavy, the cars have more holes in their mufflers. But you have to listen hard. And no matter how hard you strain your ears, you can never hear the gunshots.

Jon checked into the La Quinta along the interstate and stood at the window, looking north at the Franklin Mountains. There is a big, illuminated Texas star—missing just a few lights—outlined on the last serious hill of the El Paso side, faced off against the whitewashed Spanish urgings to read and believe the Bible across the border. The Franklin range represents the last dribble of the Rocky Mountains, and because of that, the El Paso–Juarez corridor has always been the natural conduit between east and west, that southern low point where you can navigate the Continental Divide without battling too many inclines. The semi-truck traffic along the I-10 is constant, especially when you factor in all the 18-wheelers coming over the bridges from Mexico to join the flow. You get a fair number of travelers coming through as well; the city is as close to L.A. as it is to Houston. While many of them stop for the night at the motels lining both sides of the freeway, they rarely stick around come morning. The name of the town itself says it all: *El Paso.*

Nobody moved to El Paso by choice. They were either born in the city or got transferred by the Army, which has two massive bases—Fort Bliss and White Sands—in the area. And then there are the NAFTA folks keeping the extended-stay motels in business, using El Paso as a staging ground for their daily sorties into Juarez. Most of the big manufacturers rotate these *maquila* specialists out every three months or so. El Paso is to these plant managers what Port-au-Prince is to Foreign Service officials.

By all conventional measures of civic beauty, El Paso is an armpit. Ground vegetation consists mostly of low scrub brush and knife-sharp "Spanish Dagger" agave plants, and without the mountains to protect the city, the winds scream in unabated, carrying all that dust from the Sonoran Desert and tossing plastic Super 8 shopping bags into the high branches of trees. It takes every transplant a few months to get used to the fine layer of dirt that builds up inside their homes every week despite the efforts of cheap Juarez housekeepers and Costco triple packs of Pledge. When the wind shifts, you get a good whiff of the burning garbage in Juarez. It's blisteringly hot in the summers—the sun crushing you under its glare so brutally that sometimes you can't even determine where the goddamn ball of solar fire is positioned in the sky—and snow-cold in the winter. The majority of homeowners have given up trying to keep a lawn; it cooks off in the heat and freezes dead in the winter. Instead, people spread reddish volcanic rocks around in front of their houses and call those yards. Others paint their cement driveways green.

But for industrial real estate purposes, El Paso is perfect, as close to actually living in Mexico as you're going to get and still be able to drink water out of the tap. Ever since NAFTA went through in 1994, it seems like the only structures getting built across the river are the *maquiladoras* and the mansions for the guys who own them. In the United States, the industrial areas are the blighted parts of town, but it's the opposite in Mexico. In Juarez, the neighborhoods look like they just got bombed, but the office parks on the east side are impeccable: country club lawns, paved streets, new Kentucky Fried Chicken franchises, drive-thru Starbucks. The recent levels of violence have certainly made the manufacturing execs think twice about bringing their shops to Juarez, but a lot more Yankee, Taiwanese and Nipponese plant managers will have to get shot before it outweighs the economic incentives of moving their factories south.

Although Juarez has been ranked as the most dangerous city in the Western Hemisphere the past couple of years running (supposedly the only place deadlier than J-Town is Baghdad), year after year El Paso is named the second safest city of its size in America, just behind Honolulu. It doesn't make much sense when you first hear that, but then you realize that El Paso is essentially—like Hawaii—an island: There are only four roads out of town—north on U.S. 54 through White Sands, west or east on the I-10, or across the bridges south to Juarez. The Border Patrol has permanent checkpoints fifty miles out of town on each highway, and considering how many other law enforcement agencies work the area, you'd have to make one hell of a run through some very barren landscape to get away from a bad deed.

But as Jon stood at the window of his hotel room that first night, he probably wasn't seeing the commercial upside of the location or the public-safety value of its relative isolation. He was probably thinking *armpit*.

Jon didn't leave the hotel for two days, opting instead to order pizza and watch pay-per-view movies. The only time he ventured out of the La Quinta was to walk to the Circle K to buy a six-pack of Diet Dr Pepper and a *Penthouse*. He visited the pool the afternoon of the third day, taking half an hour to recline on a wobbly chaise lounge and go through all the paperwork accumulated from the cops, the consul and the private eye about my disappearance. Since no ransom demand had come in, the consensus among the authorities was that I was either decomposing in an east Juarez ditch or drunk as a loon in Cancun. Jon returned the papers to his briefcase and eased into the pool, keeping his nose and eyes above the surface like an alligator.

He came back to the room and ordered another pizza before getting in the shower. The maid had neglected to replace the bath towels, so he had to dry off with a wash-cloth. He was holding for the hotel manager in order to lodge a complaint when his cell phone rang. He saw his wife Cheryl on the BlackBerry's caller ID and let it go to message. She redialed immediately. He dropped the house phone and answered.

"How's it going?" she asked.

"Nice town."

"Really?"

"I'm kidding."

"You've been talking to the police?"

"Of course."

Cheryl sighed. "How much longer do you think it'll take?"

Jon didn't say anything.

"Jack Swanson called today," Cheryl reported. Swanson was from the firm, the guy whom Cheryl had been screwing around with since Christmas. "He wanted to know what your state of mind was."

"My state of mind?" Jon asked. "What the hell does that mean?"

"He's worried about you. Taking this leave of absence, not telling them how long you'd be gone. You're an important part of the firm."

"Did he say that?"

"In so many words, yes."

"Hold on for a second." Jon went to the door for his pizza.

"An important part of the firm," Jon repeated when he got back on the line.

"That's what he said."

Jon saw that the delivery guy had brought him six packets of red pepper flakes instead of the Parmesan he'd asked for. He told Cheryl to hold and went out to the hallway, hoping to catch the kid. He was in time to see the elevator doors slide closed.

"My brother gets kidnapped, and all Swanson can think about is when I'm going to get back there to handle his caseload." He saw the car with the pizza-delivery dome on the roof drive out of the parking lot and slapped the window. "He's freaked out because he might actually have to do some work."

"Jon, that's not—"

"Screw him."

"Be rational for a moment. What chance do you have of finding your brother down there? If he's not dead, then he's certainly not just hanging around Juarez."

"Leave him out of this," Jon said.

"Pardon?"

Jon paced the room. "I said leave my brother out of this."

Cheryl let the line hum for a moment. "What about me?" she asked in a small voice.

"What about you?"

"Jack's not going to let you stay away very long before he hires a replacement."

"Did he tell you that?"

"Yes."

"I cannot believe you people."

Cheryl abandoned the meek act. "*You* people?"

"Yeah, Cheryl, *you* people.'

"That's not fair—"

Jon accidentally knocked the pizza off the nightstand and it spilled onto the floor. It landed facedown, and bits of rug stuck to the greasy pepperoni.

"Goddammit!" he yelled.

"What's wrong?"

"I should have been a bus driver," Jon said as he scooped up the pizza and dumped it in the trash can.

"What?"

"A bus driver."

"I'm not following you," Cheryl said. "I thought we were talking about your brother."

"That's exactly what we're talking about—"

"Hold on—"

Jon didn't let Cheryl speak. "This is a family emergency, okay? So don't tell me Jack is going to replace me, because I don't care anymore."

"I have no idea what you're talking about," Cheryl said. "And it's not like you to get this bent out of shape. If you told me what's really going on, I might be able to understand."

"All you need to understand," he said, kicking the trash can so hard that it flew across the room, "is that Jack

Swanson can kiss my ass, because I'm not coming back until I figure out what the hell is going on."

Jon dropped the cell phone onto the bed, grabbed the offending trash can and flung open the door. A maid ducked behind her cart as Jon chucked it down the hallway.

"What *is* going on there?" Cheryl asked when Jon got back on the phone.

"I'm not sure yet," he said before hanging up. "But I've got it under control."

CHAPTER FIVE

The next morning, Jon took a cab to the El Paso Police Department's headquarters. He sat in the waiting area with several Mexican women who patiently knitted or jiggled sleeping babies in their laps. The television high in the corner of the room was tuned to a Spanish variety show on which a balloon-chested young woman was interviewing a green puppet. The room smelled of microwave popcorn and disinfectant, and the phones rang without being answered. A steady stream of people paid traffic tickets at a small window on the other side of the lobby. After an hour, Jon strode over to the desk sergeant with whom he'd checked in upon arriving.

"What's the delay?" Jon asked.

The sergeant looked up from his hunting magazine as the phone at his elbow rang for the tenth time. The cop sat behind a high desk protected by scarred bulletproof glass, regarding Jon through a sliding window. The edge of the counter on Jon's side was rounded from years of people leaning against it.

"Who'd you say you were here to see?" the desk cop asked.

Jon took the missing-persons report out of his briefcase. "For the third time. Detective Quintana. Carlos Quintana. I called this morning and got an appointment."

The sergeant dialed an extension. Nobody answered.

He hung up the phone, shrugged and went back to his magazine.

Jon slapped the bulletproof glass with his open palm. The sergeant's head snapped up.

"You'd better secure that shit," the cop said.

"I've been parked out *here* and I'll bet Quintana is back *there* listening to his phone ring just like you are. Now, I don't give a damn if I have to sit here all day, but my client, who's paying me $250 an hour, might take exception when he gets his bill. So why don't you just buzz open this door, and I'll go back and find Quintana myself?"

An older officer appeared at the desk.

"What's the trouble?" he asked.

"This guy wants to see Quintana, Captain. Quintana ain't in."

"What d'ya need with the detective?" the captain asked.

"Missing person," Jon replied. "Quintana filed the report."

"Well, you're gonna to have to wait, because, like the sergeant says, Quintana ain't in." The desk sergeant allowed himself the tiniest smile—just the corner of his mouth moved—but Jon saw it.

"What's so funny?" Jon asked. "I've got plenty of time here; maybe I'll get to work on a civil suit."

"Bullshit," the sergeant muttered.

"Hey, you really want to talk to a detective?" the captain asked.

"Sure," Jon said. "Why not?"

"Let him talk to Sheffield. I'll bet Sheffield's got nothing better to do right now."

The sergeant laughed. "Sure, Cap, I'll page Sheffield."

The captain pressed a button next to the phone, and the door to the right of the desk buzzed open. The captain met Jon on the other side to give him a visitor's badge. The laminate on the badge had started to bubble up and peel. "Detective Sheffield's your man." The cop led Jon down the hallway to the detective's pen.

"What's the deal with Detective Sheffield?" Jon asked, clipping the badge to his coat.

"Detective Sheffield is good police," the captain said. "He'll fit you just fine."

Jon heard the cop at the front desk laughing.

⬝ ⬝

The detectives' bullpen was lit by buzzing fluorescent tubes, which made Jon's skin look bruised. The air conditioning kicked up a hell of a racket but didn't produce much cold air. Several desk fans oscillated to make up the difference. Six desk and chair setups occupied the middle of the room, and an equal number of offices ringed the perimeter. A color-warped TV in the corner was tuned to CNN with the sound down. A bedraggled young woman in a Juicy track suit sat in front of one of the desks, being interviewed by a detective. The detective scratched under his shoulder holster strap with a ballpoint pen as he asked questions. The uniformed captain left Jon outside an office bearing Detective Iraan Sheffield's name. The captain nodded to a black guy in a Philadelphia Phillies jersey who was slumped in a chair outside the office.

"Wassup?" the black guy said as the captain walked away. He wore baggy jeans and tan Timberland boots. The door to the office was ajar. Jon looked inside.

"You waiting for Detective Sheffield?" Jon asked the black guy.

"Yeah," the guy said, pulling a red Chupa Chups lollipop from his mouth. He had gold fronts and a shaved head.

"How long?"

The detective interviewing the woman in the center of the room looked over. "Too goddamn long," he said.

"Word," said the black guy and stuck the lollipop back into his mouth.

Jon settled into a school desk. *HATE THA POLICE* was carved into the writing surface above *JUAN ROBLES SUX DIX*. The windows to the offices were frosted, so all Jon could see of the outside was the intense yellow of a hot afternoon.

"What you looking for?" the black guy asked around the lollipop.

"I'm following up on a missing-persons report," Jon said.

The man leaned his chair back against the wall. "Which side?"

"Pardon?"

"U.S. or Mexico?"

"Mexico. Juarez."

"Not good, homes."

"People keep telling me that."

"You needing a body, or what?"

"Pardon?"

"You need a body for insurance or something?"

"It's a missing person."

"You'll be lucky if you get a body."

"Thanks." Jon popped his briefcase and rummaged around.

"Hey, man. Just trying to help." The guy started cleaning the treads of his boots with the end of his lollipop stick.

Two janitors went inside the office. They took measurements of one wall and marked studs and electrical runs with a pencil.

"Okay," one of them said as he came out of the office a few minutes later. "I think we're set."

The black guy looked up from cleaning his boots.

"We'll start on that wall tomorrow morning," the other janitor said. "So get all your stuff out of there 'cause there's gonna be a lot of dust."

"All right," the man said. He slid off his chair and made his way into the office. Jon waited a minute before following. The guy stood regarding the marks on the wall. There were off-color rectangles where pictures had once hung.

"They're busting this out," he said without turning around. "Gonna make this into another interrogation room."

"You getting a new office?" Jon asked.

The detective snorted. He walked behind the desk and plopped into the creaky swivel chair.

"So what you got?" he asked. "Who gone?"

Jon took a seat in front of the desk.

"My brother. A week and a half ago. Here's the report." Jon slid the folder across. The man flipped through the pages.

"You talked to Detective Quintana?" he asked without looking up.

"I had an appointment," Jon said. "But the captain at the front told me to see you. You are Sheffield, right?"

Sheffield pushed the folder back at Jon and looked him over for a moment. He pinched the bridge of his nose like he had a headache. "What do you want me to tell you, man? It doesn't look good. Especially since his apartment got tossed. That means whoever snatched him knew who he was."

"And?"

"If they knew who he was, it means he fucked up."

"I don't follow."

"Listen, if your brother got jacked for his car or his watch or something, that'd be the end of it. They call that kind of thing a 'flash kidnapping.' The dudes are just after an ATM limit and whatever else is right there. Case closed. If it was a more serious kidnapping, then we'd have heard a price by now. Since your brother hasn't shown up at Customs in his tighty whiteys with a big prejudice against Hispanics, we can eliminate the possibility of the former. Your family hasn't been contacted for money, so it's not the latter. That leaves us with…" Sheffield shrugged.

"How come you guys keep talking like he's dead?" Jon asked.

The detective shrugged. "I think you'd be a lot better

off talking to one of our counselors." He picked up the phone and started to dial.

"I can't see how they could possibly demonstrate much more sympathy."

The detective hung up the phone. "Man, the sympathy part is not..." Sheffield stared at the ceiling for a moment. "Look, the fact that they went through his apartment after he disappeared means he probably got in the middle of a deal."

"A deal?"

"Dude, where you from?"

"Denver."

"Denver," Sheffield repeated.

"So?"

"You sure you don't want to speak with a counselor?"

"You're doing just fine."

"A drug deal, all right?"

"My brother sells real estate," Jon said.

"And that means?"

"He isn't into drugs."

"Oh, okay." Sheffield started taking things off his desk and putting them into a cardboard box. After a full minute he looked back at Jon. "And?"

Jon crossed his legs and picked at his sock for a moment. He smiled at Sheffield across the desk. "You fucked up pretty good, huh?"

Sheffield blinked one time. "Come again?"

"If they're booting you out of your office, I'm guessing you must've screwed something up pretty nicely. Those flatfoots up front were having big laughs at your expense."

"What are you talking about?"

"You tell me. I'm betting it's bad. Not like *bad* bad, but, you know, embarrassing." Jon uncrossed his legs and leaned back in his chair. "But I suppose that since you're black, they can't just fire you, huh?"

Sheffield smiled slowly, those gold teeth peeking through his lips like the sun coming up. "Get the fuck out of my office."

"It's only going to be your office for another"—Jon checked his watch—"five hours."

—▸ ◂—

Jon took a cab from the police station to the storage unit where the landlord had put everything from my apartment that hadn't been taken in the burglary. It was past noon, and the day had warmed up considerably. Jon shucked his sport jacket and dress shirt before ducking into the sweltering room. My stuff had been boxed up haphazardly, and he began to drag it into the lane that ran between the sheds. He found my straw cowboy hat on top of my old motorcycle-racing trophies, and clamped it on his head to keep the sun off his face while he worked. By the time he found the shoebox I kept my pictures in resting on top of four empty bird cages, his undershirt was damp with sweat. He pushed all the other stuff inside and rolled the door down and locked it. He called the taxi company, but hung up after a couple of minutes on hold. He could see the La Quinta on the other side of the I-10, so he popped open his briefcase and emptied all the snapshots into it. With his jacket and button-down shirt thrown over his shoulder and the cowboy hat on his head, he started for the hotel on the shoulder of the access road. If not for the copious amounts of sweat and the attaché, he might have looked like an illegal. Cars whooshed past him with their windows rolled up to keep the AC inside. Shards of broken glass in the ditch sparkled in the sunlight. He crossed the freeway via an underpass where three leathery Mexicans sat in the 85-degree shade, passing a 40-ounce bottle of Steele Reserve. They watched Jon pass without curiosity.

When he finally arrived at the hotel grounds, he used his room key to open the gate to the swimming pool. He took off his shoes, socks and trousers and slipped into the water wearing his boxer shorts. He ducked his head a few times before climbing out and drying off in the sun. Upstairs in his room, he took a shower and, ignoring the blinking red message light on the phone, spilled all the photographs out on the bed. He spent the next hour going through them. Only after he'd ordered and eaten a pizza did he check his voicemail messages. Cheryl had called twice.

"So you're going to root him out down there when the police have given up?" she asked when he called her back.

"That's the idea," he said.

"Really, are you just driving up and down the street, hoping he'll pop out of some alley?"

"How's Jack Swanson holding up without me?" Jon asked.

Cheryl coughed. "What's Jack got to do with any of this?"

"I'm starting to think the two of you kidnapped him, you're both so anxious for me to give it up."

"Jon, please. You scared the hell out of me last time we talked, slamming doors and screaming. Come home and we'll get all this sorted out. You've not been yourself lately."

"I wonder why that is?"

"Do I need to remind you that we've got bills to pay?"

"It all comes back to money, doesn't it?" Jon asked.

"Stop trying to make me look like the bad guy!"

"I'm not coming back. Not right now."

"And I'm not going to sit here as the laughingstock of the neighborhood while you screw around down there playing Magnum P.I., living off Andre's Pizza. You're going to get fat, you know."

Jon flipped the pizza box lid closed. "Andre's Pizza?" he asked.

"I see the statements online. That credit card is half mine. You know how much that stupid hotel is costing us every night?"

"I'll move someplace cheaper," Jon said. "And how's this if you're so worried about our finances? I'll pay for all my expenses."

"With what?"

"Let's just say that you won't see any more charges on the credit card or withdrawals from the bank."

"Oh, this is too much. You've got a secret Swiss account now? My husband, bounty hunter, man of mystery." Cheryl's laugh was bitter. "This is classic."

CHAPTER SIX

Jon checked out of the La Quinta that afternoon and, upon the advice of the taxi driver, relocated to a pay-by-the-week motel on Mesa Avenue, the main drag that arcs from the I-10 downtown to meet back up with the interstate on the west side of El Paso. The Vagabond Inn was a two story, olive-drab affair built in the 1960's that offered "fully furnished" rooms for $350 a month, $150 a week. At four o'clock, the parking lot was full of late-model cars and SUVs bearing license plates from all over the country. The number and quality of vehicles outside didn't seem to fit with the shabby building. Jon signed on for a week, paying in cash that he pulled from an ATM on the way to the motel.

The manager led him up a flight of concrete stairs to the second tier, where they navigated an open-air hallway littered with charred hibachis, empty beer cans and dust-coated running shoes. Surveillance cameras had been mounted at both ends of the hallway.

"What's with all the shoes?" Jon asked.

"Joes," the manager said.

"Pardon?"

"Army. They run a lot." The man started to add something, but thought better of it and unlocked the door.

The darkened room had a wall-unit air conditioner

that sounded like a Cessna engine revving for takeoff, a sagging twin bed, a particle-board bureau missing three knobs, and a dinette set next to the refrigerator. The manager handed over a key.

Jon dropped his suitcase on the bed and threw open the greasy drapes to reveal a courtyard. The pool was a murky turquoise color with a pair of desiccated floats bobbing on the surface and several beer cans on the bottom. Jon looked at the windows of the other units and saw that they were all shuttered against the afternoon heat.

He pulled the drapes and dumped the pictures from the storage shed onto the bed. He picked out a photo of me at a construction site. The photo had been taken in Culiacan and showed me standing with a group of Mexicans I'd been working with. We were holding quart bottles of Carta Blanca to celebrate a deal. Jon stuck the picture in the corner of the mirror over the chest of drawers.

He had just reclined on the saggy bed when his cell phone rang. He scanned the caller ID.

"Hi, Mom," he answered.

"Jon, Jon, Jon," she said.

"What, Mom?"

"Cheryl called."

"Uh-huh."

Mom sighed. "Jon, Jon, Jon."

"Mom, knock it off."

"I'd like to think you knew what you were doing. Do you know what you're doing?"

"Not really."

"So why stay down there when the police and

that crowd say there's no point? I'm sick to death over Christopher. But what can I do but pray and…by the way, have you visited that Moon fellow yet?"

"Moon?"

"The private detective. I just got another invoice from him. Since you're down there, you might check up on him and find out what he's doing. His invoices are so vague. I have the feeling we're being bilked."

"I'll check it out," Jon said.

"So, Cheryl. She was crying her eyes out when she called. I know things haven't been right between the two of you for some time, but that happens in every marriage. You've got to work through these times. Your father and I had a terrible—"

"Mom, stop."

"She thinks this is your way of getting a divorce. You've always been so non-confrontational."

"This isn't about my marriage," he said.

"There's no one who loves your brother more than I do," Mom continued. "Even though he decided a long time ago to follow his own path—a path, I might add, that has never made any sense to me. If he'd really wanted to work in real estate, I told him a hundred times he could have called Francis Barnhart and worked with him here in Denver. Francis makes a very nice living. Have you seen those condos he put up along the lower Platte?"

"Mom."

"I love both of you so much, but it's been almost two weeks and nothing has come up. The police have no leads. We've talked to the consulate, the FBI—your father even went to the governor's office here to try and get something done." She sniffled a couple of times. "Jon, your father and I just want you to come back. We read about all these terrible things happening down there."

"Yeah, how's Dad taking this?"

"He's mowing the lawn every day to get the lines right. I'll never give up hope, but I can't keep going like this, the chance of losing both you boys." Mom blew her nose again. "We've been talking to Doctor Ghausi."

Jon walked the length of the room. Dr. Ghausi was Mom's shrink, whom she'd been seeing on and off for a decade.

"Do you feel like it might help to talk to Doctor Ghausi?" Mom asked. "I mean, he thinks this might not really be about your brother."

Jon didn't say anything for a moment. "I thought Ghausi got his medical license pulled. Wasn't he prescribing pills over the Internet?"

"No, no. That was Dr. Ghausi's partner."

"Good for Ghausi. Mom, I've got to go."

— ◆ —

At six that evening, someone cranked a boombox in the courtyard. Jon parted the drapes to see that several young men had gathered around the pool with hibachis and beer coolers. One of them dropped a match into a barbecue, and it lit up with a *whoomp*! They turned up Kid Rock as more men emerged from the apartments with bags of ice and towels. A couple of them stood around the pool's filtration system with hands on their hips, regarding the machinery. They turned to look up, and for a moment

Jon thought they'd seen him watching. Jon pulled back behind the wall as a shirtless redhead with a flat-top haircut moved under the window.

"Major Gates!" the redhead called up. "Major Gates, are you awake, sir?"

"Get your ass out of bed, Six to Ten!" one of the others shouted.

Jon heard lumbering footsteps in the next-door apartment and then a window slid open.

"What's your malfunction, trooper?" the neighbor called down.

"The filtration system is fucked, Major. Pool's all murky again. Gotta have the pool, sir. Hot as a gnat's twat at the equator down here."

"You got to stop leaving your beer cans in there. Talk to the manager. I'm sick of fixing it."

"Yo, Six to Ten," another man called. "Get your sorry decom ass down here and help us out."

"Those beers cold, soldier?"

"Hooah, sir. I'm shipping for Eye-rack in two weeks. You think I'm drinking warm beer?"

"Give me a goddamn minute."

The redhead under the window snapped off a salute.

A few moments later, a man limped into the courtyard wearing red board shorts, flip-flops and a green-and-blue Hawaiian shirt open to display his belly. He accepted a beer from one of the younger men as he shuffled over to the filtration system. There were now twenty or thirty guys in the courtyard, igniting their hibachis with too much lighter fluid. The stench of burning briquettes wafted through Jon's window.

"How's she looking, Jimmy?" the redhead asked.

"Bring me another beer and I'll tell you. Get me that bag of chemicals and the wrench," Jimmy said.

One of the men sprinted across the faded courtyard turf as another chased him with a lighter and an aerosol can of Right Guard, shooting flames at his back.

"Okay, knuckleheads," Jimmy asked. "Who was eating the Ritz crackers last night?" Jimmy held up the clogged pool filter.

One of the men suggested that they run the system without the filter.

"Yeah, that might kill off the bad case of the clap you picked up last night at the Red Parrot, but you'd all show up to P.T. tomorrow morning with green skin. I'm sure the C.O. would love that." Jimmy got gingerly to his feet and rubbed his forehead.

"Another beer, sir?" the redhead asked.

"How many's that?" Jon overheard a guy ask.

"We're close," another replied. "I think that was five."

Jimmy ambled around the pool deck, muttering to himself. He looked up suddenly and pointed to the lawn mower sitting abandoned in the corner of the courtyard. The redhead pushed the mower over, and Jimmy started tinkering.

Jimmy removed the gas filter from the lawnmower engine and tried to work it into the pool system. It didn't fit right, and he rubbed his head again. He scanned the courtyard. Some of the guys were winging a Nerf football back and forth across the pool.

"Send me that football."

"Aw, c'mon, Jimmy, I just bought this."

His fellows called for him to give up the ball. The guy tucked it under his arm as the others swiped at it. A hulking young man sprang out of his lawn chair so suddenly that the chair flipped into the air and blindsided the guy with the football. A couple others piled on, and the ball squirted out of the jumble. Jimmy pulled a pocketknife from his shorts and started cutting a ring from the Nerf ball, trimming it down to size and then molding it around the lawnmower filter. He put the cover back on the filter system and flipped a switch. The pump whooshed to life as the men cheered.

Twenty minutes later, Jimmy declared the pool safe, and the men started throwing each other in.

—◄ ►—

By midnight, the coals in the hibachis glowed red in the darkened courtyard and the underwater pool lights cast rippling blue shadows on the walls. The soldiers brought out the bourbon. Jon ate his pizza and drank his Diet Dr Pepper while watching the soldiers sing along with the boombox and spit fire into the grills. The redhead was hanging his head over a garbage can, throwing up. The drifting smoke and ashy barbecues made the courtyard look like an aerial photo of a bomb run. The scorched bratwursts left smoldering on the grills could've been dismembered enemy appendages.

The soldiers finally dispersed at two in the morning, abandoning their bbqs, lawn chairs and coolers. Jon lay on the side of the mattress that hadn't gone completely to springs. He was just about to drop off to sleep when he heard someone outside on the walkway.

"Aw, c'mere baby," the voice cooed. "Just come over here for a second. Don't be scared."

Jon got out of bed and peeped around the curtain. He saw a chubby young blonde leaning against the walkway railing, shaking her head vigorously.

"Aw..." Jon recognized the voice of his neighbor, Jimmy. "What you so scared of? We're just gonna have one drink. You can trust me, I got two Purple Hearts."

The girl shook her head again, her bleached-blonde tresses falling into her eyes and revealing black roots. Her denim skirt was askew, and her bra strap cut into the flesh of her exposed shoulder. Jon couldn't see Jimmy, who was standing just inside the doorway of his apartment.

"You want me to bring the drink out here?" Jimmy asked. "Hey, we could go down and take a swim in the pool. I just cleaned it."

The girl hiccupped and something started to work in her throat.

"You want a Hot Pocket?"

The girl puked, spraying a watery stream onto the walkway.

"Oh, shit," Jimmy said, slamming his door against the splatter.

The girl took a few deep gasps before stumbling down the hallway. Jimmy opened his door and ran to the railing with his car keys and a towel. The girl exited the stairs on the lower level and staggered into the parking lot.

"Let me give you a ride home!" Jimmy called. "I got a new Mustang!"

The girl wobbled onto Mesa and almost got plowed by a taxi. The driver slammed on his brakes so the girl could clamber into the back of the cab. Jimmy turned and saw Jon looking around the drapes.

"You see that?" Jimmy asked.

Jon stepped out onto the walkway. The sodium lights in the parking lot buzzed.

"It's not that bad," Jimmy said, regarding the puddle outside his door. "You got a bucket?"

Jon shook his head.

"Get in here and help me find something." Jimmy walked into his apartment. Jon followed.

A narrow passage led from the door to the kitchen through layers of junk piled on the floor. The coffee table was covered with take-out bags, plastic Whataburger cups and *Maxim* magazines. A computer lay in pieces on the sofa along with a soldering iron. Jon also saw an Army helmet, three bowling balls, a set of ancient golf clubs and a spear gun. Jimmy rummaged under the kitchen sink until he came up with a goldfish bowl. He filled it with water, splashed the vomit off his doorstep, and then dropped the bowl in the laundry hamper. He looked at Jon like he was seeing him for the first time. He blinked deliberately.

"Who the hell are you?"

"Jon," he said, extending his hand.

"You an operator?" Jimmy asked.

"Pardon?"

"Delta?"

"No."

"Well, then, what the hell are you doing here?"

"I'm next door," Jon said. "Moved in today."

"You've got to be shitting me. You're not Army?"

"Why does that surprise you?"

"Jesus, man, this whole place is Army. Fort Bliss, some homo air defense guys from White Sands, the usual fuckups rotating through. Got enough military to fill up Delaware. Who the hell told you to stay here?"

"The cab driver."

"Goddamn Mex must've thought you were Army. Well, shit, how about a drink?"

Jimmy stood 5'10" with bowed legs and a wrestler's cauliflower ears. When he came back into the living room from the kitchen, Jon noticed several scars around his eyes. His light-brown hair had been cropped close to the skull, which didn't hide the fact that it was receding. Jon pegged him as about forty years old. Jimmy pushed take-out bags off the coffee table and set down two keg cups and a bottle of Crown Royal.

"Mixer?" Jimmy asked as he made a space for himself on the sofa.

"Ice is fine."

Jimmy poured three fingers of Crown into both cups and handed one to Jon.

"Welcome to the Vag," Jimmy said, raising his cup.

Jon took a tiny sip.

"I really thought I had that one in the bag," Jimmy said. "Was talking to her all night at Erin's. You ever been there?"

Jon shook his head.

"I'll take you. Cool place." Jimmy drained his drink

and poured himself another. He offered Jon the bottle, but Jon shook his head. "You running dope?"

"Not yet."

"Man, I don't care. I mean, it's cool. It's just that I can't figure out why a guy who's not in the Army would be here. 'Specially here at the Vag."

"I came to look for my brother. He's been missing for a couple weeks."

"No shit?"

"They've got him over in Juarez somewhere."

Jimmy blinked in disbelief. It looked like he had to make an effort to close his eyes, as if the skin over his face was too tight.

"You're kidding," Jimmy exclaimed. "Like in jail or something?"

"Kidnapped. I think."

Jimmy dropped his drink. "Oh, shit."

"That's what the cops say."

Jimmy crossed the room and leaned against the wall for a moment before sliding heavily to the floor. "What the fuck the police know? God, that's awful, man. I can't believe that shit. If it was my bro, I'd be down here, too. You bet." Jimmy closed his eyes and rubbed his forehead. "You never leave a man behind."

Jon heard showers start to hiss in the neighboring apartments. The commemorative Hawaiian bamboo clock on Jimmy's wall read 4 a.m. Footsteps sounded on the walkway, and vehicles began to fire up in the parking lot.

"What's going on?" Jon asked.

Jimmy spoke with his eyes closed. "P.T."

"What?"

"Physical training," Jimmy said. "They got to report to base for P.T. by five."

"After that night of drinking?"

"Hooah," Jimmy said.

Jon picked his way to the window and watched the soldiers—now in full camo uniforms—make their way to their cars. "Why don't they just live on base?"

"They're officers. Officers don't live on base if they can help it. Especially not when they're single and only got a few weeks before deployment."

He remembered the redhead calling Jimmy "Major."

"Don't you have to get up, too?"

Jimmy laid his head on a duffel bag. "I'm out. Eighty-per center."

"Eighty what?" Jon asked.

Jimmy started to snore.

Jon let himself out of the apartment. He stood on the walkway watching the last of the Army guys pull out of the parking lot. It was still dead dark, and just over the river he could see the flickering lights of Juarez.

CHAPTER SEVEN

The private detective's storefront was wedged between a chiropractor's office and the Godzilla sushi restaurant in a strip mall along Mesa. A Mexican man in jeans and a mesh baseball hat squatted in the thin slice of shade outside the office. Jon said hello as he passed. The Mexican looked up and nodded. Chimes sounded as Jon pulled the door open, and a blast of sour-smelling refrigerated air rushed to meet him. The desk in the reception area was unoccupied, and a Beretta Firearms calendar on the wall was still on the March page even though it was already two weeks into May. The sound of a clacking keyboard came from the back office. An open *Redbook* and a pack of Marlboro Ultra Lights sat on the reception desk.

Jon heard a toilet flush as he took a chair next to the nearly empty water cooler. An incredibly pregnant young woman waddled out of the lavatory. Without acknowledging Jon, she grabbed the package of cigarettes off the desk and maneuvered her girth outside. The chimes dinged and the clicking of the keyboard stopped.

"Goddammit," someone cursed from the inner office.

A thin man in cowboy boots strode out of the office and yanked open the door.

"Christy!" he said. "Put them cigarettes up!"

"I'm just having me a little drag," the woman protested.

"Gimme those." The man snatched the cigarettes and held the door open for the woman. She tossed her hair as she made her way behind her desk. She popped two pieces of Nicorette and violently turned the page of her magazine.

"Who's this?" the man asked in his thick Texas drawl. He was about 35 years old and completely bald.

"Dunno," the secretary said, not looking up from her reading.

The man rubbed his pate. "Sorry about that," he said, extending his hand. "Justin Moon. What can I do for you?"

"I'm already a client," Jon said.

"Come again?"

"Chris Lennox."

"Oh, sure, sure. You're his…?"

"Brother."

"Come on back to my office."

Pre-law texts and an LSAT guide covered Moon's desk.

"Studying for the exam?" Jon asked.

"Yep."

"Must take a lot of time."

"Sure," Moon said, marking his place in a book with a Whataburger receipt and setting it aside. "It's a hard test."

"Must not leave much time for your investigations."

Moon looked up with sad eyes. "What you shootin' at, Mr. Lennox?"

Jon brought a folded copy of Moon's last invoice from his shirt pocket. "It says here that you put in…let's see…22 hours last week on my brother's case. Three trips into Juarez. A surveillance of the location where he was last seen. That's a lot of work for somebody studying for the bar."

Moon dropped the LSAT guide into a drawer and leaned back in his chair. He steepled his fingers. "I already done received payment on that last invoice. Your folks didn't seem to have a problem with my report."

"Forget the invoice," Jon said.

"It's all in there."

"In where?"

"In the report."

Jon and the detective regarded each other.

"Okay, bud," Moon said finally. "You want this straight?"

"Since I'm already sitting here, why not?"

Moon leaned forward in his chair. "I'm afraid to say that your brother is gone."

"Elaborate."

Moon seemed a bit shocked that his pronouncement didn't have more of an impact. "How close were you to your brother?"

Jon looked at a dusty Remington reproduction on the wall. "We're brothers."

"Yeah. Sure. Well excuse me for saying so, but I think your brother might have been involved in some things not pertaining to real estate. I mean, the whole darn thing doesn't make sense. And I mean on a very basic level. Let me ask you something. What do you think of El Paso?"

"I think it's an armpit."

"I was born here, and I don't even take offense to that statement. So did you ever get to ponderin' why your brother decided not only to come here, but to stay? According to your mother, he had several better opportunities in Denver to choose from. So why El Paso? Why all the business in Juarez?"

"Aside from the fact that's where his work is, you mean?"

Moon nodded his head. "Okay, what exactly was his work?"

"For form's sake, let's use the present tense. He leases industrial real estate. In Mexico."

"How about this?" Moon lowered his voice. "I think your brother was—okay, is—a federal agent."

Jon laughed.

"Have you ever met his boss or his co-workers?"

"Didn't get invited to the Christmas party," Jon said, still chuckling.

"They're all ex-Army. Special Operations. Intelligence."

Jon shook his head. "You know what I think? I think you've been sitting in here reading law, and maybe on your break you took a couple minutes to make this shit up." Moon started to speak, but Jon cut him off. "Then again, you might've come up with this right now, on the spot. But I don't care so much about your theory as the fact that I don't think you've done one thing in regard to investigating my brother's disappearance aside from answering the phone and putting together a couple of invoices."

Moon pointed across the desk. "I resent those accusations."

The door to the office was still open, and they both

heard the receptionist let out a snort of laughter. Moon got up to close the door.

"Tell me what you're getting at, buddy," Moon said when he returned to his chair. "You want your money back? Well, you're shit outta—"

Jon raised his hand. "Forget the money," he said. "What I want from you is some good-faith information. I want you to put all this Army-secret-operations crap aside and give me the real stuff. Ten minutes of honest conversation and I'll be out of your hair."

Moon touched his head self-consciously. "But I want you to know, just on principal, that I have looked into your brother's disappearance."

"I said forget the spiel. Just give me what you've got."

Moon picked up a pencil and tapped the edge of the desk. "Okay. Your brother was on the other side to take photos for another broker when he vanished. That sounds like a semi-reasonable thing for a fella to be doing. Now, my first thought was that he got robbed, plain and simple. And over there, it's not unusual for a robbery to end up a murder. They really don't give a damn about that sort of thing. But if it was a simple robbery, then I'm sure we would've found your brother's body right away. Since we haven't, I start thinking he's mixed up with something more than real estate. If it was indeed a drug thing, the body's not going to turn up for some time. They treat the bodies like trophies over there. Well, more like signals, actually. They don't just whack somebody, they punch their card in such a way that it's clear who did it and why."

"When you say 'they,' you're talking about...?"

"The cartels. The drug cartels. There's got to be 150 gangs working over there now, but the three main ones, they've been going at it pretty bad. On one side you've got this old boy Lazaro; he's been the head honcho of the Juarez cartel for almost a decade now, fighting it out with the boys from down in Sinaloa. The Sinaloa guys aren't very organized, though, especially since their chief, sumbitch named Beltran Leyva, got knocked. The other guy is this dude they call El Animal. Jorge Cisneros is his real handle. He's been pissing on Lazaro's lawn for the past year. Cisneros is a military guy, Mexican Special Forces, so he's got a lot of ex-commandos working for him. They run around with heavy machine guns and rocket launchers, the whole catastrophe. Call themselves Zetas. These assholes are the real problem right now because they've got more guns than the Army. 37 folks got killed over the weekend. Half of them Zeta pistoleros and the other half Mexican soldiers trying to arrest them.

"Lazaro is more old-school, if you know what I mean," Moon continued. "A cowboy. Pays fellas to write ranchero songs about him. Some of the worst goddamn music you ever unfortunate enough to hear in your life. Got them accordions squeezing like a heifer with a calf coming out of her sideways and trumpets blowing like an elephant in heat—"

"Lazaro," Jon said to get Moon back on track.

"Don't get me wrong: Aside from bad musical taste, this guy is a goddamn psychopath, too. Lazaro may be getting a little old and eccentric for the game, but he isn't just gonna hand it over to these new guys."

"Eccentric?"

"Oh, I don't know." Moon walked the pencil along his knuckles. "You hear stuff like he's into science fiction and outer space. Or that when he needs to relax, he flies down to Cabo and works as a waiter in some tourist joint for a couple weeks. Everybody down here has a weird Lazaro story."

"How do you know all this?"

Moon shrugged. "You're in Dallas, you know about the Cowboys."

"Okay, but I don't see how my brother fits into that."

"I'm not trying to tell you that the violence doesn't get incredibly random, so there's the wrong-place, wrong-time, bad-luck possibility. But like I said, if that was the case, we'd have a body by now. That's the red flag: no body. They way these guys work is that they keep the bodies and then sort of strategically leave them so the message is clear."

"Example."

Moon swiveled back and forth in his chair. "Okay, here's one. A few months back, a bunch of El Animal's guys went over the wall at Lazaro's mansion, some kind of half-assed O.K. Corral shit. Well, they missed Lazaro, but they killed his pet tiger. I think it was a hand grenade or something. Anyway, the tiger got blown to shit. So for the next month, El Animal's guys start showing up dead, wrapped in those cheap-ass tiger blankets they sell on the bridge.

"Or when a *federale* they've got on the payroll screws the pooch, the corpse will turn up with a yellow ribbon wrapped around its neck. Don't ask me why it's got to be yellow. My point is that the bodies never stay where they're killed. They place them after the fact for maximum effect."

"And this is the half-assed reason why you think my brother was involved in the whole cartel thing? Or, as you said, was a federal agent."

"Look, I wish I could tell you what the hell happened to your brother, but nothing makes any sense on the other side these days. It's always been a rodeo down here: the Mexican Revolution, Prohibition, now the drug gangs. But then there was that thing with all those women getting raped and murdered a few years back. That was just pure, senseless butchery. No one ever found out who was behind it. No suspects, no arrests, nothing. It's so screwed over there that the locals trust the cartels more than they do the cops. It's the whole goddamn country, man. Down in Mexico City, a mob of citizens burned two federal agents alive because they thought they'd kidnapped a couple kids. It was on TV, man. They dumped gasoline on these cops and lit them up.

"You got this so-called corporate security specialist by the name of Batista, holds executive seminars for all the American employees who work in Juarez, gives them tips on how to avoid being kidnapped. Well, he gets nabbed a year or so ago, and nobody's heard a goddamn thing out of him since. It's like the cartel boys are just doing this stuff for shits' n' giggles sometimes. It don't make no sense."

Moon leaned over to retrieve two Miller Lites from

the little refrigerator in the corner of his office. He set one down in front of Jon.

"But hell," Moon said, cracking his beer, "there's always the possibility that your brother met some sweet *señorita* and flaked out to Acapulco, so in love that he didn't even think to call y'all. I'm not ruling that out."

"Do you ever find anyone? Or do you just come up with theories?"

"Whoa there, buddy." Moon looked hurt. "I thought we were pals now."

"Do you?"

Moon took a gulp of beer. "Bud, let me tell you what I specialize in. Rather, what I used to specialize in. Kids. High school kids. They go across for parties on the weekend. They call them—or used to, anyway—'drink and drowns.' Rent out some disco, and then for twenty bucks you get all the booze you can stomach. I get the calls Sunday morning from the parents, and I go across and check—in this order—the bathroom of the club, the closest whorehouse and the nearest police station. And if they're not in any of those places, well…. But that's completely dried up now. Even the Army won't let the soldiers cross the bridge these days, so you can sure as hell bet that every parent here in El Paso would rather have their kids set up a kegger in their living room as opposed to them going into Juarez to try and get boozed up. I get more calls these days from Mexicans trying to find their children *over here,* because not even the Mexican kids go out in Juarez anymore. Must be twenty new bars open along Mesa that used to be on the other side. Had to relocate to stay in business." Moon took another drink. "Look, you want your money back? I'll refund half."

"Keep the money."

"All right, but I offered."

Jon rolled the unopened can of beer between his palms.

"Now here's some free advice," Moon said. "If you're serious about this, if you really need to put your mind at ease, I'd do two things. First, go to Juarez and see for yourself. I know you can stand outside my office and look right at it, but you only have to walk a few blocks off the other side of the bridge to see what I'm talking about. It'll cost you thirty-five cents each way to get over and back. Remember to take your passport and forget your wallet. Just take a couple bucks. No credit cards or ATM. That way, if you get mugged, there won't be any PIN number for them to beat out of you. Secondly, I'd talk to your brother's boss, Max Bowden. And I'd do that just so you can understand that there's more than real estate going on in that office. I really do believe that your brother was tangled up in something that could've got him singled out by one of those outfits down there. Maybe it wasn't drugs. Maybe it was…hell, I don't know what the hell it might have been. Maybe he was selling goddamn anti-tiger grenades. But I think meeting the guys he worked for might put your mind to rest a little bit as far as you thinking that this was just some random occurrence."

Jon stood up and set the unopened can of Miller Lite on Moon's desk.

"And how would it do that? Put my mind to rest?"

"It might convince you that your brother really is gone."

Moon stuck out his hand, but Jon left him hanging. He pushed through the office door, and the afternoon heat caught him right in the chest. Moon's secretary was leaning against the wall smoking a cigarette, the hand not holding the Marlboro resting on the ledge of her belly.

"Good luck," she said, exhaling a stream of smoke.

CHAPTER EIGHT

That night, Jon was treated to the same mayhem in the courtyard as he'd witnessed the previous evening, a little more fascinated this time knowing that these roughhousing kids were soon to be the leaders of men in places like Iraq and Afghanistan. His neighbor Jimmy moved among them, helping fix one guy's boombox that had gotten too close to the pool and then spending much of the evening absentmindedly dismantling the ancient lawnmower. The party broke up around two in the morning, and then the Joes were up and at 'em before dawn.

Jon walked down Mesa to get the newspaper from a 7-Eleven and then sat in his dank apartment. The top headline on page three of the El Paso *Times* read: "Mexican Agents Free 44 in Raids." The victims had been kidnapped by the Gulf cartel in Neuvo Laredo and held for weeks. Since all the hostages worked for a rival drug gang, the *federales* weren't sure as to why they'd been kept alive as opposed to executed. Jon tore out the article and set it on the dresser.

He went next door to listen for consciousness. It was noon, and Jimmy had yet to stir. He knocked on the door. No response. He knocked again.

"What?!" Jimmy yelped.

"It's Jon."

"Jon who?"

Jimmy's battered face appeared around the drapes. He blinked twice, again giving the impression that it took physical effort to make his eyelids meet. He stared at Jon for a couple of seconds before he realized who it was. He opened the front door, and a strong odor of boozy sweat—sickly sweet, like soiled diapers—wafted out. Jimmy collapsed facedown onto the cluttered couch. Jon noticed a disassembled television on the dinette table along with a textbook titled "Nuclear Thermodynamics and Heat Transfer."

"Tell me your name again," Jimmy mumbled.

"Jon. Your next-door neighbor."

"Right, right. Down here looking for your brother. What the hell time is it?"

"A little past noon."

Jimmy let out a moan.

"I'll let you go back to sleep."

"You had breakfast yet?"

Jon said he hadn't.

Jimmy rolled off the couch onto the floor. He got to his knees and then used the coffee table to push himself to his feet. "Let me take a shower and we'll get breakfast, okay? You like migas?"

"Migas?"

"Mexican eggs."

"Sure."

"Oscar Mike in ten minutes." Jimmy hobbled into the bathroom.

Jon waited for him on the walkway, trying to acclimate himself to the heat. It was already ninety degrees, and sweat stains spread under his armpits. Jimmy emerged wearing shipwreck-style cargo shorts, stale flip–flops and an open *guyabera* shirt. His wraparound Oakley sunglasses were perched on his forehead. He took a swig from an amber medicine bottle and made a face.

"Want some?" he asked.

"What is it?"

"Cough syrup. Got codeine in it."

"No, thanks."

"It's the good shit. I get it from the VA." Jimmy took another slug and tossed the bottle into his apartment.

Jimmy's new Mustang GT had so much dust on it that the color was indeterminate. He had disabled-veteran license plates, and there was a foot of trash on the floor and loose wires dangling under the dashboard. Jimmy cranked it to life and peeled rubber out of the parking lot.

"They come from the factory with these chips in them that only let you make second–to–fourth shifts," he explained as he sped down Mesa. "I yanked that son of a bitch out right away."

They drove under the freeway and past several auto parts shops and liquor stores before they hit Doniphan, which runs parallel to the railroad tracks through town. Jimmy swerved into the gravel parking lot of La Riviera restaurant. He pulled around back and parked next to a dumpster.

"What you got planned for today?" Jimmy asked after the waiter had dropped off their food. He shoveled heavily Tabasco'd eggs into his mouth and chased them with a Corona.

"I was thinking about going over to Juarez."

Jimmy mopped his mouth with a napkin. "Gonna look for your brother?"

"I want to get the lay of the land."

"Shit, man," Jimmy looked at his digital watch. "If we get a move on, we can be in and out of there before the bridge traffic gets bad. Maybe even make it out before the bad guys wake up and start shooting."

"Guy said it cost 35 cents to walk across the bridge." Jon said.

"Fuck *that*," Jimmy said, signaling for the check. "We're driving. Use the car as a weapon if we have to. Everyone's saying that the only place that's worse right now is Baghdad, and I've *been* to Iraq. Besides, I need to stock up on booze. It's *beaucoup* cheap over there. We'll go back to the Vag so you can ditch your wallet and grab your passport. You've got your passport, right?"

— —

The border in El Paso sneaks up on you. You're driving along the I-10, take one of the sweeping overpass exits, and, next thing you know, you're eyeball to eyeball with Mexico. There are five bridges along the El Paso-Juarez border, and up to 200,000 people cross on a daily basis—the vast majority of them Mexicans with travel visas. Although it's rarely a hassle getting into Mexico—you can leave downtown El Paso and be in Juarez in a matter of minutes—coming back is a gridlock nightmare, especially since Homeland Security ramped up the checkpoints after 9/11. You can feel slices of your life peeling away as you inch along in the smog for hours at a time. Any U.S.

citizen who makes the crossing on a regular basis eventually sucks it up and pays $250 for a Century Pass, which lets you use the Dedicated Commuter Lanes. The wait in the DCLs is rarely longer than twenty minutes. You have to submit to an FBI background check to qualify, and you can't have any passengers in the car with you when you cross back into America, but everyone who buys a Century Pass considers it among the best investments of their lives.

The entrance to the international bridge is an estuary, the two cultures colliding in a picket of toll boxes. The Mexicans—packs of kids in school uniforms, mothers dragging roll-on bags full of toilet paper (for some odd reason, you can't get good T.P. in Juarez), yardmen in sweat-stained cowboys hats—accept the inevitable hassle of crossing the concrete frontier like most Americans accept grocery-store checkout lines. They don't seem to be as menaced by the security fortifications as the Anglo travelers. It's hard for an American not to be apprehensive, knowing that by driving over an invisible boundary in the middle of the Rio Grande, you're renouncing your rights as an American citizen. Sure, the threat of violence is one thing, but there's also the uncertainty that comes along with entering a nation where there aren't any hard and fast rules. All bets, as they say, are off. You see some American drivers crossing themselves and saying the Rosary before pulling onto the span.

As Jimmy merged with the other bridge traffic at the bottom of the offramp, he reached into the glove box and pulled out another bottle of cough syrup. He chugged what was left before chucking the bottle out the window.

"You don't have any shit on you, do you?" he asked.

"Pardon?"

"Drugs, guns, that sort of shit."

"No. Why do you ask?"

"See that?" Jimmy said pointing at a brown sign with the outline of a pistol crossed out. "The spics are bonkers about anyone bringing guns into Mexico. I've heard stories of priests who drove across the border with one shotgun shell in the trunk of the car left over from a hunting trip getting arrested for gun running. Thrown in prison for a year. The Mexis don't give a damn if it's a single .22 bullet."

The freeway splayed into several corridors of light traffic. Jimmy veered to the far right lane, where there was an empty toll booth.

"Do you have Mexican insurance?" Jon asked.

"For what? You get in a wreck over here, and the only paper that's gonna spring you is the kind with pictures of U.S. presidents on it."

Jimmy drove the Mustang past the American guardhouse—which was empty—then gunned it to get ahead of the other vehicles merging back into three lanes of traffic over the span. The sides of the bridge were protected by ten-foot-high hurricane fences topped with razor wire that curved inward. Pedestrians walked along the caged sidewalk. A woman who looked like an office secretary carried a stack of Domino's pizza boxes.

"Used to be a lot of recruits coming over here," Jimmy said. "Head straight for the Kentucky Club. M.P.'s worst nightmare. Now look at it: not a *gringo* in sight."

They crossed a metal band in the middle of the bridge,

where a tarnished plaque indicated that they had officially entered Mexico.

The roadway opened up on the other side into five lanes leading up to the Mexican entry points. Although there was no wait coming in from El Paso, the line of cars on the Juarez side heading to America stretched off as far as they could see. A traffic light flashed green as the Mustang lurched over three speedbumps.

"What are the lights for?" Jon asked.

"Green means keep driving," Jimmy said, ducking to check out the Mexican security forces standing on the curb. "Red means pull over and start paying bribes. My God, will you look at all that hardware?"

Mexican Customs agents packed sidearms while the *federales* propped FAL burp guns on their hips. Army personnel in body armor carried assault rifles and had black balaclavas covering their noses and mouths, which may have had as much to do with keeping the car exhaust at bay as with concealing their identities. "Jesus," Jimmy said, "those Army guys have SAWS and 40mm whumpers under their 16s."

Jon gave him a look.

"Grenade launchers, man. What the hell are they going to do with a grenade in this kind of crowd? This is insane."

To emphasize Jimmy's point, a *federale* Blackhawk helicopter dropped out of the smog to assume a hovering position 1,500 feet above the boulevard. Even at that height, they could spot a pair of black-clad commandos with sniper rifles dangling their legs from the open doorway. Jimmy rolled down his window and waved at the chopper.

Several vehicles were parked in corrugated-steel stalls off to the side of the checkpoint. Drivers stood on the curb as Mexican Customs officials searched the cars.

"What are they looking for?" Jon asked. "All the smuggling is going the other direction."

"Like I said, guns. But also computers. You can't get good PCs on this side, so guys go to El Paso, pick up a couple MacBook Airs and bring them back to sell for a profit. It was worse when the Joes could still come across. They used to have signs about that shit at the computer department of the P.X."

"P.X.?"

"Post Exchange. The one over at Bliss is about the size of two Walmarts. The Joes don't have to pay any tax. They'd buy a laptop for $600 at the P.X., bring it across and sell it here for $800, maybe a grand if they knew the right guy. We used to get about fifteen or twenty smart recruits each year who thought they invented the racket. They'd go to the Kentucky Club, and Pancho would come up and tell them what he'd pay for a nice Toshiba, and the next day we'd get a call from Mexican Customs, holding Private Numbnuts for smuggling."

A squad of Army soldiers manned a checkpoint consisting of stacked orange traffic cones a few yards past the Customs sheds. The soldiers had stopped a van and were tossing its contents into the street while the driver smoked a cigarette. A soldier who couldn't have been more than 17 years old waved the Mustang around the van. The kid's slung machine gun was almost as big as he was.

"Those G.I.'s were looking for guns," Jimmy continued. "They're killing each other right and left down here, but supposedly getting a piece is impossible if you try to do it through the legal channels. That's another scam the Joes used to get caught up in: Go to a gun shop in El Paso, five-minute background check, walk out with three Beretta nines and bring them over here to sell for double the money." An armored Humvee chugged past with a crew of soldiers in the back. One of the troopers had his arm draped over the .50 mounted machine gun. Jimmy whistled. "Seriously, I don't think we had this much firepower at our checkpoints in Mosul."

Jimmy eased to a stop at a traffic light. A dirty little kid held up a box of fabric bracelets for inspection. Jimmy rolled his window down and gave the kid two quarters, which attracted the attention of several newspaper vendors. The paperboys pressed copies of *El Diaro* to the window. A photo of a bullet-ridden and bloody Mercedes graced the front page. A cheesecake shot of a Mexican blonde in a string bikini ran across the bottom of the page.

As soon as the light went green, Jimmy cut in front of a graffiti'd panel truck and almost sideswiped a whirring Volkswagen. He followed the potholed street past an overgrown park and several barren soccer fields. The stoplights had the same color lights as those in the U.S.—red, yellow, green—but they didn't flash in the same sequence. They went green, then flashing green, yellow and finally red. Jimmy tried to approach each light slowly enough so that he didn't have to come to a complete stop. When he couldn't avoid a red, he kept half a car length of open space in front of him. His eyes made a constant circuit of his mirrors—passenger side, rearview, driver's side and back again.

Small four-stool, open-air restaurants lined both sides of the road, along with tin-roofed shanties and junkyards displaying mountains of used tires. Skinny dogs darted among the vehicles, their tongues lolling as if they were dying of thirst. A warehouse parking lot was full of pallets stacked high with mannequin arms.

Jon pointed at the plastic hands, and Jimmy shook his head.

The road narrowed as taller buildings began to crowd in on them. They wheeled onto Dieciseis de Septiembre, the main drag lined with street-level shops and markets. It was hard to tell if the buildings were going up or coming down, as none of them were completely intact. Every other shop had its security gates pulled down and the lights off. Through the rolled-up windows of the Mustang, Jon could see the thickness of the pollution over the city. The sunlight that came through it was the color of an old banana.

"Here we go," Jimmy said, taking a right into a plaza surrounded by open-air patio bars. A fat, middle-aged Mexican in a dirty khaki uniform waved them into a metered spot. His uniform fit so tightly that they could see the off-white of his undershirt between the stretched buttons of his tunic. The man had a laminated card clipped onto his shirt pocket beside a tin badge. He guided them toward the curb, peering down to make sure Jimmy's bumper didn't scrape. Jimmy took a quick look through the car and stuffed a tennis racket and his CD carrying case under a pile of newspapers. There were no other vehicles in the dusty lot.

"Five dollar," the Mexican said to Jimmy when they got out of the Mustang. "Parking five dollar. I watch you car."

Two little kids appeared out of a shuttered storefront with torn boxes of gum and started tugging Jon's sleeve, chirping "*Chicle.*" Jon tried to shoo the kids away. They were barefoot.

"No five dollar," Jimmy said in English with an accent that sounded more Chinese than Spanish. He walked over to the parking meter and pushed a few peso coins into the slot.

"Five dollar parking," the guard repeated. "Five dollar watch you car. *Muchos ladrones aquí. ¿Comprende?* Five dollar only."

"Piss off," Jimmy said, and pressed the button on his keychain to lock the Mustang and chirp the alarm.

The guard scowled at them as they walked across the parking lot toward the cantinas. Shops on the other side of the plaza sold serapes, piñatas and plastic Virgin Mary statues, all of which were so faded that they looked like they'd been hanging in the sun for several years. The two little kids kept after Jon, pushing their flats of gum at him. A uniformed waiter rushed out from under the awning of a bar and kicked at the kids. The moppets stepped back a couple of feet and made faces.

"Cold *cervezas*," the waiter said, gesturing toward his patio. "Only two dollars. Corona. Pacífico." The waiter also wore a laminated badge.

Another waiter wearing a Carlos'n Charlie's T-shirt

and a Cruz Azul cap started talking to Jon. "Come with me, my friend. Cold beer for one dollar. Rock-and-roll music. Hard Rock Cafe. This way." He took Jon by the upper arm tried to lead him under the plaza's awning.

The first waiter, who was still trying to get Jimmy's attention, started cussing the Carlos' n Charlie's guy. Jon shook his arm free. Jimmy followed him as the two waiters continued to argue. They took seats at a wobbly metal table. A teenage kid with a training mustache dragged an electric fan over to them. They were the only two patrons on either side of the plaza.

"*¿Cervezas?*" the kid asked.

The two older waiters scurried over. "This is no good place," the one in white said. "Beers no cold and very expensive. You come with me, my friend." He tried to seize Jimmy's arm.

Jimmy feigned a karate chop. "Get the fuck away from me."

The two waiters backed off, giving the teenager hard looks. "He no is waiter," the Carlos' n Charlie's guy said, pointing to his own laminated badge.

"Bring us a couple Pacíficos," Jimmy said, ignoring the badged waiters. The kid started for the bar, but Jimmy caught him by the shirttail. "In the bottle."

"*Sí, por surpuesto,*" the kid said.

"*¿Cuántos?*" Jimmy asked.

"Two dollar," the kid said, straining against Jimmy's hold.

"For both," Jimmy said.

"Two dollar," the kid repeated.

"For both or no deal." He looked at Jon. "Let's go." Jimmy started to stand.

"One dollar each," the kid said.

"Okay." Jimmy let go of his shirt. The kid said something under his breath as he went to the bar. Jimmy smiled as if he'd just closed an important deal.

A withered old woman in a black shawl crept up beside their table to display a felt pallet of tarnished silver jewelry. She smiled, showing toothless gums.

"*No, gracias,*" Jon said.

"*Para tu novia,*" the woman persisted.

"Yeah," Jimmy said. "For your old lady back in Wisconsin."

"Denver," Jon corrected. "And if you knew my wife, you'd know better than to give her jewelry that doesn't come in a bag that costs more than this lady's whole inventory. *No, gracias,*" Jon repeated, and the crone faded back into the shade.

"They say it's the thought that counts," Jimmy observed.

The kid came back with their beers and set the bottles on the table alongside a cracked dish of hard limes. Jimmy took a long swallow. Jon watched his beer drip condensation onto the tin table. He closed his eyes and rubbed his temples to try to drown out the noise of buses roaring down the street and the dragonfly-like whirring of the Volkswagens. The lone traffic cop in the middle of the street blew his whistle incessantly. A mariachi foursome wearing white tennis shoes strolled over to the table and began to play "La Cucaracha."

"Get outta here," Jimmy said. "Scram."

The musicians kept playing, fake smiles cemented on their faces and their eyes focused on the horizon. Their instruments rang hollow and out of tune.

"I'm not giving you a penny," Jimmy said. The mariachis started playing more loudly.

"Oh, for chrissakes," he said, searching his pockets for money. "Here," Jimmy said, thrusting a dollar bill at the accordion player. The man stepped forward and took the bill between two fingers as he kept sawing away on his creaky instrument. "Now will you please shut up?" Jimmy asked.

The accordion player smiled, said something to his buddies, and they switched to another song. Jimmy finished off his beer.

"You gonna drink yours?" he asked.

Jon pushed his full bottle across the table. Two little girls approached with wilted roses.

"You got any change?" Jimmy asked.

Jon said he only had the twenty Jimmy told him to bring.

"Sorry, girls," Jimmy said, spreading his hands. "*No más dinero.*" The girls backed away, their shiny black eyes expressionless.

Jimmy slammed Jon's beer and dropped a five-dollar bill on the table. The kid darted over to take the money. "We've got to get out of here before I kill someone," Jimmy said. "I thought I'd show you the city, but this is ridiculous. I used to come down here and there'd be people everywhere. It's a ghost town now."

"Why don't we just drive around a little bit?" Jon asked. He pulled a piece of paper and a map from his pocket. "I want to see this place called El Parque Omega. That's where my brother was heading when they grabbed him. You know how to get over there?"

Jimmy looked at the map and said it was pretty much a straight shot across town. He stood up and looked for the kid, who had vanished inside the cantina.

"That little pissant owes me three bucks," Jimmy said.

"Forget it," Jon said. "Let's get out of here."

The parking attendant intercepted them halfway across the lot. "Five dollar parking," he said again, scribbling in a notebook.

"No dollar, no pay," Jimmy said, clicking the button to disable his alarm.

"I am police," the man said, tapping his badge with his pen. "You pay."

"I am United States Army," Jimmy said, pushing past him. "I no pay."

They got in the car and backed out of the spot. The parking attendant hopped out of their way and then made a show of recording the license plate number. Jimmy fish-tailed out of the lot, heading down a driveway with a big *No Salida* sign posted next to it.

"You sure that was a good idea?" Jon asked, looking back through the rear window.

"They're all cops down here," Jimmy explained. "Every stinking taco vendor has some sort of badge. The only thing that matters is if they have a gun. If they've got a gun, then you have to pay." Jimmy went down side streets until he found Dieciseis de Septiembe, the main thoroughfare they'd come in on. "That guy," he said, "didn't have a gun."

CHAPTER NINE

Elderly women in black squatted stoically along the sidewalks with pirated DVDs of recent Hollywood releases. Other vendors pushed dented food carts, trying to attract customers with the ringing of bicycle bells. There was garbage everywhere.

"Third World," Jon said.

"How's that?" Jimmy asked.

"It's amazing how you go from America to...this."

"Makes sense why so many Mexis try to cross the border, huh? El Paso must look like goddamn Beverly Hills from here."

Jon spotted Iraan Sheffield on the sidewalk, hard to miss in a throwback Bo Jackson Raiders jersey.

"I know that guy," Jon said, tapping the car window.

"Who?" Jimmy asked.

"The black guy in the Raiders jersey. Find somewhere to pull over, down that side street there."

"You want to give him a ride?" Jimmy made to honk the horn.

"Don't honk," Jon said. "Just find someplace to park the car where he won't see us when he walks past."

Jimmy checked his watch. "All right, dude, but it's almost two. The shooting is probably going to start any minute." He hung a right at the next corner, but there were no places to park along the curb. Jon craned his neck to see out the back window. Iraan crossed the street and disappeared behind the buildings of the next block.

"Go down and over one more," Jon said.

"Who is this guy?" Jimmy asked.

"Just try to keep up, okay?"

Jimmy cranked the steering wheel to make a left so they were running parallel with Iraan. They got to the next street in time to see him cross.

"Look," Jon said, pointing. "Right behind that truck." Jimmy skidded into the spot.

"Let's go," Jon said, getting out of the car.

Jimmy gaped. "Are you nuts? I can't leave my car here. It'll be stripped clean in five minutes." A group of kids kicking a soccer ball stopped to watch them.

"Okay, you stay with the car and I'll be right back."

"Where are you going?" Jimmy asked.

"I've got to find out what that guy's doing here." Jon looked for a landmark. "If I can't figure out where he's going in fifteen minutes, I'll double back. Give me a half hour."

"This is ridiculous," Jimmy said. "Why don't we just pull up to the guy and ask him?"

"Jimmy, please. Half an hour."

Jimmy exhaled. "Yeah, yeah. Recon. Hurry up and wait. I know the drill. I'll yell really loud when I get carjacked."

Jon took his BlackBerry from his pocket and checked the signal. "I've got reception," he said, surprised.

"Man, the American cell-phone towers are just two miles away." Jimmy rattled off his number so Jon could punch it in.

Jon jogged to the corner in time to see Iraan cross the next intersection. He walked as quickly as he could without running, and by the next block, he was only fifty feet behind the detective. He slowed his pace and stayed at that distance. Sweat soaked through the back of Jon's shirt.

Iraan turned in to a storefront with a faded picture of an owl on the sign above the entrance. The entry was so dark that it looked like someone had just painted the side of the stucco wall black in the shape of a door. It was 95 degrees, and the air scratched as it went into Jon's lungs.

Jon was about to peek into the bar when Iraan stepped onto the sidewalk with a quart bottle of Carta Blanca. He walked a little ways down the street, peering at the curb, until he found his spot. He mouthed a few words to himself before pouring a measure of brew into the street. The detective then looked up into the murky Juarez sky and took a long pull from the bottle. Turning to head back into the bar, he spotted Jon. Iraan squinted as he tried to place him. Jon spun around and headed down the first side street. He ducked into an empty doorway that smelled of rotting meat. He waited for two minutes, but when Iraan didn't follow, Jon cut back to the car.

Jimmy was leaning against the hood of the Mustang with a can of Tecate while a rabble of little kids danced around him. Jimmy hid his face behind his hands and then opened them up and said, "Boo!" The little kids screamed in mock terror and ran away, screaming "¡*Feo!* ¡*Feo!*" Then they came back over and started tugging on his pants leg. There were three empty beer cans under the car.

"At least you ditched me close to a beer store," Jimmy said. "You find the guy?"

"Yeah, he's in a bar a few blocks down."

"Who is he?"

"El Paso P.D. A detective."

Jimmy reached through his open car window and scooped a handful of change from the center console. "Okay, kids, no more play," he said, handing each of the children a few silvers. The kids skipped away, kicking their soggy soccer ball. "So what's he doing down here?" Jimmy asked.

"He's drinking at a bar called El Buho. I think that means 'owl.' He poured some beer on the curb."

"Probably an informant he got whacked." Jimmy drained his Tecate. "Can we get out of here now? It's two-thirty. Traffic on the bridge is gonna be murder."

A white-and-green transit police car turned onto the street and slowed as it passed them. The cops inside looked them over.

"Definitely time to get out of here." Jimmy handed the keys to Jon. "You haven't been drinking."

They were getting into the Mustang when the police car pulled a U-turn and parked behind them with its lights flashing. Jimmy waved as he slid into the passengers seat.

"Haul ass," Jimmy said under his breath.

Jon remained standing by the open driver's-side door. "Are you kidding?"

The cops got out of their car and ambled up to the Mustang. They both wore crisply ironed uniforms under bulletproof vests that didn't quite fit.

"*Buenas tardes,*" Jon said, reaching back for his couple years of college Spanish.

The cops nodded. The shorter one with the goatee walked around to check out Jimmy. The other regarded Jon.

"*¿Hablas español?*" the cop asked.

"*Más o menos,*" Jon said.

"*¿Tienes licencía y seguros?*"

Jon pulled his Colorado license from inside his passport and handed it to the officer.

"Jonathon Lennox." He compared Jon's face to the picture on the license and smiled with one corner of his mouth. "*¿Y seguros?*" he asked.

"Jimmy," Jon asked through the window, "you have insurance? I hope."

Jimmy started to get out of the car, but the short cop on his side stopped the door with his battered nightstick, which looked like a cut-down Louisville Slugger. "*Siéntate en el coche,*" he told Jimmy.

Jimmy handed Jon the insurance papers through the driver's-side window. "These guys have guns," he said under his breath.

The cop looked at the insurance. "*Estos no son para manejar en México. Y estos papeles tiene otro nombre: James Gates.*"

"We're fuuuuucked," Jimmy sang.

"*Señor Gates está en el coche,*" Jon said. "*Yo estoy manejando.*"

The cop on Jimmy's side kicked the empty beer cans. "*¿Estás borracho?*"

"*No, señor, mi amigo bebe algunas cervezas, pero yo no.*"

"*Es muy peligroso manejar en esta ciudad sin seguros y en el coche de otro hombre.*" The cop tapped Jon's driver's license on his ticket book, which Jon noted didn't have any citation forms in it.

"We're fuuuuucked," Jimmy repeated in the sing-song voice. "How much money do you have?"

The cop winced. "I do not wants your monies," he said. "I only wants you to be safe driver. You understand?" He returned the license and insurance card to Jon. "If you have accident in Juarez with no having Mexican insurance, is very bad. Much trouble. Next time, you have insurance, okay?" He pulled the little half smile again. "Or maybe better, you no come back to Juarez. *¿Comprende?*"

The cop on Jimmy's side of the car said something in rapid Spanish that Jon didn't pick up. The officer talking to Jon shook his head. The little cop came around the back of the Mustang and jabbed Jon in the ribs with his nightstick. His partner told him to knock it off.

"Have a good day, Mister Lennox. *Ándale, pues.*" The cop nodded to his diminutive partner, and they sauntered back to their car.

"A miracle," Jimmy said when Jon got behind the wheel, rubbing his side where the little cop had poked him. "Now they'll probably shoot us and say we were resisting arrest."

The police car pulled out from behind them and turned onto the main intersection.

"There's one for the books," Jimmy said, cracking a Tecate he'd stashed under the front seat and downing half of it in one long swallow.

"How do I get to that industrial park?" Jon asked.

"Fuck the industrial park!" Jimmy sputtered. "Our luck has run out for the day. Point this bird back to the L.Z."

"You serious?" Jon asked, maneuvering around an ancient yellow school bus filled with factory workers. "That one guy was reasonable."

"*Reasonable*?" Jimmy gulped his Tecate. "Maybe you didn't hear that last part when he told you to basically get the fuck out of Juarez. At the very least, we should have had to pay them. They work it so they start to write a ticket and then tell you that you can just settle up with them right there for whatever you've got in your wallet, which always just happens to be the amount of the fine. That cop must've had a brother in Colorado or something, because the short stack wanted to beat your ass. I'm telling you, we pushed it far enough today. Make a left here."

They took a corkscrew exit off the main drag and the road narrowed into a three-lane, one-way cobblestone street lined on both sides with bars, liquor stores and piñata shops. Traffic was bumper-to-bumper, inching forward a couple feet every minute. They could see the hump of the bridge in the distance.

"Shit," Jimmy said, looking at his watch. "This could take a while."

Little kids wove through the creeping traffic, displaying their wares—Chiclets, woven bracelets, cigarettes. Two boys ferried snow cones out to the cars from a wagon parked on the curb.

"This is about as far as most of the Joes got," Jimmy

said. "The C.O. at Bliss wouldn't let them drive across, so they'd park their cars on the other side and walk over." Jimmy pointed to a bar. "There's the Kentucky Club, where most of us used to go. That or the Cave. Try to pick up on the high school chicks from El Paso. Hey, I'm going to pop into the Kentucky to see if there's anyone there, then grab a couple bottles. You mind holding down the vehicle?"

Jon told him to go ahead.

Jimmy limped through the bumpers to the other side of the street. It looked like they were going to be stuck in traffic for at least a half hour before they even made it to the checkpoint on the Mexican side. Jon looked straight ahead in an attempt to ignore the children hawking candy apples and lottery tickets. For something to do he pulled out his BlackBerry and checked messages. There were two from Cheryl and another message from Mom, both of them suggesting that he get back to Colorado, post-haste. The last message was from Dr. Ghausi.

"Jonathan," Dr. Ghausi said in his best talk-you-off-the-ledge voice. Even after twenty years in the States, the doctor still had a thick Persian accent. "I'm calling to see how you're coping with this, the loss of your brother. I understand your desire—your feelings of obligation—to search for him. I think that's a good thing. Highly com-mendable. We all wish we had a brother who would go to such ends for us. But in this case, Jonathan, I'm wondering if this action of yours is really about your brother? Now, I'm not suggesting that there is not a sincere operational base at work here—a true urgent desire to help your brother in his time of need. But talking to your mother and your wife, I think we all wonder if this might be a way for you to act out. An excuse to let out some of the emotions you try so hard to repress. I can't help but think—"

Jon pressed seven to erase the rest of the message and shut off the phone. A moppet wearing a Boston Celtics shirt and an Astros hat that covered his ears stood next to the car, staring at him. Jon rolled down the window.

"*Quiero una bebida fría,*" he said.

The kid regarded him for a long moment. "Two dollars," the kid said in good English.

"*Uno* dollar."

"One dollar for *la bebida*, one dollar *para el servicio.*"

"No," Jon said and started to roll the window up.

"Good deal," the kid said. "Super price for my super friend."

"*Quiero una* Diet Dr Pepper."

"*¿Mande?*"

"Okay, Diet Coke. *¿Me entiendes?* Diet Coke. No *regular.*"

"*Okay, magüey.*" The kid stuck his hand through the window. Jon handed him a dollar.

The kid held up two fingers.

"*Uno ahora,*" Jon said. "*Uno cuando regresas con el Coke, el Diet Coke. El Diet Coke frío.*"

The kid took the dollar and one last look at Jon before dashing through the gridlock. Jon inched the Mustang closer to the checkpoint. He was a couple blocks past the Kentucky Club and still no sign of Jimmy. There was very little honking, all the drivers seemingly resigned to the drill.

Just when Jon was about to take the dollar loss, the kid tapped on the window. He was holding a can of Coke. Regular Coke.

"I said Diet."

"*No hay. Pero es muy frío, sí?*"

The can was ten-minutes-out-of-the-fridge cold. Jon handed the kid the other dollar, and he stuffed the bill into the pocket of his greasy shorts. "You want smoke?" he asked. "You want chronic green bud?"

Jon laughed. "This close to the checkpoint and you're trying to sell me weed? This is great. I'll bet you get a kickback from the cop who busts me."

"*¿Sí?*"

"*No. No, gracias.*"

"Is no problem," the kid said. "I tell you which place to drive. The police no problem. Is very easy. No problem, my friend. Twenty dollar." He unclipped a cell phone from the waistband of his shorts. "I call for you."

"*No gracias, amigo.*"

Jon rolled the Mustang a few more feet toward the bridge. The little hustler walked alongside the car until he spotted another mark down the line. He spat on the front tire of the Mustang before running off. "Cheeeken!" he called over his shoulder.

Jon was two spots from the first checkpoint when Jimmy climbed into the car with a plastic shopping bag, sweating profusely.

"I'm telling you," he said, mopping his brow, "the only good thing about this shithole is the cheap booze. Sorry to leave you like that, but I can't sit in traffic jams. The Kentucky Club, by the way, is closed until further notice. Which means that it'll reopen when the gunfire stops."

"I thought the traffic in Denver was terrible," Jon said. "But up there at least you don't have to deal with the little kids giving you the business."

"What's that?"

"Just some kid," Jon said.

"I hate this part," Jimmy said.

"You got somewhere to be?"

"I just can't sit in a car that's not moving. I get freaked out some Haji is gonna launch an RPG through the windshield. You stop rolling for a second over there and you're Spam in a can."

"In Iraq?'

"We used to drive on the sidewalk, across the median, through somebody's fucking front yard kebab cookout. Anything to keep moving."

They pulled up to the guardhouse on the Mexican side. Jon rolled down his window and tried to show his passport. The bored guard pointed to the tin sign on the wall of his hut. BRIDGE TOLL $1.60.

Traffic was just as snarled on the bridge, with all the vehicles inching along and trying to jockey over a lane. Occasionally, a car would whoosh past in the walled-off right-hand DCL lane, provoking the same envy that you get seeing a stateside vehicle work the carpool lane to skate past a traffic accident. Jimmy started fiddling with the radio and tapping the dashboard. He kept looking in the side mirror and flinched each time a kid passed with a selection of DVDs fanned out like playing cards. Jimmy rifled through the glove box.

"Damn," he said, "I threw that cough syrup away before we crossed." He pulled a bottle of Crown from the shopping bag and took a long pull. He wiped the back of his hand across his mouth. "Remind me to never do this again, okay? Next time we fucking walk to the liquor store. In America." The end of the bridge channeled all the cars into one lane before it fanned out into a dozen queues leading to the American checkpoints.

"Over to the far left," Jimmy said, pointing to the last guardhouse, where the line was shorter.

Jon cut in front of a van, drawing a barrage of honks. Jimmy stopped sweating a little when he could finally see the U.S. checkpoint, but it still took half an hour to get to the front of the line. Before approaching the guardhouse, they had to stop in a waiting area where several cameras in hooded steel boxes pointed at the car—one aimed at the license plate, another at the passenger, and another at the side of car. The light turned green, and Jon pulled up to the guardhouse.

"Afternoon," Jon said.

The American Customs officer ducked to look at Jimmy. He furrowed his brow.

"Nationality?" the officer asked.

"American," Jon said.

"U.S.!" Jimmy barked.

"Passports."

Jon handed them over.

"How long have you been in Mexico?" the agent asked.

"Just a couple hours," Jon said.

"We went over to buy liquor," Jimmy added.

The guard took another look at Jimmy.

"You all right, sir?"

"Hooah."

The guard went into his booth to swipe the passports. He stared at the computer screen for a moment before stepping outside to return their documents and wave them through. "Register your liquor at the inspection office."

Just past the checkpoint, there were several waist-high concrete barriers set up to form a series of tight switch-backs that forced vehicles to slow down. As soon as they were out of the chicane, Jimmy leaned back in the seat and took several deep breaths. The car was filled with the acrid smell of flop sweat.

"You okay?" Jon asked

Jimmy closed his eyes.

Jon slowed down at the tax board trailer.

"Forget it. Take me back to the Vag."

"But don't we need to get the tax stamps for the liquor?"

"I said forget it. I'll pay the fine if they catch us. I need my cough syrup."

They stopped by the motel to pick up liquid codeine, and then Jimmy insisted they go to Erin's for drinks. Erin's is a Joe bar that's not much more than a warehouse with a couple of pool tables and a back patio that looks like an oversized tool shed, sans roof. It was four o'clock, and the bar was filled with officers getting off for the day. The day-to-day military is like a construction gig in that they get to work early and knock off early. Some Joes head straight to the bar after leaving base, and they can work up a fierce head of steam by the time the regular citizens arrive for happy hour. There are a lot of holes in the walls at Erin's.

The cry of "Six to Ten!" went up when Jimmy walked in. A group of officers stood along the rail with a pyramid of empty shot glasses in front of them, still wearing their camo pants and gray, sweat-stained Army T-shirts. Jon moved to the end of the bar as Jimmy slapped backs. The guys were celebrating a promotion. The bar was mercifully dark and cool, and Merle Haggard played on the jukebox. Jon overheard Jimmy relating their adventure in Juarez. A few minutes later, Jimmy came down to the end of the bar and took the stool next to Jon.

"I told those guys you were NSA," Jimmy said. "Said you were using the Vag as a safehouse. The Vag is strictly hard-core."

Jon offered half a smile.

Jimmy chucked him on the shoulder. "What's the matter, man? We hit the fucking lotto today, getting let off by those *federales*. By all accounts, we should be in the stockade right now, pissing blood."

"I'm just tired."

"It's big, isn't it?"

"What?"

"J-town," Jimmy said. "Two million people with no pattern whatsoever."

"Yeah?" Jon asked.

"It's gonna be awful hard to find your brother in that mess."

Jimmy blinked, again looking like it was something that took effort. "You can't give up. If you give up, you'll never forget it. Believe me." Jimmy rejoined the officers and they did a round of shots. The jukebox started skipping.

"Goddammit Skeeter!" Jimmy yelled at the bartender. "I thought you got that fixed."

"I called the frickin' service guy yesterday," the skinny, mop-haired bartender said. "He said he'd be out."

"Give me those pliers," Jimmy said.

"Six to Ten!" one of the officers yelled. "Hooah!"

Jimmy unplugged the jukebox, and the bartender helped him drag it away from the wall. Jimmy opened the back panel and went to work. Jon made a trip to the bathroom. There were three condom machines installed on the wall—all of them dented from punches. On his way back to the bar, one of the officers congratulated him on his luck in Mexico.

"Shitfire," the officer said in an Alabama twang, "If I was a Mex cop, I'd take one gander at Six to Ten and toss him in the darkest cell I had. Guy looks like a homo-cidal maniac." He took a swallow of beer. "Check that, he *is* a maniac." They looked over at Jimmy examining the guts of the juke.

"Why do you call him Six to Ten?" Jon asked.

The officer laughed. "We got it figured that between six and ten drinks, Major Gates over there is a goddamn genius. But get him before he's had six or after he's past ten, and he's worthless as tits on a boar. I'd say by the way he's going at that juke that he's right in the hot zone at the moment. Eight drinks." The officer finished his beer and took on a more serious tone. "But let me tell y'all something, Gates was one of the brightest officers we had in this Army. You know he graduated West Point at the top of his class?"

Jon shook his head.

"How the hell would you, way his shit's all over the place now? But I'll be damned if he didn't. They had him working on target acquisition lasers. Serious work. He was attached to a missile defense unit in Kuwait during the first Gulf War. Tell you what, they made those Patriot missiles sound like the best invention since debutante pussy, but those things were so cock-eyed that they were just as likely to bake cookies as knock down a Scud. Old Six to Ten there, fresh out of the Point and green as hell, was running from battery to battery un-fucking them all day and night. He was the only guy who knew how to fix the sons-a-bitches. Shoulda got a medal. But that would have meant that some general would've had to admit they were fucked in the first place, right?" The officer called for another beer. "Six to Ten was good Army."

"Why'd he quit?" Jon asked.

The officer gave Jon a serious look. "Quit? Gates didn't quit. The Major got hit."

— ◂—

Erin's was packed by seven o'clock, and Jimmy was definitely in the post-ten zone and showing no inclination toward going back to the Vagabond. He'd occasionally check on Jon at the end of the bar and try to feed him booze, but he was mostly absorbed by his former Army comrades. Jon could have easily walked back to the motel; instead, he nursed his Diet Coke and watched the crowd, which included a handful of valiant females. The Army fellows were so tight by the time the fairer sex arrived that Jon was privy to some horrendous pick-up lines.

"How you like your eggs in the morning?" an officer asked a chubby redhead.

"What?" she asked.

"Do you prefer them scrambled or fertilized?"

When the soldiers ran out of things to say to a girl, they had the habit of shouting "Hooah!" at their buddies across the bar, perhaps a signal that even though they might not be getting over with the chicks, they still had their Brotherhood of Man.

A woman took the stool between Jon and one of the officers who had been celebrating since earlier that after-noon. She wore jeans, work boots and a denim shirt tied off at the waist. Her jet-black hair fell to her shoulders, and the fingernails on the small hand peeling the label off her Bud Light were chipped. Jon could smell her perfume just under a soft sweat.

The officer next to her gave her the nice-girl-in-a-place-like-this line, making a deliberate effort not to slur his words.

"I like the company," she replied. "Guys in uniform turn me on."

The officer puffed out his chest.

"Do you drive a tank?" she asked.

"Sure," the officer said. "Abrahams T-39. All the time."

"Tanks get me hot."

Jon watched as she nudged her almost empty bottle of beer to the edge of the bar while the officer rambled on about the lethal merits of the T-39. The officer made a sweeping gesture, and the girl knocked her bottle off the bar. It hit the floor and broke.

"Oh, shit," the officer said. "Did I do that?"

"It's okay," the girl said, staring at the puddle of beer.

"Let me get you another one," the officer said. "God, I'm sorry about that."

The girl got her new beer and began to pick at the corners of the label as the tank commander droned on. Jon saw the man give one of the other Joes a salacious wink like he was getting over. The girl saw the wink, too. When she was almost finished with the beer, she maneuvered the bottle to the edge of the bar again, and when the Army guy tried to slide a little closer to her, she flicked the bottle to the floor.

"Goddamn!" the officer shook his head. "I'm clumsy as hell tonight."

"You sure this isn't just your way of picking up girls?" she asked.

The bartender brought over a new beer, and the girl stood to let him sweep the broken glass.

"Nice little career you've got going," Jon said in a voice that only she could hear.

The girl put her almond-shaped eyes on him as she leaned in close. "I'll screw you, too," she said, "but I'm all booked up until after church on Sunday." She sat back and smiled sweetly.

"Huh," Jon said, nodding his head. "Good one." He finished the last of his Diet Coke and pushed away from the bar. He tapped Jimmy on the shoulder as he made his way out. Jimmy was measuring a shot at the pool table. He'd been lining up for about thirty seconds. Jimmy blinked.

"I'm heading back," Jon said.

"What?" Jimmy asked.

"I'll see you later."

"Oh, sure." Jimmy's bridge hand slipped off the side of the pool table and he knocked his forehead against the edge of the table before hitting the floor. The guys whooped as they helped him back to his feet.

━ ━

Jon picked his way from strip mall parking lot to parking lot, hopping over the low concrete abutments that separated them. There were stretches between buildings where he had to walk on the dirt shoulder of the road as the sidewalks in El Paso have a tendency to end abruptly. He was halfway home when a Jetta drove past and hit the brakes. The car made a U-turn and pulled into the lot next to Jon. The driver rolled down the window.

"You lost?" the bottle-dropping woman from the bar asked.

"You might say that," Jon said.

"You too drunk to drive?"

"I thought I'd stretch my legs, but it's like an obstacle course out here."

The girl laughed. "Where you headed?"

"The Vagabond."

The woman looked at him for a moment. "The

Vagabond Motel? On Mesa?" Her English was perfect, but she pronounced the word "Mesa" with a definite Spanish accent.

"That's the spot," Jon replied.

"You want a ride?"

Jon got in the Jetta, and the woman chirped the tires.

"They sure as hell don't make it easy to get around here," Jon commented.

"Yeah, they sort of forgot to finish the sidewalks, didn't they?" she said. "You been in El Paso long?" she asked.

"Almost a week."

"You notice the signs? The neon signs?"

"What about them?"

"They're worse than the sidewalks. Almost every one of them is missing a letter. Look at that one." She pointed to a Denny's restaurant. The second light behind the red "n" was blacked out.

"That's not neon," Jon said.

"Ugh. Okay, how about that one?" She indicated an Albertsons grocery store missing the "t" and the "n."

"That's not unusual," Jon said.

"Oh, yes it is," the woman said. "I'll bet you my car that there are more broken neon signs here than any other place in the country."

"I'll take your word for it," Jon said.

"It's like that guy who discovered the germ," she said. "What was that guy's name? French dude."

"Pasteur," Jon said. "Louis Pasteur."

The girl smiled. "Right. It's like as soon as you start looking for something, you see it everywhere. And now that I've noticed this crazy neon thing, it's obsessive. I drive around and get pissed off at the owners for not fixing them. Look!" she pointed at a Gold's Gym sign missing the first letter. "'olds Gym.' What kind of business is that?"

"I'm right there," Jon said.

The woman turned into the Vagabond parking lot.

"I can't believe you're staying here," she said.

"It's different."

"Different like skid row." She reappraised Jon. "You look a little old and dignified for this."

"It's a long story," Jon said.

"You're not some kind of hush-hush Army guy, are you?" she asked. "No," she added quickly, "you don't have the look. Really, I'm fascinated. You want to get another drink and you can tell me all about the secret mission you're on?"

"How about a rain check?" Jon said. "It's been a long day, and I'm kind of worn out." He looked at the motel. "Besides, all the guys are at the bars right now, so if I'm lucky, I can get a couple hours of sleep before they get back and turn the place upside down."

"My name's Sway," she said, extending her hand.

Jon raised an eyebrow.

"Short for Consuelo," she explained.

"Jon." He shook her hand. "Thanks for the ride."

Sway rolled her window down. "Fridays they have a good happy hour at G2 on Cincinnati Street. I break a lot of bottles."

Jon smiled. "I'm sure you do."

Jon stood in the parking lot as she backed into the street and tore off down Mesa. He scanned the signs along the street in her wake. She was right about the signs; every marquee was missing at least one letter.

CHAPTER TEN

The offices of Bowden-Everitt were located in a low-slung steel-and-glass building on the west side of town. A well-watered lawn surrounded the building, a barrier of green trying to hold off the scorched brown scrub brush beyond the parking lot. Even at 5:30 on a Friday afternoon, the lot was filled exclusively with late-model American SUVs or luxury sedans. Old Boy Bowden insisted not only that his employees stick it out until six on Fridays, but also that they buy American; penance I suppose for the company's specialty of exporting American jobs. The company's biggest deal, for example, had been the relocation to Mexico of the factory that manufactured the dashboards and interior panels for Chevy Suburbans. These same Suburbans were then regularly stolen in Texas, driven back into Juarez and stripped by the Mexicans. The unemployed auto workers in Michigan would call that justice.

The truth of the matter is that the United States instigated the southerly flow of manufacturing—and the corresponding reverse flow of drugs—a long time before Bowden-Everitt opened shop. Sending all our boys off to fight World War II left huge swaths of agricultural land unattended, especially in the West. To keep the crops from rotting in the field, the U.S. government got together with Mexico to set up what they called the Bracero

Program, which allowed Mexican workers to legally enter the United States to fill the void in the workforce. They shut the program down and deported the Mexican workers when the G.I.s got back. This stranded a huge labor pool in northern Mexico without anything to do until some genius came up with the idea of having American companies open factories just across the border to take advantage of these displaced workers. The deal was sweetened with tax breaks. Zenith opened the first major *maquiladora* in Juarez in the late '60s, and pretty soon Mexico became as popular with American manufacturers as it is with college Spring Breakers today: it's close to home and, more important, cheap. Foreign companies operating in Mexico only have to pay "value-added" tariffs, which means that if they bring $100,000 of raw material to their factories in Juarez and the finished product is worth $200,000, they only have to pay tax on the difference. If you're assembling your vehicles in Flint, Michigan, you have to pay tax on both the materials and the finished product. You combine that tax break with the dirt-cheap Mexican labor and it's no wonder Detroit has become an industrial wasteland.

When NAFTA passed in 1994, it really opened the floodgates. Not only did it kick up *maquiladora* production by almost 20 percent, but the constant back-and-forth flow of raw products and consumer materials across the border made huge drug shipments a hell of a lot easier to conceal. NAFTA hubs like Juarez, Reynosa and Laredo soon became just as valuable to the cartels as they were to the manufacturers. The resulting spike in gang violence was a natural consequence and makes the use of "cartels" to describe the *narcos* today a joke. A cartel, by definition, is a business that involves actual cooperation among producers and distributors; the Mexican border has turned into open warfare.

Bowden's secretary, Carol, had Jon wait in the foyer for the old boy to finish up a conference call. The office walls had pictures of Bowden posed with the usual Texas luminaries: former presidents of both the United States and Mexico, Dallas Cowboys, Tommy Lee Jones. A dozen brokers operated out of the office, and they were tucked inside their cubicles, working the phones. Bowden-Everitt had a similar office in Juarez, staffed almost exclusively by Mexicans. The company made deals in teams: One American, one Mexican. The American makes the executives from Ohio feel comfortable while the Mexican cuts through all the bullshit with the landlords on the other side.

Bowden kept the office like an icebox so his brokers had to wear their sport coats at their desks to ward off the chill, and then they had to cross the parking lot to their cars as quickly as possible to avoid heatstroke. Bowden, of course, had his Caddy parked a couple feet from the door and all the spots around it "reserved" for clients.

Max Bowden strode toward Jon shaking his head in a manner he must've thought portrayed his sincere regrets for the calamity that had befallen Jon's family. Instead, it looked like he was trying to clear his head after taking a blindside hit. Bowden had played football at West Point and kept his 6'4" frame in good shape aside from the obligatory West Texas Beer Gut. He wore a nicely tailored tan suit, silver bolo tie and cowboy boots, but somehow he made the country-Western outfit seem as starched and formal as a full military uniform. The whole office had that sort of regimental vibe, almost barracks-like.

Jon put down the *Field & Stream* he'd been reading and stood to shake hands with Bowden. The old boy was a real believer in putting the hurt on people with that handshake. He'd let his hair go silver, but other than that, he looked younger than his sixty years.

"Sir," Bowden said, taking Jon's hand in both of his, politico style, "we're all real sorry to hear about your brother. Come on into my office." Bowden set Jon down in a chair and then scooted his own high-backed, padded leather swivel around so the desk wasn't between them. An inscribed photo of George W. Bush hung prominently on the wall.

"Can I get you anything to drink?" Bowden asked. "A bottle of water? Coke-Cola?" Bowden smiled. "Cold beer?"

"I'll take a Diet Dr Pepper," Jon said.

"Diet Dr Pepper…" Bowden mused. "Well, sir, let's see if we've got any of that around here. Carol!" he shouted through the open door. "We got any Diet Dee Pee in the icebox out there?"

Carol peered around the corner. "What?"

"Diet goddurn Dr Pepper," Bowden barked. "Christopher's brother is thirsty as hell in here."

"I don't think we even have any regular Dr Pepper," Carol said.

"Well, then get down to the store and pick some up, for chrissakes!"

"That's all right," Jon said. "I'll take a bottle of water."

"I apologize about that, sir," Bowden said, his leather chair creaking like a saddle as he leaned back.

"Jon, please."

"Sure."

The whole "sir" thing is a Texas colloquialism, and it doesn't mean much as far as respect goes. The old boys call everyone "sir", and depending on their inflection, they can make it sound like "piece of shit."

"Now, are you Christopher's older or younger brother?" Bowden asked.

"Older."

"You ever come down to visit before?"

"I wouldn't really consider this a visit."

"It's a goddamn shame about your brother," Bowden said. Carol came in with the bottle of water and made a soft clucking noise in agreement. "I'll tell you what, though, we've got every man working on it. The entire staff is down there asking questions, and I guaran-god-damn-tee you that we'll find something before the police do. I don't know if Christopher told you about this, but we've got a lot of men here who were in the Army—like me—and we don't take kindly to losing one of our own."

"You make it sound like a war," Jon said.

"Just look out that window, sir." Bowden's office had a view of a vast expanse of undeveloped scrub brush to the south. In the distance, especially at night, you could see the slum suburbs of Juarez across the no-man's land. "We got two million Messicans two miles from here living like it's the goddamn Wild West. You been over there?"

Jon nodded.

"You see downtown?"

Jon nodded again.

"It's a Third World country. Now, did you get over to the east side? The industrial zone?"

"I was meaning to," Jon said.

"Well, go take a look at that, sir. Fantastic. Paved streets, streetlights that work, no garbage all over the place. Commercial activity going full tilt."

"So what happened?"

"Well," Bowden ever so slowly rolled his chair back behind his desk. "We don't know anything for sure. He was headed over to Omega complex when we lost him."

"What was he supposed to be doing?" Jon asked.

Bowden waved his hand as if a fly was buzzing him. "Standard B.O.V. Taking a look at a facility to see if it'd work out for one of our clients. But the reality of it is that he probably never made it there before they carjacked him."

"Carjacked?"

"Sure, them Messicans held him up for his vehicle."

"So they killed him for his car?"

Bowden pulled a sad face. "I'm sad to say it happens too much."

"You don't think there's any other explanation? I mean, if they shot him for his car, where's his body?"

"Son," Bowden lowered his voice, "the fact that we can't give Christopher a proper burial is a disgrace." Bowden smacked his fist on the desk. "And I'm not going to let up the heat on the Messican officials over there until we get some action on their part to help…um, recover the body. Your brother's body. I've got a lot of important contacts over there, but not even they can keep the *federales* focused. They got this goddamn 'Single Window' thing going on down there ever since Peña Nieto got elected, so everything we pick up on our side has to go through one goddamn Mexican with a fax machine down in Dee Effay."

"Pardon me?"

"The Mexican capital, son. The District-o Federal. Mexico City. So now that they got themselves a couple scalps doing it that way, they think they invented criminal justice.

"It's a goddamn travesty, son. And I hate to say it, but I feel personally responsible. I know how dangerous it is for our boys over there. But dammit, that's part of the business. I wouldn't send any of my boys over there if I wasn't willing to do it myself."

"You don't think my brother was involved in drugs?"

Bowden set his hands flat on the desk and leaned forward. "Pardon me, son?"

"Well, the way I understand it is that he may have been caught up in some sort of drug business."

Bowden stared hard at Jon, then spoke in a lower voice. "Son, this is your brother you're talking about."

"The way I hear it is that when the cartels kill somebody, they take the body with them. Like a trophy. That was how it was described to me."

"By who?"

"By the people I've been talking to."

"You've been talking to the wrong folks." Bowden looked at his watch. "Son, I'm ten minutes late for a meeting I was supposed to be at an hour ago." He stood up. Jon finished his water and set the bottle on

Bowden's desk. Bowden looked at the offending piece of trash on his mahogany as he grabbed his Stetson off the hat rack.

"I'm real sorry about your brother," Bowden said, crushing Jon's hand. "Now, y'all be careful. Like I said, it's the goddamn Wild West out here. You give us a call if there's anything we can do for you. In the meantime, we'll keep tickling them wires." Bowden released Jon's hand and ushered him into the foyer. "You know how to get back to town?" he asked.

"I'll call a cab."

"That's fine." Bowden clamped on his hat and pushed through the glass doors.

"What about birds?" Jon asked.

Bowden paused in the doorway, looking up as if he could see his paid-for cold air rushing out of the building like $20 bills. "Pardon me?"

"I found a bunch of bird cages in my brother's storage."

"Son, I've got no idea about any of that personal stuff." He let the doors swing shut behind him.

Jon stood in the foyer, flexing his hand. He went back to Carol's desk.

"Could you call me a cab?" he asked.

"Sure, honey." She dialed. "We're all real sorry about Chris," she said while on hold with the cab company. "He was the nicest young man, and a real hard worker. He went over to Mexico almost every day. I bet you miss him something awful."

—◄ ►—

The taxi exited the I-10 at the Sun Bowl, the University of Texas El Paso's football stadium. The college is derogatorily referred to by some locals as "Taco Tech" because of the predominance of Mexican nationals going to school there. UTEP is in fact the only public university in Texas where students qualify for in-state tuition if they're from the neighboring Mexican state of Chihuahua, which pissed off the anti-immigration folks something fierce. The cab driver cruised over to Cincinnati Street, the one-block drag that passes for hip in El Paso. The cluster of bars on Cincy attracts young NAFTA executive types and rich Mexican kids. Despite the poor reputation El Paso has for being a dustbowl, there's quite a bit of money in town, and it's never more obvious than in the parking lots along Cincinnati Street on a Friday or Saturday night. Mercedes, BMW and Range Rover are all represented, and there are even a few Ferraris and Aston Martins thrown in for variety. Although it isn't hard to guess where the money for most of these whips originated, there are a few legitimate fortunes in town that sprang from real estate and manufacturing; the company that makes Brut cologne has its headquarters on the west side of town. If you drive through the Coronado Country Club or up along Rim Road and see all the mansions, you might even be fooled into thinking you're in Newport Beach, California—except, of course, for the fact that almost everyone is Hispanic.

As the violence across the border has intensified, more and more wealthy Mexican families have relocated to the safe side of the border. Even though the cartels aren't above coming across to snatch someone who's done them wrong, for the most part El Paso is a sort of sanctuary. Going to the shopping mall now, you see just as many Chihuahua license plates as you do ones from Texas, and if you want to work retail in the Dillard's, you'd better be able to speak Spanish because the *fronchis* (from the combination of *Frontera* and *Chihuahua*) bring their money with them and like to throw it around. Stories circulate all the time about folks showing up at local banks with suitcases full of currency, looking to open an account. When questioned by bank authorities as to the provenance of a duffle bag containing $350,000 of well-worn $20s, one Hispanic gentleman claimed that he'd been working in his backyard and dug up the loot by accident. That caper didn't work out so well, but El Paso still has one of the highest reported records of cash transactions in the nation. The majority of the cities rounding out that cash-money list also have predominantly Spanish populations.

The Mexican kids—"Juniors," they're called—who congregate on Cincinnati Street or downtown in the warehouse district with their tight Ed Hardy T-shirts and distressed denim have become a real nuisance. They're all about 5'8" and mope around the clubs alternately scowling at their Christina Aguilera-looking girlfriends or checking their iPhones, thinking they've made it to Miami Beach. Still, they're easier to take on the U.S. side than they'd been back when Juarez was swinging. J-Town had some very nice restaurants and clubs, but when the *narcos* really started going at it, you were taking a serious risk being there after dark. It wasn't that you were going to be singled out for violence because you were American; it was more that the gangsters doing the drive-bys hadn't quite figured out the trigger control on their AK–47s. When they busted into a nightclub and started spraying bullets, you were truly *en los manos de Dios*. Still, the one thing the Mexican city does still have in much larger quantities than El Paso (aside from drugs, murder and general mayhem) is beautiful women. These chicks with their tight jeans tucked into their tall boots will knock your socks off, but as soon as you're able to get a little rap going, some *fronchi* Junior will sidle up and pretend he has a .45 tucked into his waistband. Seventeen percent of the time, he does, which is pretty awful odds if you consider it.

Jon spotted the G2 and told the driver to let him out. The G2 is the hippest of the Cincinnati Street clubs; all of its blue neon lights are usually operational, it plays trance music that's less than six months old, and the cocktail waitresses wear black. The place was packed with the after-work crowd, but Jon found himself a single barstool and confounded the bartender with his usual request for Diet DP. He got a DC instead and was taking his first sip when he heard the sound of a bottle breaking. Sway smiled at Jon across the bar as a young guy in a suit apologized and motioned for another beer from the bartender. A few minutes later, Sway worked her way over. Jon let her have his barstool.

"¿*Qué Pasó?*" Sway asked.

"Stopped in for a drink on my way home."

"You sure that's it?"

Jon leaned over to speak into her ear. "Don't break any bottles on me, okay?"

"I only did that to get your attention."

"I thought it was about the free beer."

"I have a job."

"Breaking bottles?"

"You meeting someone?" she asked.

"I doubt it."

"I don't get it."

"For a pretty girl, you're quite forward."

"It's a small town," she said. "A girl's gotta take her shot when she spots some new blood."

"I still don't see how breaking bottles fits into that."

"That's about the free beer. You want an ice cream?"

"I'm married," Jon said, showing her his ring finger.

"What does that have to do with ice cream?"

They backed away from the bar and wove their way outside. Sway drove them to the Baskin-Robbins on Mesa next to a shuttered Blockbuster video store. As they approached the door, Jon noticed a black guy wearing a Chicago Bulls shortset leaning against the stucco wall next to an outline of a payphone that had once been installed there.

"I'll meet you inside," Jon told Sway.

"You really having a ball down here, ain't you?" Iraan said when Jon got up to him. "Got yourself a Messican girlfriend and everything."

"Working hard tonight?" Jon asked.

"Oh, yeah."

"I saw you in Juarez yesterday," Jon said.

"Boy, that was top-notch surveillance work you was pulling." A beat-up Toyota pulled into the lot filled with four white kids in their early twenties. Iraan watched the car as he continued talking to Jon. "Ducking into doorways like a real pro. Maybe we ought to sign you up for the Academy. We need more white police down here, 'specially ones that know how to tail as good as you. You'd be chief of police in two years. Hold up a sec."

Iraan pimp-rolled over to the Toyota, holding his baggy shorts up with his left hand, as the driver lowered his window. Iraan leaned into the car and made an exchange. As he walked back to Jon, he muttered something into the collar of his basketball jersey. As soon as the Toyota pulled out of the lot, two police cars lit it up with their flashers. A cop on a mountain bike appeared from behind the ice cream store and pedaled up to Iraan. Iraan handed him a wad of crumpled bills.

"Forty," he said.

The bike cop looked at Jon. Iraan shook his head. The cop rode to the other officers, who were giving the kids in the Toyota the full treatment.

Sway came out of the store with three ice cream cones.

"You," she said to Jon, "seem like a French vanilla. And you," she said to Iraan, "look like a sherbet." She handed over the cones, keeping a mint chocolate chip for herself.

"Appreciate ya," Iraan said, taking a lick.

"You're welcome, officer."

"Detective," Jon corrected.

"You sure you're not a cop?" she asked Jon.

"Oh," Iraan said, "I can say for sure that this dude ain't police."

"Then what is he?" she asked.

"I'll let you know when I find out," Iraan said.

"My ice cream is melting," Sway said. "I'm going inside."

They watched Sway push open the door.

"You something else, man," Iraan said, shaking his bald head.

"How's that?" Jon asked, trying to keep the ice cream from dripping onto his hand.

"You're supposed to be down here on a manhunt for your brother and instead you running around with a fine piece of J.Lo-lookin' ass like that. You a real fucking hero, man."

Jon threw his cone into the trash can. "I see you're putting a serious dent in the drug trade tonight."

Iraan laughed. "You love to flip it on a brother, don'tcha?"

"I think you got a major problem off the streets just now. Kudos to you and the entire force. Five cops, probably all pulling overtime, to bust four college kids for an eighth of weed. Really top-notch."

Iraan crunched the last bite of his cone. The police handcuffed one of the kids and stuffed him into the back of a squad car. A tow truck materialized to put the hooks on the Toyota. The bike cop cruised past them.

"You gonna make another call?" the bike cop asked. Iraan nodded.

"Grab your girl and get on out of my way," Iraan said.

"Oh, yeah, I forgot I was standing in the middle of a major operation here. Wouldn't want to get caught in the crossfire. The next bunch might be looking for NoDoz." Jon started inside.

Iraan spat on the curb. "You're a fucking phony," he said.

Jon turned around.

"Yeah, you heard me right. You probably just down here making sure your brother *is* dead so you can collect the life insurance." Iraan smiled, showing his gold fronts. "That's it, ain't it? You just down here for a body. You get the body and then you get paid."

Jon took a step toward the detective. Jon stood 6'1" and weighed about 190 pounds, but the shorter detective didn't look the slightest bit nervous.

"Oooh," Iraan said, "you gonna bring it now? You stupid hick. We got five police right here, and you gonna take a pussy-ass swing at me?"

Sway rushed out of the store to step between Jon and Iraan.

"Guys," she said.

"How 'bout this, homeboy?" Iraan said over the top of Sway's head. "I get off here in an hour. You still want a piece, you meet me over at Hemingway's." He looked at Sway. "You know that spot, right?"

"You boys are ridiculous," Sway said.

"Have J.Lo drop you at Hemingway's and then we can sort this out real quick. What you say to that, whiteboy?"

"Who the fuck are you calling J.Lo?" Sway asked over her shoulder as she pushed Jon toward her car.

Iraan leaned back against the wall and laughed.

"Go home, boy," he called after Jon, pulling out his cell phone and scrolling through his numbers. "You'll get your money eventually."

"What the hell was that all about?" Sway asked.

Jon didn't reply.

"I really know how to pick the weird ones," Sway muttered.

"Take me to Hemingway's," Jon said.

Sway stopped at a red light. "You've got to be kidding."

Jon opened the door.

"Wait." Sway grabbed his arm. "I'll take you to the place. Just tell me what this is all about, okay? Is that fair?"

"I'll tell you when we get there."

＊ ＊ ＊

Murals of Papa had been painted on the walls of the bar, depicting the man in the various stages of his life. The artist showed the aging process by adding facial hair to his basic picture of Hemingway—first clean-shaven, then the mustache, then the big white beard—and changing the scenic background from Paris to Spain to Havana and finally Key West. Idaho, Papa's last stop, was not portrayed.

The crowd on Cincinnati had swelled since they'd left the G2. Cigarette-smoking kids now spilling onto the sidewalks outside the bars, but Hemingway's was only half full of middle-aged men in sport shirts. Sway led Jon to a small table in the back by the dartboards and asked him what he wanted to drink.

"Diet Dr Pepper," he said. "And a double shot of tequila."

Sway came back with the drinks, and Jon offed the tequila in one gulp. His gullet worked like he was going to spit it up, but he managed to keep it down. He chased with the soda and made another face.

"No DP," Sway explained. "Not diet, anyway. Why is your favorite drink the hardest one to find?" Sway laughed. "I guess I just answered that for myself." She took a pull off her beer. "Okay," she said. "Spill."

"One more drink."

"Not if you're going to get drunk and try to fight that cop. He'll kick your ass."

"Relax—the cop's not going to show." Jon pulled a twenty from his wallet. "And a beer, too."

"Okay," Sway said, "but you look like you're about to puke already."

Sway returned with two more shots and a pair of Tecates, and this time she knocked back a tequila with Jon. Five minutes later, Jon was shaking his head and grabbing the table like the room was tilting.

"You don't drink much, do you?" she asked.

Jon burped. "Alcohol doesn't agree with me."

"That's an understatement. So, you're really down here to find your brother's body?"

Jon pushed himself up in his chair and blinked a couple times. People have always been surprised by how quickly booze makes it from my brother's stomach to his brain. "So, okay, my brother. Chris. Christopher. Total fuckup, okay? Comes down here to get away from the family, right? Takes this job selling factories in Mexico. Mom's freaking out. She only gets to see him at Christmas. I don't think it's a big deal. Dad never says anything about it. Dad never really says anything anyway. More of a fax/email man, if you know what I mean. Great legal mind, zero people skills."

"Your brother," Sway reminded.

"Right, right." Jon took a sip of beer. "So a week and a half ago—make it twelve days—Chris is over in Juarez taking pictures or something for work. Bam!" Jon clapped his hands. "Gone. Cops can't find his car, can't find his body. No ransom note, nothing. Cops tell my folks that all they can do is wait, see if something turns up. Mom blames it all on Chris not going to law school. I went to law school. Law school is the key. Gotta know the law."

"That's awful," Sway said. "So you decided to come down here and find out what happened?"

"Do I have to have a reason for everything?" he asked.

"It's just a question."

Jon tried to focus on the wall murals. "I'm getting another drink."

Sway held Jon by his arm. "I think you've had enough," she said. "Finish your beer."

Jon shook her off. "I'm sick of everyone telling me what I've had enough of!" He upended his chair and stumbled to the bar. When he got back, he put his head down on the sticky table. Sway rubbed the back of his neck.

"You're a serious lightweight," she said.

"That's what Dr. Ghausi says. He says that I'm down here because it provides an emotional release."

"I said lightweight, not emotional release. You need emotional release from what?"

Jon didn't reply, and Sway thought he might've passed out.

"I'm a lawyer," Jon said, his head still on the table.

"You told me that. What kind of lawyer are you?"

"I drive a Mercedes."

Sway spoke like she was talking to a small child. "I'm sure it's a very nice Mercedes."

"I hate that fucking car."

"I'm sure. A Benz can be such a pain."

"You wouldn't understand." Jon closed his eyes. "You sound funny."

"What?"

"Your accent," Jon mumbled. "It's like you're speaking Spanish, but in English."

Sway laughed. "You think I'm bad, you should hear my cousin. She and I go *completamente pocha* when we get together. Nobody can figure out which one of us is talking or what the hell we're saying."

Jon took a couple of deep breaths and passed out.

"Looks like Cinderfella turned into a pumpkin early."

Sway looked up to see Iraan walking over with a Styrofoam take-out container. He pulled up a chair and opened his box of hot wings. "I thought the cracker might crumble, so I brought dinner. What happened to him?"

"Why don't you take your fake Bulls jersey and chicken wings and get out of here?"

"Whoa, this jersey is NBA-authenticated," Iraan said. He pulled the collar around to show her the hologram tag. "I ain't trying to buy none of that knock-off shit they selling at the bridge."

"Great," Sway said. "Take your ugly NBA *authentic* jersey and your dinner and get lost."

"Sheeeet," Iraan said. "Homeboy over there was the one who called me out. What's his story? He passed out?" Iraan took his gold fronts out and put them in a small case.

"Nice girl like yourself don't need to be running around with a fruitcake like this."

"Those things come out?" Sway asked, nodding at the case.

Iraan looked at her for a moment, then pushed the take-out container across the table. "*¿Pollo?*"

Sway shoved the wings back to the cop. "His brother disappeared on the other side," Sway said. "He's down here looking for him."

Iraan wiped his fingers on a wad of napkins. "I know the part about his brother going missing. I read that report. The thing I don't know about is this guy here actually looking for him. It seems to me like he's down here on a lark."

"Why do you say that?" Sway asked.

"Baby, I've been a detective for a lot of years—"

"Could've fooled me."

Iraan laughed. "So maybe I'm not at the top of my game right now, but I've been on the job for a lot of years, and I've worked my share of missing-persons cases. This guy doesn't fit the profile of the grieved relative. Usually they're all up at the police station, camped out like little Billy is gonna pop out of the Coke machine or something. Or if they're not pressing us at the station, they're out on the street putting up a million fliers. Offering rewards, shit like that. This dude," Iraan pointed a stripped drumstick at what was left of Jon, "ain't doing none of that. He's just walking around looking lost, talking smack and hanging out with you."

"What's he *supposed* to do?" Sway asked. "It sounds like every person he talks to tells him to forget it and go home. Should he go over to Juarez and start asking people on the street if they've seen his brother? I mean, really, what are you cops doing about it? All those women. Hundreds of little girls raped and murdered not two miles from here, and you're hanging around the Baskin-Robbins busting college kids? Give me a break." Sway put her hand on the back of Jon's neck.

Iraan closed his take-out box and carefully wiped his fingers. He picked up Jon's almost full Tecate and took a drink. "First of all," he said, "don't assume you know anything about my current situation, okay? You feel me?"

Sway didn't say anything.

"Now, as far as your boy goes, I honestly can't figure out what he's up to. Dude was following *me* down in J-town the other day. I'll agree with you that the authorities here aren't very helpful when it comes to this kind of thing. But I've seen a lot of folks who've lost people, and this guy just doesn't feel right to me. Is he really passed out?"

Sway leaned down to look at Jon's face pressed against the table. His eyes were still closed.

"I think so," she said. "He did a couple shots of tequila, and I don't think he drinks."

"Okay, I don't have any idea who the hell you are or why you've taken such a shine to this clown, but I looked at his brother's file. He worked for this real estate company—"

"He told me that."

"Yeah, well, I ain't saying this guy's brother was into some mischief, but given the fact that we haven't found a body, I'm thinking he got caught up in some business he shouldn't have been in. The kind of biz that gets you dumped in a 55-gallon oil drum with a dose of milk and then dropped along the side of *el camino numero dos* outside of Juarez."

"Dose of milk?" Sway asked.

"That's what they call quicklime," Iraan said. "To keep the smell down. But these *narcos*... hell, you're from here. You know what I'm talking about. For the most part, they don't go around knocking American biz-types. More biz means more traffic, more cover for them to get their product in. Last thing they need is a crackdown. And if it was a kidnapping, we'd have heard about a ransom."

Sway took a sip of beer. "You don't think he's trying to figure anything out?"

"I don't know. That junk I said about him just being down here for the insurance money, I was pulling that to get a reaction. But dude didn't say shit; he just looked like he wanted to knock me on my ass. Didn't try to justify. But I don't know...he seems a little cool about the whole thing, right?"

Sway considered that for a moment. "You could say that."

Iraan smiled. "He make a try for the cookie jar yet?"

"None of your business."

"I guess that's a no."

They regarded Jon.

"Well," Iraan said, putting his gold fronts back in, "it doesn't look like the Great White Hope is gonna get in the ring tonight. You know where he lives?"

They grabbed Jon under the arms and dragged him

out the back door of Hemingway's. Jon regained consciousness in the parking lot.

"That cop ever show?" he slurred.

"Yeah," Sway said.

"Did I kick his ass?"

They pushed Jon into the backseat of Sway's Jetta.

CHAPTER ELEVEN

Iraan and Sway hoisted Jon out of the car and lugged him up the Vagabond Motel stairs.

"Why in the world is he living in this shitbox?" Iraan asked. "Dude looks like he's got a couple bucks in his pocket."

"Something about his wife," Sway said.

"Screwing a married man, huh?"

"*Cállate.*"

Jon was trying to walk, but he was like a puppet controlled by a drunk puppeteer. His head hung loose on his neck.

"Which room is yours?" Sway asked.

"Two-fourteen," he mumbled.

Sway fished through his pockets for the key. She let Iraan support Jon while she unlocked the door. Just as the door swung open, Jimmy popped out of his apartment wearing yellow dish gloves, brandishing what looked like a large Super Soaker squirt gun. Iraan dropped Jon and went for the pistol in his waistband. Jimmy pulled the trigger and there was a sound like a clock spring snapping. Two small darts popped from the barrel of Jimmy's gun and hit the detective in the torso. Thin wires connected the prongs to the gun. Iraan went down in a heap next to Jon. Jimmy's gun then shorted out in an audible crackle of electricity. Jimmy's eyes rolled back in his head and his knees buckled. Sway screamed. The lights along the hallway flickered once and went out. The smell of singed hair filled the corridor.

A pair of Joes appeared at the end of the walkway, one of them the redhead who had helped Jimmy fix the pool filter.

"What the hell's going on?!" the redhead hollered, shining a flashlight down the corridor. "What did you do to the major?"

"What major?" Sway asked.

The redhead checked Jimmy's pulse. "Major Gates? Can you hear me?" The redhead looked up at Sway. "Did he just fire this weapon?"

"Weapon?" Sway asked.

"The stun gun, this thing."

"He shot the cop."

"Which one is the cop?" the other Joe asked. "The black guy or the drunk guy?"

"The black guy."

The redhead checked Iraan's pulse. "He's alive." He lifted Iraan's basketball jersey to reveal the gun and badge clipped to his shorts. "And he's a cop."

Jon made a slow crawl into his room.

"For Christ's sake," Sway said. "Help me get these guys inside."

They dragged Jimmy and Iraan into the apartment.

"Should we call the police?" the redhead asked.

"An ambulance?" the other Joe suggested.

"Are these guys going to be okay?" Sway asked the redhead.

"I think so."

"You *think?*"

"Well, yeah. They just got the bejeezus shocked out of them, but they'll come around pretty soon. They have strong pulses. I can't believe Six to Ten actually used that thing."

Sway told them to get the lights back on.

Iraan and Jimmy were both stirring when the current started running again.

"You sure you're okay?" the redhead asked, poking his head into the room.

"Go!" Sway said.

Iraan came to with a start, popped up to his knees and pulled his gun.

"Hold on!" Sway yelled.

Iraan laid his Glock on the floor and took several deep breaths. "What happened?"

"This guy stun-gunned you," Sway explained.

Jimmy lifted his head from the carpet. He blinked twice. "What happened?"

"You just assaulted a cop, asshole," Iraan growled.

"Who's a cop?" Jimmy asked.

"This guy is wasted," Sway said. "Are you okay, Iraan?"

"Goddamn, that hurts," Iraan said, getting to his feet. "I feel pins and needles all over."

Jon made it to the bathroom and vomited.

"What the hell's going on?" Jimmy asked, still lying on the floor.

"We brought him home," Sway explained.

"Who?"

"Jon, you idiot," Sway said. "What was that thing?"

"What thing?" Jimmy asked, standing unsteadily.

"That laser gun you shot the detective with."

"Who's the detective?" Jimmy asked.

"Right here," Iraan said, peering down the front of his jersey to see where the darts had stuck him. "Man, you put holes in my Derrick Rose."

Jon emerged from the bathroom with a wet towel wrapped around his head.

"I thought you were rolling him," Jimmy explained as he peeled off the dish gloves. "A Mexican chick and a gangster drag my passed-out ass home, I hope somebody does something about it." He examined his arms. "Shit, I fried all the hair off my forearms. You got anything to drink?"

"Diet Dr Pepper," Jon croaked.

"I'm going to get a drink." Jimmy staggered to the door.

"Hold on," Iraan said. He turned to Jon. "Who is this dude?"

"My neighbor. Jimmy, meet Detective Sheffield. Detective Sheffield, Major Gates."

"Lie down," Sway said. "You're sick."

"Let me see that thing," Iraan said, following Jimmy out of the apartment.

The door to Jimmy's place was still open and the stun gun lay in the entryway, an extension cord connecting the gun to a blackened wall socket. The plastic gun was partly melted.

"Damn," Jimmy said. "I was afraid that might happen."

"That was more than 110 volts," Iraan said.

"Yeah," Jimmy said. "There's this generator thingy in here that pumps the voltage up to 220. Pretty good jolt, huh?"

"Knocked my ass out," Iraan said. "What you got to drink?"

—◄—

An hour later, Jon lay on his rump-sprung bed with a Ziploc full of ice pressed to his forehead. Jimmy and Iraan sat at the dinette, halfway through a bottle of Crown. Sway sprawled on the floor with a pillow.

"They're all after what they call 'The Plaza,'" Iraan explained. "It's not like some shopping center or shit like that, but the corridor they run all the drugs through, the clearinghouse. They've got similar deals in Tijuana, Nuevo Laredo, on down to Reynosa. But because of how central Juarez is along the border, it's always been the prime spot for the *narcos*. Plus, you've got a serious amount of legitimate traffic coming through here to cover the shipments."

"But it hasn't always been this terrible," Sway said. "In high school, we went over to Juarez every weekend. Nobody was freaked out then. We still used to go over for dinner last year."

"How about drink 'n' drowns?" Jon asked.

Sway looked puzzled. "How do you know about that?"

"I have sources."

"The Juarez boys and Beltran Leyva had it locked tight," Iraan continued. "The problem now is that nobody's in control. From a law-enforcement standpoint, you don't necessarily want these guys organized, but if you're looking at keeping the violence on the down low, it's a good thing to have one main shot-caller. As it is now, you've got the two big cartels and then these Army dudes shooting it out. And *Presidente* Peña Nieto deciding not to look the other way like Fox and Calderón did makes it even worse."

"Satellites," Jimmy said. He was several drinks past ten.

"What?" Sway asked.

"Satellites," Jimmy repeated.

"This guy," Iraan said, jerking his thumb at Jimmy.

Jimmy blinked twice.

"Isn't there anything you guys can do?" Sway asked Iraan.

"About the *narcos*? Yeah, we could get all the dot. commers in California to stop paying $80 a gram for their blow."

"Not that. I'm talking about his brother."

"Listen, beyond putting out bulletins and letting our friends across the border know that we've lost this guy, no. Like I said the first day, a missing-persons case is tough anywhere."

"Okay, great," Jon muttered. "Since it's a hopeless case, you can all go home."

"But for the sake of argument," Sway said, ignoring Jon, "isn't there somebody you know who could find out for sure what happened?"

"Well, if we're talking hypothetically, I'd say look for the man who knows what's going on in Juarez."

Jon adjusted the ice bag. "And who's that?"

"Chuy Lazaro," Iraan said. "I mean, what the hell? If you're gonna start knocking on doors, might as well start with the penthouse, right?"

"I thought you said there wasn't anybody running the show."

"He's the guy who's got the most turf," Iraan said, pouring himself another drink. "As of this week, that is. He's the *jefe* of the Juarez gang. Might as well tickle his wires to start with."

Jon closed his eyes for a minute to fight off a wave of nausea. "What does 'tickle the wires' mean?"

"It means you start monitoring their phones and e-mails," Iraan explained. "Where'd you hear that?"

"I think my boss's brother said something about it."

"You mean your brother's boss," Sway corrected. "You're still drunk. My cousin runs around with one of his guys."

"Whose guys?" the detective asked.

"Lazaro's."

Iraan put down his drink. "Bullshit."

"It's not like it's something to be proud of," Sway muttered.

"Has she actually met him?" Iraan asked. "Lazaro?"

"To tell the truth," Sway said, "I think I saw him at El Babylon once."

"Oh, now I know you're lying. You saw him at the hostess club?"

Sway shrugged. "That's where my cousin works. But you know how it is: Everybody's seen him and then nobody's seen him. But he might've been in there one night, because my cousin's boyfriend was scared to death. He used to box. Real tough guy, likes to knock people out. He's usually a total *super-chulo*, but that night this guy came in and Lalo looked like he was going to piss himself. The creep came by the table, but I can't say I'd recognize him again if I saw him. I was kinda drunk."

"You don't know what Lazaro looks like?" Jon asked.

"No," Iraan said. "Not even the guys over at EPIC have a picture they're sure of."

"EPIC?"

"El Paso Intelligence Center," Jimmy said. "Satellites."

"This guy must've been hell on wheels in the Army," Iraan said. "What were you, a general?"

"Hooah."

"Gives you faith in the military, doesn't it?" Sway said.

"Hooah." Jimmy put his head down on the table.

"Fuckin' A, bubba." Iraan patted Jimmy's shoulder. "Anyway, EPIC is the DEA's op center outside of town. They run all sorts of intel through there. DMV, Customs, FBI, Interpol. Access to everything. If you get pulled over for running a red light in Seattle, most likely your info goes from the cop car on the side of the road down here for processing then back up north. They probably know where you had lunch yesterday. But my guy over there admits that they don't even have a clear description of Lazaro." Iraan took a drink. "And since we're all telling tales out of school tonight, supposedly Lazaro built one of his mansions across the river so that when the DEA guys go out to their cars in the EPIC parking lot, they're able to see it."

"'Fuck you,' huh?" Sway said.

Iraan nodded. "I think that sums it up."

"Wait a minute," Jon said. "You know where this guy lives and you still can't catch him?"

"I don't work for DEA."

"But they do?"

Iraan swirled his Scotch. "Well, it's not that…well… yeah, basically."

"Ridiculous," Jon said.

"Look," Iraan said, "you don't know what you're talking about. This guy is *the guy*, get it? He supposedly got the president elected last time around. I mean, literally paid for the Mexican presidency. And even though the motherfucker has killed more people than cigarettes, the locals love his ass. You can't get close to him without setting off his whole network. El Paso has a rich history of this kinda nonsense. Take Pancho Villa. Homeboy used to kick it here back in the day, and there were plenty of cats—on both sides of the river—who wanted his ass dead. But they never got him. Not here, anyway. Dude used to take his old lady out to get ice cream right in plain day. Everyone knew where he was, but they never touched him."

"That was a hundred years ago," Jon pointed out.

"I kind of remember him being a slob," Sway said.

"Pancho Villa?" Jon asked.

"Lazaro," Iraan said. "Some say he's a fat guy. Then you hear he's this real handsome cat with class who has plastic surgery every five years to change his look. I've heard so many descriptions, it's unreal. I know a couple guys who'd call it a career if they were just able to get one clean look at the dude."

Something heavy was tossed into the pool, and they turned to the window.

"Those Army boys really get after it, don't they?" Iraan said. "Okay, here's a story you'll like. A few years back, just for laughs Lazaro decides to go along on a run on our side. Somebody sells that to the DEA, so the feds track the truck to this warehouse, and they get confirmation that Lazaro is inside. They get their perimeter all set up, but have to wait because the honchos need to chopper in to get a piece of the credit. Classic DEA caper. So they're out there in the dark, waiting to raid this warehouse, and this little guy comes out and gets into a station wagon and drives away. They jump the car as soon as it's down the road and the *bracero* driving confirms that there's a bunch of *narcos* in the warehouse. He's just the janitor, so they kicked him out because there was some important shit going down. So the feds let him drive off in his junker station wagon, and ten minutes later, they come down on the warehouse and bust in on a hundred tons of coke. They line all the guys up and start sorting them out, asking where Lazaro is."

"And he's the guy who just drove off in the station wagon," Sway said.

Iraan tapped his nose. "Some dudes took early retirement on that one."

"So how do you propose to find him?" Jon asked.

Iraan shot Jon a look. "I didn't propose anything of the kind."

"But if you wanted to get ahold of him?"

"Call 411 and ask for his number. I mean, you've got a thousand federal agents over here who can't figure that part out. You'd be better off asking homegirl's cousin."

Sway sighed. "Second cousin. And I don't even know if she's dating that punk anymore."

"Forget that," Iraan said. "You're not going to go over there and have a stripper introduce you to Lazaro."

"Hostess!" Sway corrected.

"Why not?" Jon asked.

Iraan pondered that for a moment. "Shit, maybe it could be that simple. But I'd bet you'd get your ass shot off if you even went over there and said his name out loud."

"And Qui-Qui is scared to death of him," Sway added. "Like Iraan said, she doesn't even use his name."

Iraan looked at his watch. "Look, kids, I got to get up in the morning. It's been real. It's been fun. It's been real fun. Thank the General for the Scotch when he comes to."

"That's it?" Jon asked.

"I thought you wanted me to get lost?" Iraan made his way to the door.

"Since I'm already down here and all, I figure I might as well act useful."

"I think you better ask yourself if this is really something you want to get into before you start going around asking any more questions. I mean, coming in to fuck with me is one thing…"

"Humor me," Jon said.

Iraan scratched his head. "This isn't a can of worms I'm particularly interested in opening up again."

Jon lifted the ice bag. "Again?"

"I'll think about it. Meanwhile, why don't you stop wandering around like Mr. Magoo? Go play golf or something."

"I don't play golf."

Iraan paused to look around the apartment. "You're some piece of work, man." He closed the door behind him.

Sway rolled onto her stomach and pushed herself off the floor. "I've got to be at work in five hours."

"You really work for the phone company?"

"Yeah."

"In the office?"

"I'm in the field. I climb the poles, got the truck with the lights and everything. Well," she said, stretching and showing her flat brown belly, "it's been an interesting night." She nodded at Jimmy. "You gonna be able to deal with him?"

"I'll be fine."

Sway checked her hair in the mirror and saw the picture Jon had pulled from the storage shed. She un-wedged it from the corner of the frame to examine it more closely.

"I assume this is your brother in the middle," she said. Jon nodded.

"He's pretty cute. Who are the guys he's with?"

"I don't know. Mexicans?"

Sway rolled her eyes. "I can see that. They look like *narcos*."

"How can you tell?"

"Check out the pointy cowboy boots." Sway put the picture back. "So," she said, "what are you going to do now? Hunt down Lazaro and find out what happened to your brother?"

Jon shrugged. "I paid a full week's rent."

"Has anyone ever told you that you're a weirdo?"

"You're the one who picked me up."

She smiled. "Yeah, but that was when I thought you were just a secret agent. *Buenas noches.*"

Jon dumped the remnants of his ice bag into the sink. He checked to make sure Jimmy was still breathing before turning out the light and lying back down on the sagging bed.

CHAPTER TWELVE

Jimmy was gone when Jon woke up late the next morning, head jack-hammering from his tequila hangover. After a long shower in the tiny bathroom stall with the thin linoleum floor that felt like it was about to cave in, he checked his messages. Cheryl was on there again, predicting dire consequences should he not return, posthaste, as was Mom, unable to mask the fact that she was under a handful of Valium, courtesy of Dr. Ghausi. Jon pulled the drapes to see 90 degrees and the sun riding high. It was only nine o'clock.

"Fuck it," he said, letting go of the drapes.

He called a taxi and packed his garment bag.

The taxi driver raised his eyes to the rearview mirror when Jon slipped in the back seat.

"Airport."

The driver nodded.

Jon paid the fare with most of his remaining cash and then checked in for a Frontier flight to Denver leaving in two hours. He charged the $800 last-minute ticket on his corporate AmEx card. The airport teemed with uniformed soldiers—both inbound and out—duffel bags over their shoulders and cammies tucked into their desert boots. After passing through the security corral where two Border Patrol agents lazily scanned the files of passengers,

Jon proceeded to the gate to find it packed. There was a bar across the way, so he took a stool.

"What'll it be, hon?" the bartender asked, dealing a cocktail napkin. Her ponderous breasts rested on the edge of the bar.

"Diet Dr Pepper?"

"Sorry, babe. We got Diet Coke."

"That'll do."

Jon typed a message to Cheryl on his BlackBerry. *Arrive DIA 4:40pm. Frontier #625. Pick me up?*

"You want to start a tab?" the barkeep asked as she set Jon's drink down.

"I'll pay you."

Jon flipped the check over and reached into his pocket for change. He pulled out his room key for the Vagabond along with a few quarters. He'd forgotten to drop the key before getting in the taxi.

"You have any Advil?" Jon asked when the bartender collected his money.

"Sorry, hon. Gift shop is right down the hall."

Two men in jeans and matching company polo shirts took the bar stools next to Jon. They ordered beers and took the bartender up on her offer of three-dollar side shots. The one sitting next to Jon had a shaved head and a goatee and the other wore glasses and a short beard. They both looked to be about forty.

"Here's to getting out of this hellhole," the one in the beard said, raising his shooter.

"Fuckin' A," the other replied. He had a dense East Coast accent.

They knocked back their shots and called for two more.

The one with the shaved head turned to Jon. "You coming or going, bud?"

"Going."

"Going is the only way. Ain't that right, Tommy?"

"Right-o."

"You want a drink, bud? Celebrate getting the hell outta here?"

"Thanks, but no. I'm feeling a little under the weather."

"Irish flu?" he asked.

"Pardon?"

"Hangover," the one named Tommy explained.

"You could say that."

"Thank God for booze. Name's Jason." The guy with the shaved head extended his hand. Jon shook it. "And this piece a work is my man Tom. You been down here for business?"

"Not really."

"Count your blessings for that, bud. Me and Tommy been working over Juarez past two months. What a fuckin' nightmare."

"I hear."

"Yeah, lemme tell ya. It's worse than anything I ever seen. And me an' Tommy seen some shit. Ain't that right, Tommy?"

"Right-o," the one named Tommy said.

"We been setting up a production facility for Mitsubishi. Makin' wind blades. Supposed to be Japs doing the job, but they got a guy snatched six months ago and now none a the Japs will come over, so we gotta set the whole thing up for them. Ain't that right, Tommy? Japs got wise?"

"Smarter than us," Tommy said.

"And that's not sayin' much."

"You've been living in Juarez?" Jon asked.

Jason recoiled. "Hell, no!"

"Red Roof Inn," Tommy said after taking a slurp of beer.

"Yeah," Jason continued. "We catch a van every morning right there at the Santa Teresa bridge and it takes us to the shop. Might as well have 'Kidnap Us' written on the side of the goddamn thing. Put in our twelve hours, catch the fuckin' van back to the border. I don't think we even set foot in Juarez. Bridge, factory, bridge."

"Red Roof, Chili's, Village Inn," Tommy added.

"Yeah, Jesus, one more fajita plate at Chili's and I'm gonna kill myself."

"Sounds rough," Jon said, pushing his empty glass across the bar for a refill.

"And it doesn't inspire a lotta confidence when you show up to the shop the first day and instead of showing you around the floor, they take you right to the fuckin' panic room. Explain to you how all that works." Jason laughed at the memory. "Tommy and me are looking at each other, like, c'mon? We got 200,000 square feet of shop to work, how you suppose the both of us gonna be able to get to the panic room when the bad guys bust in? Remember that first day, Tommy?"

"I do."

"Say by the love of Jesus the both of us lock ourselves

in the panic room? Then what? The cops gonna come save us? Probably the cops holding the joint up! I'm telling ya, this is the most fucked-up place we ever worked. But does that stop me from havin' my old lady come down for a couple days?"

"Oh, buddy," Tommy laughed.

"True story," Jason said, twirling his finger for the bartender to set them up with another round. "My old lady comes down here from Providence—Rhode Island, right?—and I don't know what the hell the dizzy broad is thinkin' 'cause she says she wants to get her hair done. Are you kiddin' me? You come all the way down here for the weekend and you wanna get your hair done? You been going to the same hairdresser for fifteen fuckin' years and now, first time in El Paso, you wanna get your hair cut? But what the hell? I'm so happy not to haveta look at Tommy's ugly mug every morning that I'm like, okay, babe, whatever. So my old lady finds this hair salon—I dunno, she looks it up in the Yellow Pages or on Yelp or somethin'—and she heads over there one day while I'm in Juarez. True story. So she's in there getting her hair done or whatever, and there's some fancy lady in the chair next to her going off about the drug cartels and all that shit. Yap, yap, yap, these guys are ruining the city, they should all be shot, they're a disgrace to Mexicans. So she's going off for ten, fifteen minutes, and then all the sudden this guy over the other side of the salon, he gets up outta his chair—got the fuckin' sheet or whatever they call it still snapped around his neck—and he comes over to this fancy lady and pulls a fuckin' gun. I swear to God, this is a true story. I mean, my wife is five feet away from this, okay? So the guy with the gun points it not at the lady who's talking all this shit, *but at the poor fuckin' hairdresser who's doing her hair.* And he goes, 'Shave it.' Swear on my mother's grave. He says, 'Shave it.' So, I mean, what's the hairdresser supposed to do? Guy's got a fuckin' nine-milly pointed at her head. She whips out the clippers and shaves the lady's fuckin' head. Bald. Guy puts his gun away, takes off the sheet or whatever they put around you when you're getting a haircut, and walks out the fuckin' door. Next day, where am I, Tommy?"

"Airport."

"Fuckin' A. The old lady is done with El Paso forever. True story. I mean, my old lady flaps her gums as much as the next, but on this one she's dead serious. I mean, she's scared out of her fuckin' mind."

Tommy nodded. "I heard it right from the horse's mouth."

"Who you calling a horse?"

"I see certain equine similarities."

"Ah, fuck you. What time is it?" Jason asked.

Tommy looked at his watch. "Finish this drink."

"Sure as hell don't want to miss this flight, know what I mean? Anyway, so after all that goes down, I not only gotta deal with going into Juarez every day—I mean, we want this job done, right? We're in there Sundays— thinking I'm gonna end up with a sack over my head, but I got the old lady callin' every half hour to see if I'm still a free man. You're taking those calls every thirty minutes, you start wishing they would come and get you just so's you don't have to talk on the phone anymore. The wife, God bless her heart, she just don't have any idea what it takes. Thinks a magic rabbit fills the bank account up every two weeks."

Jason and Tommy finished off their drinks.

"All right, bud," Jason said, standing. "It's been good talking to ya. You have a safe flight home, okay?"

Jon shook hands with the men and watched them gather their carry-ons and walk out of the bar. The bartender took away their glasses and wiped down the bar. She caught Jon's eye and shook her head.

Jon checked his BlackBerry and saw a text message from Cheryl. *Take a cab.*

Jon went to the gate to see about his flight. The board above the check-in counter showed a half-hour delay. The agent standing behind the desk asked if there was anything she could do for him.

Jon considered the boarding pass in his hand before stepping up to the counter.

"Is this ticket refundable?"

———

When the taxi dropped Jon off at the Vagabond, Sway was standing next to a parked Southwestern Bell utility truck. The rig was loaded down with ladders and coils of heavy cable. She had been writing a note.

"You're keeping the taxi company in business," Sway said by way of greeting. "Why don't you rent a car?"

"Finances."

"Exactly. A rental would be cheaper."

"I wasn't planning on staying this long." The cab

driver handed Jon a credit card slip. "You weren't kidding about the truck," Jon said.

"Lunch?" Sway asked.

"Let me put my bag away."

His room was in the same shambles it had been when he'd left; the empty bottle of Crown and dirty glasses on the dinette, vomit crust on the toilet seat and the bedsheets in a massive twist. Jon optimistically hung the placard for the maid to make up the room even though he had yet to see a housekeeping cart during his stay.

Sway reached across the console to unlock the passenger door of the utility truck. "Were you at the airport?"

"Kind of."

Sway shook her head.

"Where are we going?" Jon asked.

"There's this new seafood place I want to try out."

"Seafood?"

"*Cállate.*" Sway moved a stack of paperwork to the floor to make room for Jon.

"If I tell you to duck," she said as they turned into traffic, "duck."

Jon gave her a puzzled look.

"Supervisor," Sway explained. "I'm not supposed to give rides to anyone."

Jon shuffled through the bank cards in his wallet. "Can we stop at an ATM?" he asked.

Sway told him there was a Wells Fargo on the way.

"No can do," Jon said. "How about Bank of the West?"

"What's the matter with Wells?" Sway asked, looking over. "You've got a card right there."

"It's not working."

"Overdrawn?'

"You might say that."

Sway let out a long sigh as she made a U-turn. "You're really a pain in the ass."

"If you truly have to know," Jon said, "I can't use the Wells Fargo because it's a joint account."

"I see. So this Bank of the West is your little slush fund?"

"You could call it that."

"Why didn't you say so in the first place?"

El Pescador was located in the corner of a shopping mall just off the I-10 on the east side of town, its exterior festooned with thick ropes and nautical knickknacks that were supposed to be brass but were actually painted plaster of paris. Twenty people waited outside on the patio, and the parking lot was full.

"You sure about this place?" Jon asked. "Looks like a crowd scene."

"We get real excited about anything new," Sway said. "And with all these Juarez joints opening up on this side, you gotta hit them quick."

"Before they go out of business?"

"Before this goddamn war ends," Sway corrected. "The restaurants can't stay open in Juarez because nobody goes out at night anymore, so they're closing down and setting up shop here. We got the Cristomo burritos, Maria Chuchena's, Aroma—"

Jon peered through the windshield at the restaurant marquee. "El Pescador."

"When the *narcos* get their act together, we're going to have to start going back to Mexico for this."

"Imagine."

"Hey, man, I don't know what it's like in Wyoming, but it's kind of nice to be able to get a good meal without crossing an international border."

She parked in a red zone and grabbed two orange safety cones from the back of the truck. She handed one to Jon. "Put this by the front bumper."

"You're gonna leave this right here?"

"Why not?"

Sway was dressed in jeans, a denim shirt with her company's logo stitched on the pocket, and work boots. She had her hair pulled back into a ponytail, highlighting her high cheekbones. She grabbed Jon's hand and led him through the crowd outside the restaurant. Two teenage hostesses were decked out in sailor hats and capris. They handed Sway a beeper, and she and Jon went back to the patio to sit in a corner of shade on the fake pier.

"No wonder you phone company people are always running late," Jon said.

"Hey, this is a special occasion. I usually eat in the truck."

Jon watched as a mall guard in a golf cart cruised past the phone truck in the no-parking zone. "You can really just dump that thing anywhere, huh?"

"You ever seen a phone company truck with a ticket on the windshield? As far as parking is concerned, it's better than a cop car or an ambulance. If I didn't have to take it back to the yard every night, I'd drive that thing everywhere."

"This is ridiculous," Jon said, nodding at the crowd. "This place is a glorified Long John Silver's."

"Don't be such an elitist," Sway said.

"Your pager is buzzing."

They put in their order with the waiter and sat through a few moments of silence as Sway mixed six packets of sugar into her iced tea. The waiter returned with watery chowder and crackers.

"So what's the special occasion?" Jon asked.

"I talked to my cousin this morning."

Jon gave her a blank look.

Sway leaned toward him. "The one who dates that boxer."

"The guy who works for Lazaro?"

Sway grabbed his wrist and hissed, "Keep your voice down."

Jon started to laugh, but remembered the story from the factory workers at the airport bar that morning. He scanned the faces of the diners around them, seeing admins, nurses in hospital scrubs and mothers with children. "So," Jon said in a low voice, "what did she say?"

"She said she was still with him, but she was being pretty ploy."

"You mean 'coy.'"

"Whatever."

The entrees arrived. Jon looked at his platter of deep-fried fish fingers, two roach-like crawfish, a breaded piece of something and a couple steamed clams. Sway started in on her salad.

"You're not going to eat?" Sway asked.

"I lost my appetite. So, you thinking about tapping your cousin's phone?"

Sway put her fork down.

"You can do that sort of thing, right?"

"You're kidding."

Jon shrugged.

Sway pushed her salad away. "First of all," she said, "I don't think she even has a land line. Second, it would be illegal. Third, you're talking about my frickin' cousin. Fourth—"

"You're the one who brought it up."

"When did I say anything about a phone tap? I can't believe you'd even think that I'd pull a stunt like that. I mean, not even considering what they'd do to me at work if they found out."

"Okay, okay, stop. I'm sorry." Jon looked around for the waiter. He waved for the check. "Let's start over. Why did you call your cousin?"

"You want that boxed up to go?" the waiter asked.

"No," Jon said.

Sway waited until the waiter had cleared their plates. "I called her because I thought you wanted to know about your brother. Iraan's right about you. You don't make any sense. I thought you'd be excited."

"I am excited," Jon protested. "I'm just not sure about what."

"Let's go," Sway said, getting up.

"What about dessert?" Jon asked.

They picked their way through the crowd out to the truck. Sway pulled the cones and they started back to the Vagabond.

"I can't believe you," Sway said.

"I don't understand what I said that was so upsetting. The part about tapping your cousin's phone?"

"You never think about anyone else, do you? I thought that I might be doing you a favor, and then you've got to suggest something stupid like that. I figured maybe the fact that you had a law degree might mean you were smart."

"You ever look up 'Attorney' in the Yellow Pages?" Jon asked. "It's not really an exclusive club."

Sway gripped the steering wheel and didn't look over at him. "This is exactly what I should expect offering to help somebody. It's the same shit over and over. You try to be nice and they walk right over you. And you know what?" She didn't give Jon a chance to answer. "It's my own damn fault every time. I get bored out of my ass and run into some charity case and next thing you know I'm taking out a fucking loan to help them open a pet store. You know why?"

"Maybe it's—"

"*¡Cállate!* It's because it's so much easier to take care of someone else's problems than to figure your own shit out. I know all this, and yet here I am once again fucking up because—"

"Hold on," Jon interrupted. "You opened a pet store?"

Sway stopped the truck at a red light and turned to give Jon such a furious glare that he stopped talking.

They got back to the Vag and Sway didn't turn the engine off.

"Okay, then," Jon said. "I guess I'll see you around." He got out of the truck and climbed the stairs to his room.

A couple minutes later, he heard angry pounding at the door. Sway stood in the walkway, her nostrils flaring.

"I just came up here to tell you to—"

Jon cut her off with a deep kiss. He grabbed her by the shoulders and pulled her into the room.

"—go to hell," Sway finished when they broke the clutch.

Jon kicked the door closed.

—— ——

Sway got out of bed and walked naked to the bathroom.

"This place is a real dump," she said as she ran the sink.

"You mentioned that before," Jon said.

"But, really, what's the point?"

"The point is that my wife canceled my credit cards. I'm working on a limited cash supply." Jon stared at the brown water marks on the ceiling.

Sway came out of the bathroom and stood at the foot of the bed. Rays of sunshine came through the slants of the shades and cut lines across her body. Sway cocked her hip, letting Jon get a good look.

"So?" she said.

"What?"

"Do you feel bad?"

"About what?"

"About committing adultery."

"I hadn't really thought about it."

"You have a picture?"

"Hand me my phone." He started scrolling through photos. "Don't you have to be somewhere?" he asked.

"Trying to get rid of me so soon?" Jon handed her the phone and Sway straddled him. Her breasts rode high on her chest, the rather large nipples still erect. "This one? The *güera?*"

"Cheryl."

"She's pretty."

Jon yawned. "That's the problem."

Sway threw the phone on the bed and leaned down to nibble Jon's earlobe. "One more?" she whispered.

"Not today."

Sway ground her hips into Jon's groin. "C'mon, I gotta go back to work and I'm still horny."

"It'll go away."

"You're such a dick." Sway rolled off the bed and stepped into her panties. "Why is it that I'm always attracted to mean guys?"

"You mentioned something about being bored and pet stores."

"You are the most annoying person in the world, you know that?"

"So let's go back to what you were saying at the restaurant," Jon said, ignoring her comment. "Why'd you call your cousin?"

"I thought," Sway said, running a brush through her hair in front of the mirror, "that I'd see if she was still dating that guy. If she was, then I figured maybe I'd get together with her sometime and see if he's said anything to her that might have anything to do with your brother.

But then you had to go crazy and suggest that I throw a phone tap on her."

Jon's cell phone rang.

"How was it, whiteboy?"

"What?"

"C'mon," Iraan laughed. "You got that Messican chick up there. I'm parked next to her truck."

"Right."

"Who's that?" Sway asked.

"It's Detective Sheffield," Jon said, covering the phone.

"Get your ass dressed," Iraan said. "We got a meeting."

"I need a shower," Jon said.

"Fuck that," Iraan said. "The guy we're meeting will dig it that you smell like pussy."

"I heard that in a movie," Jon said, getting out of bed. "I'll be down in five minutes."

"Roger that."

Sway went to the window and pulled the shades as she buttoned up her denim shirt. She spotted Iraan in the parking lot and shot him the finger. She laced her boots and turned to watch Jon running a wet comb through his hair. He caught her eye in the mirror.

"Has it always been like this for you?" she asked his reflection.

"Like what?" Jon replied.

"People falling all over themselves to help you out?"

Jon slipped into his loafers. "I'd say it's probably been the exact *opposite* of that. But from now on I promise not to jump to any conclusions."

"Is that your way of saying sorry?"

"It's my way of telling you I won't ask you for any money to open a pet store."

"The pet store was actually a pretty solid concept. Unfortunately it was a total gee-pay."

"What's that Spanish for?" Jon asked, opening the door.

"It's English. GIPE: Great Idea, Poor Execution."

CHAPTER THIRTEEN

The main attraction in downtown El Paso used to be the live crocodiles in San Jacinto Plaza, but the city had to shut it down because people kept killing the crocs by feeding them bad flan. A few modern buildings have gone up over the years as the Chamber of Commerce has tried to gentrify the area with the Museum of History and renovations to the Plaza Theater, but downtown is still plagued by high vacancy rates, and window displays in the shops look like they haven't been changed since the 1950s. Foot traffic is comprised of police and lawyers moving between the courthouse and assorted federal buildings, and the gaggle of Mexican nationals walking to the Sun Metro bus terminal by the library. The only businesses that do any kind of consistent trade are the dollar stores set up for these Juarez commuters. There's been a plan in the works for a while to build a new minor-league baseball stadium downtown, and the only remaining hitch seemed to be that in order to accommodate the new ballpark, City Hall would have to be demo'd. It says a lot about the city that many folks don't see why that would be such a problem.

AAA ball would have a hard time eclipsing the last time downtown had any real draw, which was when Pancho Villa slugged it out with General Huerta in the battles for Juarez in 1911 and 1913. Folks watched the

Mexican Revolution from the rooftops. Those were serious ringside seats, because looking into Juarez from downtown El Paso is still like looking over a backyard fence. A bit of elevation must have enhanced the view dramatically.

The Camino Real Hotel retains a bit of its grandeur from when it was constructed in 1912 (perhaps in hopes that Villa's revolutionaries would continue to provide spectator sport for the paying guests), and it continues to represent a hopeful luxury that no one seems willing to take seriously. Despite the Italian marble floors in the lobby and the Tiffany skylights over the hotel's Dome Bar, the Holiday Inn and Doubletree a couple blocks away are always busier. Still, the hotel lounge with its stained-glass, aquarium-like ambience is not too shabby. At night, when the lights are dimmed and the house band is putting out half-assed Sheena Easton hits, the joint can almost pass as elegant.

It was late afternoon when Iraan and Jon arrived, and the Dome Bar was a quarter full, mostly with men in business suits coming over from the convention center for an early pop. Iraan looked like a rapper in his saggy jeans and Washington Nationals jersey. He led Jon to a corner where four chairs had been set up around a low coffee table. A large movie screen hung crookedly from one of the balconies with a faded-out telecast of a golf tournament projected onto it. The cocktail waitress eventually wandered over to them, and by that time Iraan had eaten most of the stale nuts that had been set out on the table. He ordered a Hennessy XO. The waitress asked if they wanted to pay cash or run a tab, and Iraan pointed at Jon. Jon handed over his corporate Amex.

"Like I told you," Iraan said, taking another handful of cashews, "this is gonna get expensive."

"Who are we meeting?" Jon asked.

"A guy I used to work with. You know, word around the campfire is that your boy Lazaro used to own this place."

"I still don't get it," Jon said. "This dude is right on top of you, and you can't touch him."

"Imagine how he feels. The cocksucker."

The waitress returned with the drinks and another bowl of nuts.

"I thought you were going to stay out of this," Jon said.

"Let's just say that you got me thinking about this guy we're going to meet. I figured I might as well hit him up to see what's shaking. Call it networking."

"Who is he?"

"Depends on what day it is," Iraan said. "Technically, he's a *federale*. Federal Security Directorate. Sort of like our FBI. But I heard he switched over to the AFI, which is supposed to be the new incorruptible task force. The Mexicans are like us that way: When something gets too fucked up, they start a new department with a different name and hope it takes. But you never know with these guys. They get paychecks from a lot of different offices."

"And you thought you'd bring me along."

"Keep your ass outta trouble."

Jon pondered that for a moment. "Do birdcages mean anything to you?" he asked.

"Come again?"

"I found a bunch of birdcages when I was looking through my brother's stuff."

"Too bad there wasn't a talking parrot in one of them. We'd have had this deal wrapped up yesterday." Iraan's phone rang and he walked to the other side of the room to take the call. Jon scrolled through his e-mails to see if Cheryl had missed him yet. Nothing.

Iraan was about to sit back down when a portly man in a cowboy get-up trundled across the room, his arms spread for an embrace.

"Keep your mouth shut," Iraan warned Jon. The detective stepped up to give the man a bear hug.

"¡*Ay, papi chulo*!" the man exclaimed. "How are you, my friend? Still wearing these ridiculous sports outfits, I see."

"Look who's talking," Iraan said. "You look like a Puerto Rican Lincoln salesman. Check out all the new bling."

The man wore a diamond-encrusted Rolex on one wrist and a heavy gold bracelet on the other. A thick crucifix nestled between his flabby pecs, visible because the man had the top three buttons of his snap-button shirt undone. He set his pristine straw cowboy hat on the chair next to Jon and took the other seat without acknowledging him. He then went about unburdening himself of his various cell phones: A BlackBerry, an iPhone, a Motorola Razor and a cheap burner that they sell at Walgreens with pre-paid airtime. The waitress appeared as the man lined the phones up along the edge of the table and silenced the ringers on each one.

"How are you, my little beautiful princess?" he asked, looking up with a smile. He casually patted her on the rump.

The girl laughed as she wiggled out of his reach. "*Ay,* Don Paulino," she said. "A married man going around slapping girls on the ass."

"A man may be married and yet still appreciate such beauty as you possess," he said. "I tell you, if that *maricón* boyfriend of yours ever strays, you know that Paulino is here to take care of you."

"I'm sure," she said. "The usual?"

"Of course," he said. "And bring my friend Detective Sheffield another of those awful brandies."

The waitress regarded Iraan. "A detective, huh?"

"Do not be fooled by his garish appearance," Paulino said with a smile. "He is a very high-ranking official. *Muy importante.* If you ever have any legal troubles on this side, this gentleman is the one to talk to."

"Yeah, sweet pea," Iraan said, showing his gold fronts, "and for anything else, too."

"I'm sure," she said, uncharmed.

"Please walk very slowly so we might appreciate the sublime beauty of your movements," Paulino said.

The waitress shot him a smile over her shoulder.

"So," Paulino said, slapping the upholstered armrests of his chair and raising a faint puff of dust. "I was pleased to receive your phone call, my friend."

Iraan picked a piece of nut from between his teeth. "I'm surprised I was able to get ahold of you." He nodded at the array of telecommunications. "You ever have problems keeping those things charged?"

Paulino laughed. "The phone rings enough so that I can hear that they are not making things easy for you on this side."

Iraan shrugged. "You know how it go."

"Your superiors are *hijos de putas*. I have always said this. They make a good detective like yourself into their enemy, for your good works expose their incompetence. It is like this in any profession when those at the top have the sense of goats. But we all have our problems, no? I must work for devils and then go home to deal with the biggest tyrant of all."

Irann smiled. "The old lady still breaking your balls?"

"Breaking?" Paulino said, spreading his legs. "My friend, can you not see that they have already been broken and scrambled? I will survive a hundred gunshot wounds, but it will be an unkind word from my wife that kills me."

The waitress returned with the drinks. Paulino slipped her a folded twenty-dollar bill as she left the table. He raised his glass to Iraan. "To you, my friend. May the bastards never get to our souls."

He and Iraan drank. Paulino had still not given Jon so much as a glance.

Paulino pulled a handkerchief from his pocket and blew his nose before he started asking Iraan questions about the Dallas Cowboys' chances for the upcoming season. They talked football for half an hour, during which time they drank two more cocktails apiece. Jon saw that the Scotch the bartender poured for Paulino was from the top shelf of the circular bar in the center of the room.

After Iraan and Paulino had reached the conclusion that the Cowboys wouldn't win more than five games that season, Paulino leaned back in his plush chair and tilted his head in Jon's direction. Iraan nodded.

"Well, my friend," Paulino said. "I do not suppose we came here to meet after so many months to talk about the *pinche* Cowboys. How can I be of assistance?"

"It's your world, Don Paulino." Iraan said, "I'm just living in it. What can I do for you?"

"My friend, it is already done. It is good to be seen with the American police from time to time. It means that you are doing business, no? You have already done your favor to me. What is it that you require?"

Iraan leaned forward. "Do you recall that real estate guy going missing a couple weeks back? The Bowden-Everitt guy?"

Paulino winced. "Unfortunate."

"Was it business?"

"I have given that much thought, as the Americans were up our asses with a flashlight. The consulate, the FBI, your El Paso police. The mayor of Juarez came to my boss's office and made a grand show of concern. Thirty of us are getting killed a day—on both sides of the street, you understand—but one *gringo* gets lost and they make such a terrible noise. The mayor says it is bad for business with the Americans. He speaks, of course, of the free-trade business. Of all the work done in the Parque Industrial and the new Parque Omega. Of all the dollars that we will lose if the Americans and Orientals fear bringing their investments across the river. The mayor also spoke of the tourist dollars lost after such an unfortunate incident. What dollars, I ask? Twenty dollars spent by these so-called tourists for cheap tequila and to see a donkey fuck a fat woman? It is always like this when an American becomes lost."

"They still have the donkey shows?" Iraan asked.

Paulino laughed. "Only when I remove my pants."

Iraan swirled the brandy in his snifter glass. "So it was a mistake?"

Paulino smiled. "Ah, there are also such things as business mistakes, no? But all this talk dries my throat. Let's have another." Paulino motioned for the waitress.

"The Cowboys will never be the same until they find a leader like Troy Aikman," Paulino said. "Without the quarterback, there is no chance. This Romo. Too busy chasing pop singer *panocha* and playing golf. He still acts like one of those young back-up players, these…what is the word?"

"Rookies," Iraan said.

"Yes. Rookies. They are in the business. They are paid professionals. But that does not mean they know the rules of the game. It is very dangerous, football. People who do not know what they are doing, people whose coaches do not tell them the correct plays, they oftentimes get hurt, no?"

The waitress dropped off two more drinks.

"There is very little mercy in football," Paulino continued after taking a sip. "Even if the opposing coach knows the rookie has not been given the correct plays, they do not hold their players back from catching and hurting him. It is the principle of the game. And if the two coaches do not like each other, perhaps there is even more incentive to hurt those who do not know. Sometimes these things are between the coaches."

"I hear you," Iraan said. "It's like that in any business. If your boss doesn't tell you shit, and you don't know what you're doing, you're in trouble."

"Yes," Paulino nodded. "But in this game, even those who are professionals sometimes get unlucky. And then, what do they do? They stand on the sidelines crying for more money, telling everyone they want to play for a new team. With that in mind, I will take a moment to offer a salute to our old friend Don Shannon, a professional. Not one to do such ridiculous things."

"Thanks," Iraan said, looking into his snifter.

"It has been almost a year now, no?"

"This week," he replied.

"To Don Shannon," Paulino said, raising his glass. "A professional."

The two men drank them off.

"So," Paulino said, "where were we? Ah, yes, the real estate man. This man's brother, I presume." For the first time since they sat down over a half hour before, Paulino looked at Jon. "Allow me to introduce myself," he said, standing. "Paulino Villareal."

Jon stood and shook hands.

"I see that you do not drink alcohol or feel the need to talk," Paulino said, tapping his temple as he eased himself back into his chair. "One must always be careful of the man who keeps the clear head and is silent when he has nothing to say."

"And it's a good goddamn thing," Iraan said. "Dude got drunk last night and it wasn't pretty."

"Yes," Paulino said, "it is unfortunate that more of

those who cannot handle their liquor do not abstain. I am sorry about your brother."

"Thank you," Jon said. "Where did you learn to speak English so well?"

"Oh," Paulino said, smiling, "I pick it up here and there. In school I studied it. It is very formal, no? But even though I speak in such a formal manner, believe me, I am a crude man." Paulino fingered the crucifix on his necklace. "Your brother. That is difficult to say for certain. It has been a question that troubles me as well, because usually in such instances it is very clear. A person is killed and they find the body, and perhaps there is a symbol to indicate why it was done. And if there was no reason for it, then there is no reason to take such cares to ensure that the body is not found. We do not often talk about things like this, for if we do not understand them, it is meant to be that way."

Jon started to say something, but Paulino raised his hand to cut him short.

"Do not ask me to elaborate, because I cannot. I do not know why those in places much more elevated than my own humble position do or do not do things." Paulino turned to Iraan. "As you very well know, things are not as they should be on my side of the river as of late. We have men of will who fight for the same thing. Things have happened which have no precedent. And the elder of these men, well, he shows signs of being tired. It is said that he has become fascinated with the occult, life in outer space. And talk such as that gives his younger rivals the courage to try and take Juarez for themselves."

"He's been on top for a long time," Iraan said. "It

figures someone would eventually come along to knock him off."

"Yes," Paulino said. "That is the law of nature. But these mercenaries and the *pendejos* from the beach—*puta madre*. They have no regard for human life. I think everyone agrees that these animals must be stopped. It is not like the old days, when at least there was some...*¿como se dice?*...some honor." Paulino shook his head.

"Peña Nieto's plan seems to be working," Iraan pointed out.

Paulino laughed. "Oh, sure. They got one of the beach boys and El Pelón, but do you really think they were not offered up by someone inside? You know that there are others to take their places already. This system they have made for themselves is like the dragon with twenty heads. One cannot cut fast enough."

"I guess it's all up to us *gringos* to stop hittin' the pipe, huh?" Iraan asked.

"It's not even that anymore," Paulino said. "Although most of the *jefes* are simple men like myself, they can see the future. Have you been to the grocery store lately? The price of limes is up 50 percent! Why? Because the *jefes* are taxing the poor citrus farmers! This is no longer a drug problem; this is a crime problem. The hippies can legally smoke all the *mota* they want in California now, yes? Have we seen any peace because of it? Of course not. If you legalize all drugs tomorrow the dragon would find a way to survive."

"I guess you can't legalize kidnapping," Iraan said.

Paulino seemed a bit embarrassed by his short speech, so he and Iraan went back to their drinks for a moment.

"In any event," Paulino continued, "the only thing I can suggest regarding the American would be to look into that thing we once spoke about. With the man who enjoys bowling so much."

"That's still going on?" Iraan asked.

"The man owed a lot of money," Paulino explained. "Therefore, there were many favors to be performed. Of course, I may be very wrong. This man's brother may be buried in the sand dunes, and it is a very simple thing. That was another good thing about Don Shannon: He was never distracted by the complex answer until he had looked at the simple one."

"Yeah," Iraan said. "That was Don."

"So perhaps the bowling man is a waste of time," Paulino said. "But you recall how he was used in the past. And this might be one of those times." Paulino looked at his watch. "*¡Ay, papi chulo!* I have enjoyed your company so much that I have neglected my appointments. I must say goodbye."

The three men stood and Paulino gathered his cell phones, tucking them away in various pockets.

Paulino shook Jon's hand. "I'm sorry I cannot offer more information than I have."

Paulino turned and hugged Iraan.

"I do not envy us our jobs," Paulino said. "So many questions and so few answers. But it is our life, no? It is like Don Shannon once said: We work in the darkness and are judged in the daylight. Goodbye, my friend. I hope we meet again soon."

Paulino started to walk away, but turned back.

"I would be a very bad friend if I did not say that I

hope that you have forgotten about the past and are pursuing this matter for business reasons, not personal ones."

"*Vaya con Dios,*" Iraan said.

Paulino stopped to whisper something in the waitress's ear that made her laugh, and then he pushed out the doors into the late-afternoon sunlight.

"What the fuck was that all about?" Jon asked.

Iraan drained his snifter.

"The guy talks about the Cowboys for half an hour and then makes some mysterious comment about bowling?" Jon said. "You sure he doesn't work for Parks and Rec?"

The waitress dropped the check. Jon opened it and saw a tab for $250. "Jesus Christ. His drinks cost fifty bucks a pop."

"I told you it would be expensive," Iraan said, heading to the door.

Jon signed the credit card slip and caught up with him on the sidewalk. Buses disgorged cargoes of Mexican domestics who trudged across the street, heading for the border. Aside from the Metros, there was no other vehicular traffic. It was that time of the evening when the sky turned on its wonderful watercolors. Even on the dingy and cracked cement of downtown, there was an ethereal light.

Jon's BlackBerry chimed with a text from Cheryl. *Where the hell are you?*

→ ◄

Iraan drove his Trans-Am straight from the Dome Bar to his duplex without asking Jon if he wanted to be dropped off. Jon followed him inside and watched Iraan pour himself another drink.

"I ain't got no diet D.P."

"I'll have water."

"You can get it yourself."

Delicate Japanese anime figurines had been evenly spaced on the living room shelves, and the walls were hung with black-and-white Ansel Adams landscape photographs. A small white cat curled up on a tatami mat in the corner. It raised its head when they came inside but didn't bother getting up. Two futons and a low bamboo coffee table constituted the living room furniture.

"Quite the G-Unit pad," Jon commented.

Iraan didn't respond, so Jon sat down and flipped through an *Architectural Digest*. The detective sipped at his drink, staring off into the middle distance. After a few minutes, Jon dropped the magazine back on the table and said he would hail a cab.

Iraan told him to take a seat.

"We're getting into bad country here," Iraan said.

"The man who likes bowling?" Jon asked.

"Well, that's the easy part," Iraan said. "A few years back we got a tip that Lazaro was using this mortician here in El Paso to bury his bodies. I mean, if you want a guy to really disappear, what better place to stick him than an actual graveyard, right? This guy fucked up some deal with Lazaro, and instead of knocking him off right away, Chuy gave him the choice of taking care of some 'special' bodies or becoming a corpse himself. Chuy supposedly gets a little Monty Hall at times."

"Pardon me?"

"You know, *Let's Make a Deal*? Give some poor fucker a choice of getting capped or let him work it off. It's not usually much of a decision."

"What do you mean by 'special' bodies?" Jon asked.

"Cops, judges, drug guys. People who needed to vanish…forever."

"Americans?"

"Mostly Mexicans, but there were a couple El Paso guys who we were never able to find."

"What does bowling have to do with it?"

Iraan shrugged. "The dude liked bowling. He had a league going on the east side that he was fanatical about. Anyway, when you wanted to find him and he wasn't at the funeral home, you could always catch him at the bowling alley."

"So what happened?" Jon asked.

"Nothing."

Jon paced the room. "You guys are unbelievable."

"I don't want to get all spooky on you, but the first thing you have to understand is that there's no incentive for anyone to put a stop to the drug business. Once you get over that hump, things will make a hell of a lot more sense. There's too much money at stake. The cartel guys get their loot and we get our budgets to chew through. Seriously, if the drug game was up, what the hell would DEA do? They've got their bureaucratic existence to consider. But it's a two-way street, because if the shit was legal, then the drug lords would have to go back to rustling cattle or strong-arming lime farmers like Paulino was rapping about. But no matter what Paulino says, they ain't gonna make the kind of paper they are now by price-fixing citrus. So the cartel guys throw us a bone every once in a while to make it look like we're doing something about the 'drug problem', and in return we let them shoot it out among themselves, as long as they keep it on their side of the border and it doesn't fuck with NAFTA or any other legitimate business."

"What I want to know is who Paulino works for besides the *federales* and the AFI."

Iraan smiled to himself. "That's the great thing about Paulino; you never know which angle he's playing. If I had to guess, I'd say he's moonlighting for Lazaro. But that's just a guess. I trust Paulino about as far as I can throw him, but he owes me." Iraan paused. "And he owes Don."

"Who the hell is this Don Shannon guy?"

Iraan took his empty glass into the kitchen. "He was my partner."

"What happened to him?" Jon asked.

"Manny Sanchez happened to him, that's what."

"Okay, so who the hell—"

"Man, will you just give me a fucking second?" Iraan rubbed his temples. "Manny was an El Paso guy who came out of the Academy with me and Don, but he ended up over at DEA. Manny was kind of a superstar for a bit. I'm talking huge busts—tons, 727s full of coke—and that got him on TV, and Bush held him up as an example of how well our drug interdiction policy was working."

"I'm still not understanding how this applies," Jon said.

"I was good friends with Manny, but he and Don were real tight. So a few years back, Manny got on the trail of a shipment coming through Juarez and figured he'd bring me and Don into the mix, try to get us some suction, you know? Paulino was our *federale* liaison on that job, 'cause you can't make a move unless the Mexicans are in on it, too. Anyway, they were handing this one to us on a platter. A cargo plane coming down just on the other side of the border, and then they were going to ferry the coke across the river. We'd bust them as soon as they delivered to our side.

"Well, you could tell from the start that everyone was way too savvy. Adding to the problem was the fact that somebody forgot to tell the guys on the plane they were supposed to roll over. And then there were a couple trig-ger-happy Mexican cops who popped out of the bushes too soon. Before you know it, we're in the middle of a full-scale clusterfuck.

"Old Paulino managed to get himself pinned down behind this little mesquite tree. You've seen Paulino, so you can imagine his fat ass trying to hide behind this stick, yelling out to the cartel guys that everything is okay, things have been arranged, don't worry about the cops you shot, etc." Iraan smiled at the memory. "Well, me and Don and Manny were in the truck, having been told that under no circumstances were we to make any sort of move until we're on the American side of the creek; we're just there to take half of the credit when the bust goes down. So the cartel guys are moving in on Paulino—he's got his .45 with about two rounds left, and they've all got AK-47s. Don and Manny don't think it's a very fair fight. I'm telling them to hold tight, but they jump out of the truck and charge right into the middle of it. So, to make a long story short, they saved Paulino's ass."

Iraan's cat got up, stretched and meandered into the kitchen. Iraan followed it in and poured food into its bowl.

Iraan continued from the kitchen. "As soon as the smoke clears, it becomes obvious that we busted the wrong party. The load belonged to Lazaro, and Lazaro was pissed. Not only had some of Paulino's *federales* double-crossed him, but one of the cartel guys who got shot was his brother-in-law. As soon as they ID'd the body, Paulino knew we were in trouble. Manny and Don thought it was no big deal. They got the coke, killed some bad guys—including the big man's brother-in-law. All's right in the world. You've got to understand that part of the bravado came from the fact that an unspoken deal in all this is that cartel guys don't kill U.S. cops."

"They made that deal with who?" Jon asked.

"Hell if I know," Iraan said. "It's not written down or anything. It's just the way it works, okay?"

Jon nodded.

"Well, two days later Manny is back in Mexico City working another harebrained deal. Some *federales* pick him up from his hotel. That was that."

"Paulino handed him over?" Jon asked.

"I don't think so," Iraan said. He stared at the wall for a moment. "But Paulino had to have made a deal with *somebody*, because you just paid for his drinks."

Jon cut in. "So the *federales* blamed Manny for screwing up their bust?"

"For an attorney, you're pretty slow. *Federales*,

Lazaro—the same thing, okay? And it wasn't just that deal. Manny had been doing way too much freelancing for a DEA agent. It's one thing to make a couple of independent busts here and there, but you start getting greedy and that throws everything out of whack.

"Well, not only did they kill Manny," Iraan continued, "they fucking tortured him. For three days. Power tools, ice picks...the cartel guys made tapes of it so we'd know exactly what they did to him. I'm sure you remember this. It was all over the news. The DEA goes batshit, the President is calling for heads, but that's all just smoke. I think a lot of guys in high places were relieved to have Manny out of the picture."

"That sounds a bit far-fetched," Jon said.

"Fetch whatever you want, but it's true. The DEA aren't a bunch of Boy Scouts. Especially when you get them out of the office."

➖ ➖

Iraan's window faced south, so they could see Juarez come to life, 60-watt bulb by 60-watt bulb. Iraan's cat twined through his legs until Iraan got up and opened the door. The cat poked its head outside, tested the air, then inched out into the hot night.

"It didn't take long for everyone to see the video," Iraan continued. "They were spread around on purpose, a warning to the rest of us not to fuck with them. It had the opposite effect on Don, and from that point on, all he could think about was getting even with Lazaro. He started going across—which is strictly not kosher for any

177

kind of El Paso cop—looking for him at his hangouts, hassling his guys. It was pure balls that kept him alive. Back here, our bosses made him ride a desk because he was completely fucking up. I tried to cover for him as much as I could, but everybody knew what he was doing. Worse than that, he started talking to the fishwraps. Told any reporter with a sharp pencil how our government was complicit in the drug trade. Any other time, Lazaro would have ignored the cop rule and shot him on the spot, but the whole thing with Manny had been such a mess that the last thing anyone needed was another dead American cop. But you can only go so far."

"What happened?" Jon asked.

"They finally killed him. He was over in Juarez, making a nuisance of himself and they'd had enough. Bunch of guys in a truck with AKs. Punched his ticket right there on the street. A year ago."

"That's what you were doing over there the other day. The anniversary."

"Yeah."

The two men sat in the darkened apartment listening to the cars whooshing past outside.

"So what did you do?" Jon asked finally.

"Nothing," Iraan said. "Absofuckinglutely nothing. But my chief didn't care. I guess they figured that even if I didn't do anything right away, I'd eventually get around to it."

"Thus the 31 Flavors," Jon said.

"Thus the 31 fucking Flavors."

"Okay," Jon said, "what does all this have to do with my brother?"

Iraan sighed. "I don't know."

"Paulino was obviously telling you something. What about the mortician?"

"That was one of the ways Don was causing such a ruckus. He never got anywhere with Claude; it was just a hunch."

"Claude the mortician?"

"Claude Terry. Anyway, the theory was that Lazaro was using this guy to get rid of the bodies he never wanted found. You kill as many people as Lazaro does, you make some mistakes, and it doesn't do him any good to have those bodies show up again. What Paulino was saying is that maybe your brother got killed by accident. Maybe they thought he was in the game and only realized he was a citizen after the fact. Have you been over to the industrial parks?"

Jon shook his head.

"Man, you go over there and think you're in Irvine, California. It's completely different from the rest of town. Guys like your brother show the executives from Detroit the regular Juarez and they put the checkbook away. But they take them to the industrial side and the suits feel better about bringing in their business. Especially when they can pay the workers three bucks a day. But like everything else on the other side, you've got a couple different elements at work. I'm sure Lazaro's got his fingers in that pie somehow, and I wouldn't doubt it if El Animal does, too."

"So that's what Paulino was talking about with the football stuff?"

"It means you should look into the Bowden guy. See if he's got anything else going on the other side besides industrial real estate. Follow the money, see whose pockets got full."

"You're not going to help me?"

Iraan shook his head.

"How can you do that?"

Iraan laughed. "You haven't heard a goddamn word I've said, have you?"

"Your partner gets killed," Jon said. "You know who's responsible. The guy who did it lives two miles from here."

"Two miles away is a different country."

"So?"

"You're still not getting the picture. You can't take the fight to them. The only reason I went across the other day was for Don, and I was scared shitless the whole time. I'm surprised you didn't get killed yourself."

"I got pulled over by the police," Jon said.

Iraan set down his glass. "What?"

"The cops pulled us over. Me and Jimmy. They let us go with a warning."

"Then you just got your free pass, whiteboy. I suggest you cash it in and get your ass home. That won't happen twice."

"What about my brother?"

"Well, he's either dead or he's alive. If he's dead, there's nothing you can do about it. And if he's alive… well, if he's alive, then he'll turn up eventually. Maybe they're holding him for a reason. A negotiating chip down the line."

"So what am I supposed to do?"

"Go back to Denver, sue somebody and screw your wife."

"And that's it?"

"Listen, man, you seem like an all right guy. I don't know what's riding you, but whatever it is, you ain't gonna figure it out here. If you don't want to go home, go somewhere else. Whatever you decide to do, you've come to the end of all this."

"You're serious?"

"What else do you want?" Iraan asked. "You wanted me to help you find out if your brother is alive or not. I got you a 'maybe.' In this game, a maybe is pretty good. Take that maybe and go home."

CHAPTER FOURTEEN

"You're still there?!" Cheryl exclaimed. "What happened to your flight?"

"Something came up."

"The real something coming up is Laura asking what she should do with the stuff in your office. They're going to fire you. You know that, don't you?"

"What did you tell her?" Jon asked. Laura was his paralegal at the law firm.

"I told her you'd be at work today!"

"I'll give her a call."

"Better yet, go in and take your goddamn job back."

"I've got a couple loose ends to wrap up here."

"I hate to tell you this," Cheryl said, "but your whole life is going to be one big loose end if you don't get your act together very soon."

"You told me to take a cab," Jon said.

"Pardon me?"

"From the airport."

"Don't give me that shit, Jon." Cheryl hung up.

Jon's next call confirmed Cheryl's report. Laura told him that not only had they started clearing out his office, but his corporate AmEx had been canceled, as well.

"Have they assigned you to anyone else yet?" Jon asked.

"No," she reported. "You taking off like this is great. J. Crew has a monster sale going this week."

"Well, I hate to interrupt your shopping holiday, but would you mind looking up a few names for me on LexisNexis?"

Laura called back an hour later. Most of the articles she'd found about Max Bowden referred to how Bowden had been a high-ranking U.S. Army intel officer and had parlayed that background into the third-party real estate operation, bringing industrialists from the U.S. together with factory owners in Mexico. This was all company-line stuff, Old Boy Bowden's assertion that a military background resulted in a tighter, more efficient corporate ship.

"Anything from his time in the Army?" Jon asked.

"I'm getting to it," his assistant said. "It's pretty old stuff, but it looks like he was mixed up in something about an Iran-Contra. What's an Iran-Contra?"

"You don't remember that?"

"I was in kindergarten. Anyway, he was doing stuff with a guy named Colonel Oliver North in the 80s. Bowden only gets mentioned a couple of times, but he's in there. It refers to him as a military advisor in Nicaragua. After all that happened, he did some joint operations with the Mexican Army, drug-interdiction stuff. There was an article about how back in '88 they found a huge pot plantation in Chihuahua—like 10,000 peasants working the fields, it was so big—and the U.S. Army went in to help burn the place down. The pictures make it look like they dropped a bomb. Anyway, Bowden's name was on that thing, too. Was Fawn Hall really that viral?"

"I don't think that's the way we would've put it back in my day. But, yeah, she got the *Playboy* treatment when it still counted for something. She had to testify before Congress."

"Not bad," Laura said, obviously looking at a picture on a website. "Serious 1980's hair. You bought this *Playboy*?"

"It wasn't free back in the day like it is now. I dropped five bucks on that one. Tell me about Stan Everitt."

"The only stuff I got on him was strictly company PR. He was also in the Army. A few years younger than Bowden. He ran supply chains and logistical stuff like that. He handles all the location-scouting in Mexico, finds the factories and warehouses, and then Bowden works the U.S. side of the deal, getting the investors to relocate. That's all I found about him."

"And Cisneros?"

"Jorge Cisneros—*El Animal*—was pretty much what you told me to expect. High-ranking officer in the Mexican army, ran the paramilitary special-forces stuff. Under President Fox, he was supposed to be using paratroopers to wipe out the drug cartels, but it looks like he took over their routes instead of getting rid of them. When Fox went, so did he."

"Anything else?"

"Jennifer Aniston is either getting a divorce or pregnant. What does all this have to do with your brother? By the way, I'm really sorry about that. I hate it when people say that, but I am."

"Aside from the fact that he worked for Bowden-Everitt, I really don't know."

"It all sounds pretty crazy. Hold on for a sec." Laura covered the mouthpiece to speak to someone in the office. "So," she resumed, "are you coming back?"

"I don't know."

"I don't think Mr. Swanson is going to take 'I don't know' for an answer. If they really clear out your office, what should I do with your things?"

"I don't know."

Laura sighed. "That's your big line these days, isn't it?"

— ◂ ▸ —

Jon went next door when he heard Six to Ten Jimmy up and moving. His knock was greeted by the usual hungover bark. Jimmy cracked the door and blinked a couple times. His boxers had a rip down the side. He shielded his eyes from the sun.

"What's up?" he croaked.

"You have plans this evening?"

"What time is it?"

"Half past five."

Jimmy groaned. He left the door ajar as he staggered back into the gloom of his apartment. If possible, it had gotten messier. Jimmy scavenged through the detritus on his coffee table and came up with his cough syrup. He pried the cap off and took a gulp.

"Hit?" he asked, wiping his lips.

"No, thanks. So, this evening?"

"I ain't going to J-Town again. Especially after dark."

"Strictly El Paso. You know where the big bowling alley is over on the east side?" Jon had called the Terry

Funeral Home earlier that afternoon and, when the re-ceptionist said Mr. Terry was not in, he pretended to be from "the league." She mentioned the name of the bowling alley.

"Bowling?"

"I thought we might roll a few frames."

"That's more like it," Jimmy said. "Lemme see if I can find my ball." He kicked piles until he unearthed a scarred purple ball that had been hacked at like a coconut. "This little mother is gonna work like a charm." He dumped the ball into a Jose Cuervo backpack. "We gotta stop by the bank first so I can deposit my welfare check."

Jon raised his eyebrows.

"My disability check. It's around here somewhere. Every month. Eighty fuckin' percent."

"Eighty percent of what?"

"Of my salary when I was in the Army."

"What does that come out to?"

Jimmy handed him the check while he rummaged for clothes. Jon saw that it was for more than three thousand dollars.

"Nice number."

"And the cough syrup is free."

—◆ ◆—

It was league night at the East Side Lanes, and the alley was full of pot-bellied men with gold retirement watches being waited on by weary cocktail waitresses with bad teeth. The waitresses slalomed through the crowd with trays of pin-shaped beers and microwaved nachos as the clatter of strikes echoed above the noise from the banks of TVs—one set above every pair of lanes—spewing ESPN gibberish. Jon and Jimmy made their way to the register and asked for a lane.

"Not until nine," the lady behind the desk said. "League play only."

"Look, ma'am," Jimmy said, leaning against the counter, "I'm a disabled veteran."

"We appreciate your service," the woman said, punching buttons to reset the scoring screens, "but the league has the place reserved for the next five hours."

"I need to bowl," Jimmy said. "It's part of my physical therapy." He smiled. "C'mon, you've got to have one lane open."

The woman shot aerosol disinfectant into a pair of rental shoes. "How about this," she said. "We've got a couple incomplete teams right now. If any of them forfeit, I'll let you bowl a frame before the next round, okay?"

"Hey, that's great," Jimmy said. "I'll be in the bar."

"I bet you will be," the woman said.

"You see that?" Jimmy chucked Jon in the ribs as they took seats along the rail in the lounge. "Disabled veteran. Gets them every time." Jimmy ordered himself a White Russian.

Jon swiveled on his barstool so he could watch the bowlers. "What exactly is wrong with you?" he asked.

"Where do you want me to start?" Jimmy wiped half-and-half from his upper lip. "I got two busted knees. My right elbow won't extend more than 65 degrees. I can't hear out of one ear. I get migraine headaches all the time."

Jimmy gulped his drink. "An IED will mess with your program like that."

"So you got discharged?"

"I fucking hope so."

"And you stayed here."

Jimmy looked around. "What can I say? I like the atmosphere." He nodded toward the far lanes. "You know that guy?"

It took Jon a couple seconds before he spotted the bald dome of Justin Moon. The skinny private detective was sitting next to a rack of 10-pound bowling balls trying to look like he was working a crossword.

"That's the guy my family hired to find my brother."

"He was at the Vag yesterday," Jimmy reported. "Saw him talking to the manager."

"You sure it's the same guy?"

"I may be a drunk now, but I was a combat officer. Shit, the reason I drink so much is because I can't help *but* notice everything. I'm telling you, it's the same guy. If he's a private eye, he's not very good. You could spot that dome of his from orbit. He should invest in a hat."

Jon slid off his stool. "I'll be back."

"Check with the lady about our lane while you're up."

Jon was making his way along the platform above the bowling pits when Moon looked up. He cut his eyes quickly to the exit.

"How's it going, bud?" he asked when Jon got up to him.

"Taking a break from the LSAT?"

"Yeah, I was going to meet a couple guys, but it looks like they ditched me. What are you up to?"

"The same."

Moon nodded a few times before folding his newspaper. "You ever make it over to Juarez?"

"For a little bit."

Moon looked at his watch. "Hey, I gotta run. I'll see you around, okay?"

"Has anyone ever told you that you're not cut out to be a private eye?"

Moon paused for a second. "Bud," he said, finally, "why do you think I'm studying for the goddamn bar exam?"

"You want my job?"

Moon laughed. "Anyone ever told you you're not a very good attorney?"

"Today, in fact. I hate to crush your dream, but being a lawyer isn't as great as it might seem."

"To hell with that noise," Moon said. "I got a buddy who's in personal injury. Just caught himself a case where an old lady got run over by a stray shopping cart in a parking lot. Guess what his cut from that was?"

"Tell me. Our fee schedule might be different in Colorado."

"Twenty-five hundred bucks!"

"Solid case."

"Goddamn right, bud."

"Okay, since you have your new revenue stream all sussed out, how about dropping the surveillance on me?"

"Man's got to pay his bills in the interim, bud. Besides, your folks' checks clear. I'll be seeing you around."

Jon headed back to the lounge, scanning the scoring monitors as he went. Southern Maid Donuts, West

End Trucking, Brentt Insurance. He stopped at lane twenty-two. Terry Funeral Home versus Montana Landscaping. They were into the sixth frame of the match. Jon checked the names on the Terry scorecard until he saw CT's turn come. He watched as a wiry little man delivered a candy-colored tangerine ball with a lot of action. The ball slid toward the right gutter before catching up with its spin and snapping back at the center pin. It hit the pocket square and exploded the pins for a strike. Claude Terry pumped his fist as he spun around to slap fives with his teammates.

"*¡En los cables!*" Terry yelled.

Jon felt a tap on his shoulder and looked around to see Jimmy.

"We're on," he said. "Lane two. Go get yourself some rental kicks."

Jimmy had two pitchers of beer set up by the time Jon made it over with his shoes and ball.

"Check this out," Jimmy said, stepping onto the deck with his beat-up purple ball. He took two big strides and chucked the ball down the lane. It wobbled like an egg as it ran straight down the center and hit the pins dead on, busting a neat hole in the middle of the frame. The outer pins didn't even tremble.

"You see that?!" Jimmy crowed.

"Your ball is lopsided."

Jimmy winked as he waited for it to come up on the conveyor.

"I wasn't sure it would work," Jimmy said. He grabbed the ball and lined up for the 2-4-7 on the left side. He let the ball fly, and again it wobbled in a straight line to knock down the pins. Jimmy let out a yelp.

"I don't see what you're so excited about," Jon said. "You left two pins on the right side."

"The ball, man! Did you see the ball?"

"Your ball is fucked, Jimmy."

"My ass. It has a gyroscope in it."

"What?"

"A gyroscope." Jimmy grabbed the ball and handed it to Jon. "Roll it."

Jon gave it a toss, intending to make it hook, but the ball ran straight into the gutter.

"What's the point?" Jon asked. "I can't get any action on the thing."

"That's exactly the point," Jimmy said. "The gyroscope rolls the ball dead straight."

"That's great, but you're going to leave yourself a nasty split every time with that thing."

"So?" Jimmy asked.

"So you're not going to score any points."

"So?"

"The point is to knock all the pins down."

Jimmy blinked. "I know how to bowl."

"It's fantastic, Jimmy. Why don't you keep rolling, and I'll be back in a minute?"

"Hoo-whee!" Jimmy yelled as he threw another line drive.

——

After finishing off the landscapers, the morticians retired to the cocktail lounge for a team meeting. Jon took a seat at the bar and watched Terry launch into a frame-by-frame assessment of the squad's performance as the team ordered drinks.

"Whatcha drinking, sir?" Jon turned to the young Mexican behind the bar. He asked for a Diet Coke, conceding that his usual was out of the question.

The bartender wiped the bar down before setting Jon's drink on a cocktail napkin. "How'd you do tonight?

"No bowling for me."

"That's too bad. Bowling is fun." The bartender looked over his shoulder to see if anyone was listening. "When I got this job I thought it was crazy white-people shit—no offense."

"None taken."

"But we get to bowl for free after the place closes sometimes, so I tried it out. I don't know, it's like something feels good when you throw that ball down the lane and it smashes up all those pins."

"Cathartic, huh?"

The bartender smiled. "I'm not sure what that word means."

"It means an emotional release."

"Yeah, that's it. You can have a terrible shift, and then you go out there and smash some pins and it feels better. You should try it out. I mean, if you're frustrated or something. You don't even have to keep score."

"I thought the score was the whole point." Jon gestured to the bowlers. "They seem to take it pretty seriously."

The bartender refilled Jon's glass with ice and soda. "Well, maybe they have bigger problems than me and need this to make the other shit seem less serious. For me,

I just like to hear the ball hit those pins. *Wham!* It's just good to break things every once in a while. I tried golf, but the only thing I wanted to break was the damn clubs. Can I get you anything else?"

Jon asked for the check, but the bartender waved his hand. "Coke's on me."

Jon swiveled on his stool to watch Terry and his teammates. Terry struck Jon as the kind of guy who probably became a mortician because he'd look less squirrelly in a black suit.

After the team meeting wrapped, Terry excused himself and headed out the side door with a huge, three-ball bag. Jon dropped a couple of bucks on the bar and followed him to the parking lot. Terry's truck was a jacked-up Chevy 250 Silverado with dual rear tires and tinted windows. Jon watched Terry monkey up into the vehicle. He noticed Jon standing a few feet away as he was about to shut the door. He turned the engine over and backed out of the spot, catching Jon in the headlights. Terry pulled to a stop a couple feet short of him. Revving the engine, he leaned out the driver's window.

"What the fuck do you want?" he asked over the V8 rumble.

"Are you Claude Terry?" Jon asked.

"Who else would I be, jerkoff? I seen you sitting there at the bar watching me. You a process server? If so, you can damn well come see me at my office. Until then, piss off!"

He shot Jon the finger before swerving around him and out of the lot. Jon waited for Terry's taillights to disappear before heading back into the bowling alley.

When he got back to his lane, he saw Sway taking a roll with Jimmy's ball. She wore an SBC bowling team jersey and white Capri pants. Jon couldn't help but notice the outline of a thong.

"You're right," she said. "It stays right on line." Jimmy had polished off both pitchers of beer and was sitting back on his plastic chair with a wide smile on his face.

"Gyros," he pronounced. "God's gift. Where you been, man? I drank your pitcher."

Sway smiled at Jon and rolled her eyes.

— ◆ —

Sway knew a place where they could get tacos after they dropped Jimmy off at the Vag. Jimmy had launched his bowling ball down the lane one too many times, and it had split where he had originally sawed it in half to install the stabilizing device. Not only did this crack the ball, but it jammed up the return conveyor to such an extent that they'd had to postpone four league games. The manager of the alley was not pleased, disabled vet or not. Jimmy had gotten so inebriated that Jon had to drive his Mustang back to the apartments.

Chico's is a little dive on the east side favored by drunk high-schoolers because they stay open late. The place could've doubled its revenue had they sold Pepto as a side dish. Jon took a hard plastic booth while Sway ordered for them.

"That was Iraan's idea?" Sway asked, folding her paper napkin into increasingly smaller triangles. "That sounds too stupid for even a cop to come up with."

"It was the Mexican guy who brought it up."

"So you thought you'd just go up to this funeral director and ask him if he buried your brother?"

"The thought crossed my mind."

Sway flicked her little triangle of napkin across the table at Jon. "That's about the dumbest idea I've ever heard. I think you, Iraan and Jimmy need to go back to sixth grade and start over. No wonder your wife is pissed. If you were down here doing something productive, I might be able to understand. But following a mortician to a bowling alley? C'mon."

"I thought you wanted me to leave you alone?"

"What can I say?" Sway pulled another napkin from the dispenser and started in on it. "Aside from the whole underlying tragedy of the situation, it's sort of interesting. Excitement excites me."

Jon rubbed his eyes. "I'm glad someone is enjoying it."

Sway flicked the napkin, and this time it got Jon square in the forehead. The counterman called their number and Sway slid out of the booth to get their tray. She doused her tacos with hot sauce. Jon took a bite of his and a dribble of grease squirted out the side. He set it back on the plate and watched Sway eat.

"You don't like it?" she asked, wiping her mouth.

Jon shook his head. Sway hooked his plate with her finger and pulled it to her side of the table.

"So that's it?" she asked.

"That's what?"

"You give up? Forget the whole deal and head home?"

"I don't know what else to do. You ever been in a situation where you can't go back and there's no way forward? You're just sort of stuck in the middle?" Jon looked at the sloppy-drunk kids eating around them. "And it looks like I've found one hell of a middle."

"Are you talking about what's going on here, or life in general?"

"The whole thing."

Sway went for another napkin, but Jon pulled the dispenser out of her reach. It was attached to the wall by a thin chain.

She stared at Jon for a moment. "Do you still want me to talk to my cousin about her boyfriend? The boxer guy?"

"What's the point?"

"The point is that I'm going to suspend my disbelief for two seconds and pretend you actually want to get to the bottom of this. But there's one condition."

"What's that?"

"You've got to come with me. To El Babylon. That's where she works."

"The strip club?"

"C'mon, my cousin may be trashy, but she doesn't hump poles. El Babylon is more like a regular bar. Sort of. Anyway, she works tomorrow night, but if we go early and get out of Juarez before it gets dark, we should be okay. Most of the shootings happen at night. What do you say?"

"You think it's worth it?"

Sway pointed at Jon. "You mean are *you* worth it."

"Okay. Am I worth it?"

Sway popped the last corner of taco into her mouth. "I guess we're going to find out." She winked at Jon. "Maybe you can start showing me how grateful you are tonight."

CHAPTER FIFTEEN

El Babylon (or "El Bobby" as the locals call it) is supposed to look like a Middle Eastern pleasure palace with its domed ceilings and elaborate palm tree murals painted on the imitation-adobe walls, but like everything else in J-town, the whole project ended up looking slapped together, built on the cheap, and although it's still fairly new, patches of rebar have started to poke through the exterior stucco. As Sway pointed out, it isn't technically a strip club. The girls who work there never disrobe, but the way they act, they might as well be pole dancers. Like Juarez's other big product, they import some of the ladies from South America, places such as Bolivia and Colombia. The uniform of tight jeans and tube tops, slinky skirts and three-inch heels, however, is all show and no go. Before the violence got completely out of hand, El Bobby was a popular hangout for American businessmen working in Mexico; it's upscale enough so that they didn't have to worry about getting jacked, and since it isn't technically a strip club, they didn't have to fret about offending skin-sensitive clients. Now it's mostly a hangout for gangsters.

The bar girls each have their own section, maybe two or three tables, and you can see them determine which table in their area has the most financial potential. Once they decide where the loot is, they tend to forget about their other customers and end up in the rich guy's lap for the rest of the night. Busboys shag drinks for the less desirable patrons.

Cadillac Escalades, BMWs and Hummers had already jammed the parking lot when Jon and Sway arrived an hour before sunset. The attendants waved Sway's Jetta to a far corner, and she and Jon hoofed it to the unmarked front door. They were met by two security guards who wore their jackets loose to give the impression that they were packing heat. The doormen frisked Jon with rough hands and leered at Sway before stepping aside to let them through. Sway had tarted herself up for the field trip in a short skirt and a low-cut blouse that showed off her chest. Her hair was curled and dropped to her shoulders in waves. They proceeded down a narrow hall that opened up onto an archway where two more security apes gave them the once-over before passing them off to the maître d'. The host sported a suit jacket with a mismatched pair of trousers, the top four buttons of his silk shirt undone. He registered them as inconsequential and showed them to a tiny round table next to the bathrooms. Run-DMC's version of "Walk This Way" blasted out of the stereo system.

"Nice place," Jon said over the music. He picked an almond from the bowl of nuts on the table and examined it on all sides before popping it into his mouth.

"*Cállate*," Sway said, looking around for her cousin.

"What does that mean?" Jon asked.

"It means shut up." Sway squeezed his thigh under the table.

They were the only patrons in their hostess's section,

but the girl sat at the bar for a few minutes chatting with her colleagues before making a production of heaving herself off the stool and doing the catwalk hoof over to their table. The hostess had long black hair, green eyes and pneumatic tits that were hugely disproportionate to her slender frame. She stood in front of their table with her hip cocked and her eyes on the doorway. Sway ordered a mojito for herself and a Diet Coke for Jon. The girl went back to the bar and plopped down on her barstool.

"Is she going to bring us the drinks?" Jon asked.

"In a few minutes. These South American bitches like to keep you in your place. She might be nicer if you were alone. Since I'm here, she knows there's no chance."

"Is that right?"

"It better be."

The bartender set the mojito and soda in front of the waitress, but she waited a couple more minutes before deigning to bring them over. She dropped them off without saying a word. As she was making her way back to the bar, the maître d' loosed a sharp whistle, and she turned to see him leading three Mexicans to a corner booth. The men wore cowboy boots, big belt buckles and thick gold chains with diamond-crusted AK–47 pendants. The waitress clip-clopped back to the bar on her high heels to get them a bottle of Dewar's and a bucket of ice, all of a sudden hustling like a Denny's waitress on a Sunday morning after church. Jon noticed a pair of men trailing the three guys into the club, and, after exchanging professional courtesies with the house security mooks, they took positions along the wall beside the booth. They caught Jon looking and gave him a hard stare-down. The waitress had the busboy carry the booze to the table as she took a seat between two of the men and started getting kittenish. The busboy backed away from the table practically bent in half as he scraped and bowed.

"Who the hell are those guys?" Jon asked.

"Rich," Sway said. She grabbed the busboy and asked where her cousin was. He said he'd get her.

"They look like jukebox repairmen."

"That's the *vaquero* look," Sway said. "Very popular with the *narcos*. Notice the pointy boots. Pretty soon this place will look like a rodeo."

A diminutive girl with a pug nose and bottle-blonde hair came over to the table, and Sway stood up to embrace her. Sway's cousin was wearing stretch pants and heels, but compared to the lanky thoroughbreds along the bar, she looked like a stable pony. Sway introduced Jon to her cousin, whose name was Qui-Qui. The cousin threw her bar towel over her shoulder and pulled up a chair. The girls talked family. While they chatted in their unique Spanglish, more high rollers arrived, and the hostesses peeled off the bar like Formula One race cars out of the starting grid, their busboys scurrying along behind them with buckets and bottles. The perimeter of the room was soon crowded with seconds in ill-fitting suits, sizing each other up, chewing toothpicks and checking their BlackBerries. The DJ switched from rap to blaring *norteño* accordion music.

"By the way," Qui-Qui asked, "what the heck are you doing over here? I haven't seen you in four months—you totally skipped Uncle Frank's party—and now you're calling me to see if you can meet up? I thought you hated Juarez."

"Jon wanted to come across to see the sights."

"Likes to live dangerous, huh?" Qui-Qui said, sizing Jon up.

"What?" Jon asked, looking at Sway.

Sway pointed at her cousin. "I asked how you liked it," Qui-Qui repeated.

"Sorry," Jon said, "You two sound the same. Yeah, it's like going to the aquarium and looking at the shark tank. Anybody ever get shot in here?"

"Only in the parking lot," Qui-Qui said. "They used to make everyone hand over their guns at the door, but they kept getting them mixed up. Now they let the guys keep them so long as they agree not to shoot anyone inside."

"That sounds reasonable."

Qui-Qui grimaced. "I was joking."

"Speaking of that," Sway said, "you still dating *el boxeador*?"

"Yes. But he's acting like a total *malcriado*. He thinks just because he's working he can cheat on me with the *fresas* over at the Joker."

"Who's he working for?" Jon leaned in to ask over the music.

Qui-Qui looked at Sway. "¿*Quien es este hombre*?"

"My boyfriend," Sway said.

"He doesn't look El Paso."

"Believe me, he's not."

"Anyway," Qui-Qui resumed. "Lalo's been messing around with those little teenagers his boss is so fond of.

It's sick. And then he's always bragging about the guys he beats up. When he was fighting, he never used to talk like that. When he was boxing, he was the sweetest guy ever. Now he acts like such a *macho*."

"But you still live with him?"

"Hell, yes," Qui-Qui said. "You saw that new house he has in *El Campestre*. I'm not moving out of that place and going back to Mom's. But I'll only put up with so much, you know?"

"He's a scumbag," Sway said.

"Look who's talking." Qui-Qui turned to Jon. "You shoulda seen this one six months ago."

"Knock it off," Sway said, fiddling with the straw of her mojito.

"What was that thing you joined?" Qui-Qui asked. "The one with all those *güera* bitches."

"My cousin is referring to the Junior League."

"Whatever," Qui-Qui said. "Bunch of white girls in a carnival booth selling Margarita Slurpees for charity while their husbands stand around comparing golf clubs. Thank God you woke up and dumped that idiot before—"

"Enough, Qui-Qui."

"No," Jon said, smiling. "This is interesting. The Junior League, huh?"

"It wasn't as bad as she makes it out to be," Sway said. "Anyway, what about Lalo? Did he really quit fighting?"

"That fight you came to with me was the last one."

"He quit because he lost one fight?"

"*Prima*, they made him lose that one. He could've beat that guy easy, but some dudes had money on him. I keep telling him that he should get a new trainer and start fighting again, but he's like all these other guys." Qui-Qui nodded at the bodyguards leaning against the walls. "Just waiting for somebody to get shot so they can move up. Besides, *su jefe le dió la casa,* so I guess he doesn't have much of a choice now."

A busboy hurried over to the table and told Qui-Qui they needed her behind the bar. "I've got a regular break in a half-hour," she told Sway.

"Goddammit, Jon," Sway said as soon as her cousin left. "Stop butting in all the time with your stupid questions. If you'd just be quiet, I could get Qui-Qui to tell me something."

"What the hell does her boyfriend's boxing career have to do with my brother?"

"Don't be a dunce," Sway said.

"What's that supposed to mean?"

"It means that if you keep your mouth shut, I'll get you the information you want. Like I said, her boyfriend works for the guy you think snatched your brother. He's like his personal assistant, okay? So if anything went down, he'd probably be in on it. And being the tough guy he is, he'd tell her. Doing an American is a big deal, so she'd know something. Okay?"

"Calm down."

Sway looked at the ceiling. "How the hell can anyone help you? Let's get out of here. This *norteño* music is giving me *un gran dolor de cabeza.*"

"What about your cousin?"

"We'll come back when she's on break. Leave twenty bucks for the drinks."

"Twenty bucks?!"

Sway headed for the exit as Jon pulled a few bills out of his pocket.

"Why is everyone around here sticking me for bar tabs?" Jon called after her. "I don't even drink!"

——◆——

The parking attendants approached for their "security fee" when they reached Sway's Jetta, but Sway shot them a look that had them backtracking.

"How did your cousin end up in Juarez?" Jon asked as they pulled into traffic.

"Duh—she was born here." Sway darted the Jetta through a yellow light. "Her mom moved across when mine did, but her dad stayed. Divorce, you know? Qui-Qui got her green card, but she kept living in Juarez. Qui-Qui's mom tried like hell to get her to move across when her dad went back to Puebla three years ago, but Qui-Qui wasn't having it."

"Isn't that pretty unusual? To stay in Juarez?"

"Qui-Qui's an unusual girl. Part of it's because of Lalo, though. She got big into boxing a couple years ago, and Lalo was an up-and-comer. Featherweight. Anyway, she went kinda groupie on him, and they ended up dating. Lalo *used* to be sweet."

"Speaking of sweet…" Jon smiled. "You mind taking me over to the industrial park?"

"Yes, I do. It's on the other side of town. Why do you want to go over there?"

"That's where my brother was heading when they got him. I want to see what it looks like."

"You see a taxi sign on the top of this car?" Sway asked Jon. He shrugged. Sway made a left turn.

"Thanks," Jon said.

Traffic thinned as they worked their way toward the industrial zone, most of the vehicles now derelict school-buses transporting *maquiladora* employees back to their shanties on the outskirts of town. There were several ballfields and parks, but they were littered and unkempt. The only action was at the skate park, where teenagers in impossibly baggy pants kicked their skateboards around under the lights. Statues of Mexican heroes in the traffic circles had been allowed to oxidize and lose appendages. As they made their way farther east, the streets started to have fewer potholes and the landscaping wasn't as completely wrecked. New, brightly lit convenience stores replaced the shacks and *bodegas* that were on the corners in the center of town. They passed several American fast-food restaurants. Ten cars idled in the Starbuck's drive-thru. Then the factories and warehouses appeared—windowless hulks, occupying entire blocks and surrounded by high fences, columns of semi-trucks backed up to the loading docks. Iraan was right when he said it looked like Irvine, California. It had that same antiseptic, master-planned feel to it.

"Do you know which one?" Sway asked as they navigated the increasingly deserted streets.

"I think it was something with Omega in it."

"That's the one near the university."

"They've got a University of Juarez?"

"It's more like a technical college. Your brother and his NAFTA guys are going for the whole enchilada. They train the workers on one side of the street and then send them to work on the other. Twenty-five bucks."

"A day?" Jon asked.

"A week." Sway glanced in her rearview mirror. "You've got to be kidding me."

"What?"

"The cops."

Jon craned his neck to see the blue and red flashers of a patrol car behind them. Sway eased the Jetta to the side of the road. She looked over at Jon and her eyes were suddenly wide with fear.

"Whatever happens," she said, "don't let them take me by myself, okay?"

"Sure."

She reached over to grip his forearm. "I'm fucking serious, Jon. Don't let them separate us."

Jon watched in the side mirror as the cops got out of the police car. The shorter one approaching the passenger side held an M-16. That one hung back while the driver came up to Sway's side and rapped on the window.

"*¿Qué pasa?*" she asked.

The cop ducked to shine his flashlight at Jon and then swept the beam around the interior of the car.

"*Identificación,*" he said. "*El hombre, también.*"

Sway handed the cop both of their licenses. Jon saw a bead of sweat trickle down the back of her neck. The cop returned to his car while the other one kept watch with the machine gun on his hip.

"They can't just pull you over—"

"Shut the fuck up and let me handle this."

The cop came back and handed Sway her license.

"*Muchacho*," he said, then added in English, "out of the car."

"*Tenemos el dinero para pagar la fina.*" Sway said, clutching Jon's arm.

"Out of the car," the officer repeated. While Jon was looking at him through the driver's window, the cop with the M-16 yanked the passenger door open.

"Give them whatever they want," Sway said, moving her hand slowly to the key in the ignition.

Jon raised his hands as he stepped to the rear of the Jetta. He could see Sway's eyes watching in the rearview mirror. The officer looked at Jon's ID again and then shined his flashlight in Jon's face. The little cop with the M-16 poked the barrel of the machine gun into Jon's ribs. The other cop told his partner to back off.

"I pull you over," the tall one said in English, "because this is dangerous area at night. You and your friend should not be here. I think, Mr. Lennox, you go back to El Paso tonight and stay there. Juarez can be very bad place. You understand? Maybe you take your lady friend for a drink on the way home so she say she have a good time in Juarez." He handed Jon his license. "But this part of town not good for tourists. Okay?"

"Sure. Whatever you say, sir." Jon regarded the officer for a moment.

The little cop said something, but his partner shook his head.

"*Buenas noches, señor.*"

The smaller officer switched the rifle to his off hand.

He put his index finger in Jon's face and mimicked pulling a trigger. "*Próxima vez, hermano.*" He followed his partner back to the patrol car.

"What did he say?" Sway asked as soon as Jon got in the Jetta.

"He said this is a dangerous part of town and that we should go back to the bars near the bridge." Jon tried to buckle his seatbelt, but his hand was shaking so badly that he missed the slot on the first two attempts.

"What?"

"That's what he said. Have you ever had a gun pointed at you?"

"How much did you give him?"

"Nothing. I swear the barrel of that thing looked like a goddamn tunnel."

Sway looked at Jon in disbelief. "Nothing?"

The police car swung away from the curb and headed deeper into the heart of the industrial area. As it passed, the shorter cop turned his face away.

"Something is seriously screwed up here," Jon said.

"That's the fucking understatement of the year," Sway replied. She took a couple of deep breaths and pulled a U-turn.

"I mean, those guys looked just like the cops who pulled me over when I was with Jimmy."

CHAPTER SIXTEEN

Once they were back in the general miasma of Juarez proper, Sway swerved into the parking lot of a white-tablecloth steak restaurant called La Garufa. She marched straight past the high-heeled Penelope Lopez look-alike hostess to the bar and called for a whiskey. The sight of upper-class families eating $50 filets and teenaged Juniors in preppy Polo shirts with the collars popped seemed to make her feel safer.

"It doesn't make any sense," she said for the tenth time. "You've been pulled over twice in one week—by the same guys—and you got off both times without having to pay a *peso*? Wake up, Jon."

"How much more awake do you want me to get?" Jon asked. "I thought I was going to piss my pants. The tall one who did all the talking seemed legit, but the little bastard with the rifle just wanted to shoot me."

"Describe the short one," Sway said. "I couldn't see because they were shining the spotlight in my rearview mirror. And then when they drove past, he covered his face. How tall was he?"

"Maybe 5'5", 5'6". He had this little beard."

"Beard?"

"A goatee."

"Holy Jesus!" Sway slammed her highball glass down on the bar. "I can't believe it! The little cop. It was Lalo!"

"You're sure?"

"I only got a look at him when he pulled your door open, and I was so scared that it didn't hit me then. Now that I think about it, I'm sure it was Lalo." Sway took a slug of whiskey. "And that fucking cologne! He wears this terrible stuff called Lime Sec."

"What was he doing in a cop car?"

Sway signaled for the check. "We gotta get Qui-Qui. If Lalo is running around impersonating a police officer, then I'm sure as hell going to tell Qui-Qui about it. That little dirtbag," she snarled.

"Can't you just call her?"

"We're only five blocks away. C'mon," Sway dropped a wad of pesos on the bar.

It was close to nine p.m. when they got back to El Babylon, and the parking lot attendants had started using orange light sticks like ground crews waving in airplanes. They let loose with a barrage of whistles as she swerved around them. The Mexicans have this special way of whistling—high-pitched and two-toned, like exotic birds. Whee-*wheee*. Sway drove straight down the alley to the back door Dumpster where two heavies were smoking cigarettes. Sway jumped out of the car, yanking the front of her blouse down to show more cleavage. "Stay here," she ordered Jon before sashaying up to the bouncers. They tried to direct her to the front, but Sway convinced them to let her in. Jon sank down in the passenger seat as the guards glared at him before returning to their cigarettes. Jon could hear accordion techno bumping inside the club.

Sway had been inside for five minutes when three black SUVs glided into the other end of the alley. Their headlights were turned off, and they navigated with only their amber running lights. The club doormen pressed against the wall as the first Yukon pulled to a halt beside Sway's Jetta, hemming it in. Men in black windbreakers dropped from the first and third vehicles and spread out along the alley, scanning the surrounding rooftops. Two of them carried Heckler MP5 submachine guns. One of them peered into the Jetta. He had a tight, military haircut. He looked Jon over and then checked the backseat of the car before moving down the alley to join his partner. The Babylon bouncers, who had been acting so tough a few minutes earlier, now stood very still. The men from the SUVs took a minute to secure the alley, and then one of them went to the middle vehicle and tapped on the passenger window. A fat man in a Members Only jacket clambered out of the backseat. He unzipped his fly and took an arching piss against the wall. The man who got out of the other side of the vehicle was a little over six feet tall and had neatly trimmed blonde hair. He wore khaki pants, tan Timberland boots and a nicely cut blue sport jacket over a golf shirt. He made his own scan of the alley while waiting for the man to finish up.

The fat man shook his dick a couple times before hiking up his trousers. He joined his taller companion and they followed a flying wedge of bodyguards through the stage door. Two men stayed posted outside the back entrance. The Yukons cruised away like orcas. The El Bobby bouncers relaxed a little bit and offered the guards cigarettes, which they accepted. One of the bouncers handed over a lighter, which one bodyguard pocketed after flaming his Marlboro.

Sway and Qui-Qui emerged a few minutes later.

"You know where the place is, right?" Qui-Qui asked as she climbed into the backseat.

Sway said she did.

"That little *pendejo,*" Qui-Qui said as she wriggled out of her work clothes and started pulling on a pair of tight jeans she had in her backpack. "If he thinks he can screw around on me and get away with it, he's in for a big lesson. I know exactly which *fresa* it is, too. He said she was his sister's friend when I caught them having *un cafecíto.*"

Sway got to the end of the alley and the two men posted there blocked her path as they shone Maglites into the car. Qui-Qui rolled down the window and let loose with a torrent of Spanish. The men laughed and stepped aside.

"I hate those Zetas," Qui-Qui said, rolling her window up. "And did you see that pig Cisneros try to grab my ass when he walked past? I swear all these Mexican men are assholes. I should have known better. My mama always warned me. She said, 'Never get involved with a Mexican.' *Mírame ahora.* Getting screwed over by some pissant, tomato-can boxer and a fifteen-year-old slut." Qui-Qui thrust her head between the front seats to examine Jon. "What are you?" she asked.

"What do you mean?"

"Like Jewish or Mormon or something?"

"Episcopalian," he said.

"Whatever the fuck that is, it's better than Mexican. You got the right idea, cousin."

"Who was the other guy?" Jon asked. "The white guy."

"Never seen him before."

Qui-Qui returned to the backseat to finish dressing. Sway shot a smile at Jon. "Episcopalian? And you're giving *me* shit about the Junior League?"

"You're sure it was him?" Qui-Qui asked.

"I'm not a hundred percent," Sway answered, "but I got that feeling."

"That's how they pull it off with the ones who don't go for the *narco* thing, you know? They pretend they're *federales* so *mamá piensa que es okay.* I can just see him doing it. I'm going to find that uniform and cut it to shreds. There it is." Qui-Qui pointed at a neon-drenched club on the next block.

"Back door or front?" Sway asked.

"Front. I'm gonna walk right in and catch his ass in the act."

Jon said he'd take a taxi back to the bridge.

"*Cállate,*" Sway and Qui-Qui said in unison.

Sway parked the Jetta among the pickup trucks and American beater sedans in the lot. The girls got out, but Jon stayed put in the front seat. Sway came around and dragged him out of the car. They led Jon up to the doorman, who let the girls in for free but insisted that Jon cough up ten dollars.

"I'm not paying to get in this place," Jon protested.

The bouncer shrugged.

"Fine," Sway said. "But don't you dare ditch us. We'll be out in five minutes."

Jon looked from side to side. "Where the hell would I go?"

The bouncer shrugged again and offered Jon a cigarette. He declined and went down to the corner of the building where he could see the side alley. The smells of open-air taco stands, decomposing trash and burning rubber wafted through the night air, collecting into an odor like an old dishwashing sponge left in the sun. Looking north, Jon saw the big star on the side of the Franklin Range. A small boy sidled up to him with a ripped box of Chiclets that looked like it had been salvaged from a garbage can. Jon slipped him a dollar, and the kid melted back into the gloomy parking lot.

The sound of running high heels came to him from down the alley. He turned just in time to see a young girl in a miniskirt and a sheer bra race past as fast as her heels would allow her to run. Qui-Qui was in hot pursuit, with Sway a few meters behind. The girl made the mistake of looking back and tripped over a parking curb. She sprawled on her face, and her purse skittered across the asphalt, scattering lipstick and rouge tins. Qui-Qui leapt onto the girl's back and seized a handful of hair. She pulled the girl's head back before slamming the girl's face into the ground. The girl spit out a tooth when she screamed.

Sway and the bouncer were on the girls at the same time, and it took both of them to pull Qui-Qui off the stripper. The girl curled up into a fetal ball, her bare ass showing pale under the yellow street lights.

Qui-Qui thrashed, trying to get loose. Jon stepped over to help the girl to her feet.

"*No lo toques* that slut!" Qui-Qui yelled.

Jon knelt down to see how badly she was hurt. Blood flowed from a cut on her forehead, and her nose was mashed. The girl made whimpering noises.

"You really busted her up," Jon said. "She needs a doctor."

"I'll take her to *el depósito!*" Qui-Qui shouted.

The bouncer, realizing that the girl was an employee of the club, asked what the hell was going on. Sway explained that the tramp had been screwing around with her cousin's boyfriend. The bouncer clucked his tongue. He handed Qui-Qui to Sway and he and Jon helped the girl to her feet. Jon gathered the contents of her purse and the high heel that had gotten away from her while the bouncer gave her a handkerchief to press to her forehead. He shone his flashlight around until he found the lost tooth, and put that in his pocket. Qui-Qui continued to curse the girl in Spanish, but didn't seem so intent on assaulting her anymore. The girl wailed that she didn't know Lalo had a girlfriend.

"Did you see him tonight?" Qui-Qui asked.

The girl nodded.

"Is he still in there?" she asked.

The girl shook her head.

"Talk you little bitch! Where's Lalo?"

The girl said that he had come by about an hour before and then left suddenly, saying he had to go to El Bobby.

"Great," Sway sighed.

Jon told them he was going to head home. The girls ignored him. The bouncer gave him a sympathetic look.

"You wanna go back over there?" Sway asked her cousin.

"Ooohh, I'm gonna kill that *hijo de puta*," Qui-Qui said.

Sway asked the girl if Lalo was in a police uniform when she'd seen him. The girl said he'd been wearing a white T-shirt and tan slacks. Maybe he'd just gotten off work, she sobbed.

"Yeah, I'll bet." Qui-Qui shook loose of Sway and patted her hair into place. Qui-Qui warned the girl that if she ever touched Lalo again, she'd come back and finish the job. The bouncer led the girl back into the club. They returned to the Jetta—Jon taking the backseat—and headed to El Bobby.

"I can't believe that's the girl he was cheating on me with," Qui-Qui said. "Ugh, it makes me sick thinking they had sex in my bed. I'm going to make him buy me a new mattress!"

They were pulling into El Babylon's parking lot when a *federale* stepped into their path. He motioned for them to turn around. The parking lot was closed, he said. There were still several cars in the lot, and Sway pointed that out to him. The whistling, flashlight-waving parking attendants, however, were nowhere to be seen. The cop insisted that the bar was off limits for the rest of the night. As Qui-Qui continued arguing with the cop, Jon saw the three black SUVs pull up to El Bobby's back entrance and two bodyguards appeared at the end of the alley. Someone let loose with one of those two-toned Mexican whistles, and the cop spun around. The two bodyguards heard the whistle and brought their guns up.

"This isn't right," Jon said. "Let's get out of—"

"Lalo!" Qui-Qui screamed. Jon saw the boxer crouched behind a custom pickup with his M-16. He turned his head at the sound of his name. Qui-Qui shouldered her door open and started zigzagging through the parked cars as a barrage of gunfire spat from the alley and stitched a trail of pockmarks along the side of the truck Lalo was hiding behind. The slugs hit like icy snowballs, sprays of metal and glass kicking up into the air. Lalo triggered a three-round burst as several other men in *federale* uniforms emerged from where they'd been hiding in ambush. A second later, everyone with a gun started shooting, and one of the bodyguards by the entrance to the alley went down. Qui-Qui stopped in her tracks halfway to Lalo, suddenly recognizing the gunfire all around her. She clamped her hands over her ears and screamed. Sway fumbled for the gearshift, trying to get the Jetta in reverse.

Just as she jacked the car into gear, Jon kicked open his door and ran for Qui-Qui. Sway shrieked at him to get back in the car. Jon sprinted low to the ground, trying to shrink himself into as small a target as possible. He could distinguish three distinct levels of sound: the gunfire like a string of cherry bombs going off in a tin garbage car; bullets making *pock-pock-pock* sounds as they shattered windshields and impacted the sides of cars; and the slugs that didn't hit their targets snapping above Jon's head with supersonic whiplashes.

Qui-Qui was still frozen in place when an invisible fist punched her off her feet and flung her into the side of a yellow Hummer. Lalo was switching magazines on his M-16 and didn't see his girl go down. Just as Jon reached Qui-Qui, Sway locked up the brakes and slid to a stop next to them. She twisted around to open the rear door. Jon threw Qui-Qui inside and dove after her. Sway jammed the Jetta into first and pulled a tight U-turn.

"What the fuck is going on?!" Sway screamed over the gunfire. She hopped the Jetta over a curb and crashed into a trash barrel just as a rocket *whooshed* out of the alley and hit a sedan. The vehicle hopped three feet into the air before exploding in a fireball. The black SUVs broke out of the ambush, men firing from every window. The *federales* popped up from their positions between the parked cars to empty their rifles into the sides of the escaping Yukons. The lead SUV rammed a light pole, and a body took the entire windshield with it as it was ejected. The second SUV swerved around the accident and snapped a chain strung along the perimeter of the parking lot. The third Yukon followed, its rear doors burst open. As it took the curb, a dead gunman rolled out. Another bodyguard clung to an interior strap while wildly firing a submachine gun from the hip. The two SUVs roared down the boulevard and took the corner with screeching tires. The *federales* continued to shoot until the Yukons were out of sight, then they converged on the stalled SUV and focused all their fire on the wreck. A man darted forward to pitch a grenade through a shattered window. Sway was able to get the Jetta turned around before the grenade exploded and scoured the parking lot with a spray of safety glass. She sped off in the opposite direction of the fleeing SUVs, throwing Jon and Qui-Qui to the floorboards.

"Ohfuckohfuckohfuck!" Sway swore as she hunched over the steering wheel.

Jon struggled onto the seat.

"Slow down!" he shouted.

"How's Qui-Qui?" Sway demanded. She hit the brakes to look over her shoulder.

Jon got Qui-Qui up and saw how her head lolled to the side. He felt along her body and found a ragged exit wound on her back, about mid-torso. His hand came away covered in blood.

"How is she?!"

Jon cradled the limp girl in his lap. "I think she's dead."

— · —

Sway paced in circles around the Jetta, unable to stop crying. Jon laid Qui-Qui's body on the backseat and looked for something to cover her with. They had finally pulled over outside a 24-hour *farmacia* where a taco trailer had been set up in the corner of the parking lot. Four men sat on stools in front of the cart, observing them. Jon's shirt and the front of his pants were stiffening with Qui-Qui's blood. In the distance they could hear a cacophony of sirens.

"Oh, Jesus Christ," Sway moaned. "*Madre de Dios.*"

Jon grabbed her as she passed in her orbit around the Jetta.

"We've got to take her to the hospital."

"The hospital?" Sway's attitude shifted from grief to disbelief. "The hospital? She's already DEAD!"

Jon let go of Sway's arm. "What I mean is that we can't keep her body in the backseat. We'll never get across the border. And look," Jon pointed to several bullet holes in the side of the car. "They're going to stop us for sure. We might as well give the hospital a try."

"I'm not leaving her here by herself," Sway said, resuming her circuit of the vehicle. "We've got to get her back to her mom."

"There must be someplace we can drop her off. We'll come back and get her tomorrow."

Sway screamed at him over the hood. "I'm not leaving her!"

"Well, I'm sorry! I've never had to figure out what to do with a body before!"

The men at the taco cart murmured among themselves.

"Fine," Jon said. "You think of some way to get her body across the border without landing us both in prison. I'm going inside to get a shirt."

The clerk behind the desk of the *farmacia* looked up when Jon walked through the door, checked out the blood all over him and went back to his magazine. Jon found lime- green shorts and a Juarez *Indios* soccer T-shirt. He asked the clerk if there was a bathroom. The clerk pointed to the back of the store. When Jon emerged, having been able to clean some of the blood off himself, he found Sway sitting on the hood of her car. Her hair hung in her face, and her eyes were so puffy that they were almost swollen shut.

"What do you want to do with Qui-Qui?"

"I told you—"

"I know," he cut her off. "We're not going to leave her. But how do you propose to get her across the border?"

"We'll do it like the wets," Sway said.

"Come again?"

"We'll take her across the river. I got her into this, and now I'm gonna get her back to her family."

"Sway."

"Thousands of people cross this border every day, and you don't think we can do it?"

"This is nuts. What about the border wall?"

"We'll drive south, down to Guadalupe, and we'll cross there. The fence doesn't run that far. We'll put Qui-Qui on a raft or something. Then one of us will come back for the car and pick the other two up."

"You're serious?"

Sway got into the car and started the engine.

—— • ——

It was after two in the morning when they reached Guadalupe, 45 minutes southeast of Juarez. It wasn't so much a city as a collection of shanties. A bridge crossing was lit up with spotlights, but the security was nothing like the spans between Juarez and El Paso; no razor-wire-topped fences, no concrete abutments, no squadrons of heavily armed Army soldiers. Even with his mind spinning about what he and Sway were about to attempt, Jon couldn't help but think of the Great Wall of China and how one of those Mongols the barrier was supposed to have kept at bay must've taken one look at it before deciding to ride a few more miles to simply go around the end.

They drove along the closest road to the river until they saw a spot that looked crossable. On the way out of Juarez, they'd stopped at a Walmart to buy an air mattress. Sway had gone completely silent. Jon had started to think they might have a better chance putting the body in the trunk and hoping the guards at the border were slacking. The interior of the Jetta was dark blue, so the bloodstains on the upholstery weren't that apparent. The bullet holes posed a problem, but again, Jon thought they had a chance of slipping through without getting searched. As they got closer to their destination, he even suggested that they come right out and declare the dead body, explain what had happened. Sway remained steadfastly silent.

Sway pulled off the road. They could see a few lights upriver in Fabens, Texas, but opposite of where they stood, there was nothing but open ground. A three-quarter moon allowed them to see fairly well once their eyes adjusted.

They wrapped Qui-Qui in a beach towel, and Jon hefted the body over his shoulder. He followed Sway into the low shrubs. They were able to stay on a clearly marked trail to the river. When they reached the bank, Jon laid Qui-Qui's body down, and he and Sway took turns inflating the pool float. The river rippled faintly in the moonlight.

"How deep do you think it is?" Jon asked.

"Three, four feet. It's pretty low, and the current doesn't look too—"

Jon dropped his voice to a whisper. "Look." He pulled Sway to the ground beside him. Fifty yards down the river, six figures emerged from the brush, quiet as deer. The people glanced over at them before wading into the water. They held plastic bags over their heads as they started across.

"I told you," Sway said. "Let's wait and see if they get picked up on the other side."

It took the group five minutes to cross the river. They came out about a hundred feet down the bank on the other side, took their shoes out of the plastic bags and disappeared into the night.

Sway and Jon waited for a few more minutes before putting Qui-Qui's body on the raft and dragging it to the bank. With one of them on each side, they waded into the tepid river. The current was slow, and the fetid-smelling water only came up to Jon's thighs. They beached on the U.S. side and dragged the raft into the bushes. They crouched there, catching their breath.

"Now what?" Jon asked.

"Pick her up and follow me," Sway said.

Jon followed Sway through the shrubs on another game trail. Looking down, he saw several shoeprints. About a hundred yards up from the river they hit a rutted dirt road. They stayed in the bushes.

"Now go back and get the car and meet me here."

"How the hell am I supposed to find this?" Jon asked.

"Keep your voice down. Look, once you get across, take a left on the first road and follow it until you hit this."

"There's no way—"

"Just keep taking left turns until you get to this road. When you find it, keep the lights off and go slow until you see me. The *migra's* got motion sensors all over the place, but they might not spot you if you keep the lights off." Sway looked around. "Look, count the exits along the I-10." In the distance they could see big rigs passing on the highway. Sway figured they were between the third and fourth exit on the freeway before Fabens. She told Jon to use that as his mark.

"And what happens if they won't let me across the border?" Jon asked.

"You're a lawyer. Negotiate. How much money do you have?"

Jon had left his billfold back at the Vag, bringing only his passport, license and forty bucks in his shirt pocket.

"Don't worry, they'll let you across. If they ask about the car, say you hit a deer or a dog."

"And the bullet holes?"

"Make something up." Sway gave him a shove. "Get moving."

"But what are you going to do out here with this body if I *don't* make it across?"

"You'll make it," Sway said.

Jon jogged back to the river.

➤ ◄

It figures that Jon didn't get any sort of hassle at the Fabens checkpoint. Some guy wearing 99-cent-bin lime-green shorts cruises up to the border at 3 a.m. in someone else's bullet-ridden vehicle, the backseat soaked with blood, and they wave him right through after swiping his passport. An old lady pulls up at high noon in a Lincoln plastered with Jesus stickers and they take five hours dismantling her car panel by panel. Then again, they'd probably find a few pounds of off-the-plane quality blow in a trap under the old lady's dashboard.

Jon followed Sway's instructions and started taking

left turns outside of town. He hit several dead ends before finally coming upon the dirt road running parallel to the Rio Grande. The lone access gate to the road was locked, but since Sway's car was already trashed, a few more scrapes on the front bumper wasn't a deterrent to ramming through the three-strand barbed-wire fence and bottoming out in the low ditch. He turned off the headlights and idled slowly down the road until Sway stepped out of the undergrowth. Without speaking, they loaded Qui-Qui's body into the backseat.

They had just closed the back door when they spotted headlights jouncing down the road toward them ahead of a powerful V8 engine. The driver spotlighted them with a high-power beam as he slid to a stop. A pair of men hopped out of the truck bed. The driver turned off the ignition, and for a moment it was so quiet that they could hear the ticking of the engine. A cloud of dust engulfed them for a moment before drifting away.

The two men had deer rifles slung over their shoulders. The driver climbed out of the cab. A bulky set of Army-surplus night-vision goggles hung around his neck.

"This is a citizen's arrest," the driver said in a thick Texas accent. "Y'all are in the custody of the Fabens Minutemen. ¿*Me entiendes?*"

"Oh, fuck this shit," Sway said.

"What's that?" the driver asked as he stepped into the headlights. He was a skinny old guy of about sixty wearing a denim shirt and suspenders. "Y'all speak English?"

"We're American citizens," Jon said, shielding his eyes to avoid the headlight glare.

One of the men with a rifle spoke up. "Then what the

hell y'all doing down here on the river, huh?" He looked over to the driver. "They's picking up wets, Danny."

"In a Volkswagen?" Jon asked.

The one called Danny chewed that one over for a moment. "Well then s'pose y'all tell us what you're doin' down here? This here's a private road."

Jon stepped towards the men. The two with rifles tensed.

"Y'all just stay right where you is," Danny said.

"Gentlemen," Jon said, holding up his passport like a badge, "I understand what you're doing, but in this case, you've got the wrong folks. We're American citizens."

"Where you from, boy?" Danny demanded.

"If it's illegals you're after, we saw half a dozen come through here a couple of minutes ago. They can't have much of a lead on you."

"Y'all running dope?" Danny asked.

"Not even close. If you want to call the police, I'd be glad to explain our situation to them. Short of that, I'll bid you gentlemen goodnight." Jon turned to get into the Jetta.

"Hold on there, boy," Danny said. "Y'all don't go turning your back on me. I said y'all are under citizen's arrest, and I mean it. Y'all can just come on back into town with us and we'll let Sheriff Gammon figger this out. Get in the back of the truck."

"You don't have the authority to detain us," Jon said. "This bullshit might work with the Mexicans, but it doesn't with me. This is illegal confinement."

"I said get in the truck."

Sway stepped forward. "You wanna shoot me?!" she screamed. "Then go ahead and fucking shoot me and get it over with! I swear to God if you motherfuckers don't get out of my way I'll rip out your eyeballs!"

Danny and the two other men took several steps backwards.

"C'mon, you pussies! Shoot me full of fucking holes! You redneck honky faggot cocksuckers!"

Jon tried to stop Sway as she advanced on the men. She pushed him so hard that he fell onto the road. "Get the fuck away from me!"

"I'm calling the goddamn sheriff," Danny said as he and his men made a hasty retreat to their truck and reversed down the road.

Sway screamed obscenities after them as they made a three-point turn and sped off. She dropped to her knees and began to dry-heave. Jon tried to get her to her feet.

"C'mon," he said, "we've got to get out of here."

"I can't take it," Sway wept. "I just can't take another second of this."

Jon led her back to the Jetta and put her in the passenger side. Sway curled up against the door. Five minutes later, they were heading west on the I-10, back to El Paso, the damaged front bumper of the car scraping against the road every time he changed lanes.

"What do we do now?" he asked.

Sway didn't respond.

"Any ideas at all?" he asked.

"Take us to the hospital," Sway said.

Jon looked at her hunkered in the passenger seat.

"What are you going to tell them? She's been dead for five hours."

"If they want to throw me in jail, fine. All that matters is that I got her across." Sway pulled the collar of her filthy blouse over her face and continued to cry silently.

CHAPTER SEVENTEEN

Jon offered to accompany Sway to the emergency room, but she thought there would be fewer questions if she went alone. News of the shootout at El Babylon was already on AM radio, and Sway hoped the police—the cops would have to get involved—would understand why she felt so strongly about getting her cousin's body back to the States. If they went to the surveillance tapes at the Fabens crossing and saw Jon driving her car across alone... well, then she'd have to do some more explaining. But at 5 a.m., with the sun creeping over the horizon, the hospital seemed like the easiest thing to do. Back at the Vag, Jon took a scalding shower to wash the Rio Grande and Qui-Qui off himself, then climbed into bed. He lay on his back staring at the ceiling, replaying the night's events, too tired for unconsciousness. His head buzzed from the gunshots and fatigue.

Realizing he would never be able to fall asleep, Jon took another shower and called a taxi. He directed the driver to the storage unit he'd visited upon arriving in El Paso. He had the cab wait until he found what he was looking for—an old color prospectus from Bowden-Everitt that Jon had seen the other time he'd looked through the shed. The company had since changed their info packets, but on the front of this dated one was a picture of Bowden and Everitt standing in the middle of the international bridge. Jon tucked the brochure in his pocket and closed up the shed. He told the driver to take him to Moon's office and to wait outside while he spoke with the private investigator.

"What the hell happened to you?" Moon asked when Jon appeared in front of his desk.

"Long story."

"Listen, man, I didn't send any more invoices to your folks. They just wanted me to make sure you were okay."

"This is my family, remember? What did you tell them?"

"Listen, bud, I don't want to get in the middle of this jackpot, okay?"

"Too bad. Triple cherry. I need you to check up on a person. A mortician. Name of Claude Terry."

Moon scribbled the name on a Post-It note. "What does he have to do with your brother?"

"I'm not sure. Just check him out. You owe me that much."

"But what the hell am I looking for?"

"See who he owes money to. Find out if he's got double mortgages on his house. You're the border blood-hound; you figure it out."

"You could've called," Moon said.

"I wanted to see how your secretary was doing with the cigarettes. Where is she?"

"Maternity leave. A boy."

"Give me a shout after you look at Terry."

"Man, you ought to check yourself out in the mirror. El Paso doesn't appear to be agreeing with your constitution."

———

Six hours later, Jon was tossing and turning in bed when three loud raps on the door startled him from his light slumber.

"Who is it?" Jon asked from bed.

Whoever it was knocked again, this time using a fist. Jon pulled on his pants and looked around the blinds to see two men on the walkway. The one with the mustache wore jeans and a pink Polo shirt. The one standing off to the side sported sloppy gray sweatpants and a wind-breaker. Jon looked around for a weapon, but all he found was a chair.

"What do you want?" Jon asked through the closed door.

"Mr. Lennox?" Polo shirt asked.

"Yes?"

"Pretty late to be in bed," he commented.

"What do you want?"

"I'm Detective Marx," he said, holding his badge up to the peephole. "This is Detective Burmudez. We're with the El Paso Police Department. We'd like you to come to the station with us."

"What for?"

"Why don't you open the door?"

"How do I know you're really cops?"

"Because we knocked."

Back in the familiar detectives' pen, Marx and Burmudez led Jon into one of the outer offices. Marx had kept up a steady, mindless banter while they'd driven over, but his partner had yet to say a word. They sat Jon in a plastic chair and wheeled an ancient TV/VCR set into the room. Burmudez flicked off the lights. The black-and-white video showed a scratchy surveillance-camera view of a parking lot.

"You know where this is?" Marx asked as he took a seat on the edge of the desk.

Jon shook his head.

"Check out that truck over on the other side of the lot. See that thing? Now who the hell would drive a monster truck like that?"

Jon didn't say anything.

"Would you believe a mortician drives that piece of shit?" Marx asked. "To a funeral home? Go figure, right? This is getting boring; let's fast-forward a little bit. Okay, here we go."

The tape showed a Buick pulling into the parking lot.

"Recognize that guy?" Marx asked, pointing to a bald figure making his way into the building.

Jon stared at the screen.

"Well, it's hard to tell because this tape is so shitty, but that's some private eye named Moon. Ever heard of him? No? Okay, so let's fast-forward a little more."

"Is there a payoff coming?" Jon asked.

"Oh, yeah." Marx pushed "Play" on the remote. "So Moon's inside there for about five minutes. Secretary said he was asking to speak to the boss man. Boss isn't around, she said. Been AWOL for a whole day at that point. So here he comes out of the office. The dick's heading back to his car, then he spots the monster truck. Looks kinda out of place. He thinks he might want to check it out." Marx spoke to his partner. "This guy is tight, huh, Detective?"

Burmudez grunted.

"Now watch this," Marx said. "This is the good part."

The video showed Moon circle the truck. Then he climbed up on the high running board and pulled the driver's-side door open.

"Whoops!" Marx said.

Moon recoiled from the door as if he'd been electrocuted. His foot caught on the running board and he landed flat on his back. Despite the fall, Moon rolled onto his stomach and scrambled away from the 4x4 on his hands and knees. He must've hollered, because a woman ran out of the building. She went over to Moon, who was lying on the ground, and then to the open door of the truck. What she saw sent her screaming back into the building. Marx stopped the tape and his partner hit the overhead fluorescents, which took a moment to buzz to life.

"Now here's the big question," Marx said. "What the hell was in that truck?"

Burmudez dropped a stack of photos in Jon's lap. They were hard to make out at first because they were close-ups. Jon looked at three before he knew what he was seeing. He let them slide off his lap and averted his eyes. He took a couple of quick breaths.

"They call that a 'Juarez Blowjob,'" Marx explained, gathering the photos from the floor. "They cut your pecker off and shove it in your mouth. You ever seen anything like that?"

Jon walked to the window.

"Now you're wondering why we woke you up from your nap and brought you all the way over here to show you this, right? Well, guess who this dick—no pun intended—said he was working for?"

"Call Detective Sheffield," Jon said.

"Sheffield?" Marx said. "What do you want Sheffield for?"

"Just call Detective Sheffield."

"What the hell?" Marx said after a moment. "Call super cop." They left Jon in the room by himself with the crime-scene photos spread across the desk. As soon as they left, Jon swept them into a desk drawer

A half-hour later, Jon heard the detectives talking with Iraan in the hallway outside the office. Iraan opened the door halfway.

"…guy in the truck sucking his own dick and this one in here asking for you. He hired the private investigator. Paperwork was right there on his P.I.'s desk when we checked his office. Your guy was at that roach motel over on Mesa that all the soldiers use to party. Asleep."

"Great," Iraan said. "The video show the hit?"

"Nope. They broke in and took the first tape, but were kind enough to replace it with a fresh one so we could see this wonderful show. Coroner's guessing it happened last night."

"You know this guy?" Marx asked, looking inside the office.

"Give me a minute," Iraan said.

"Just don't go messing up his statement," Marx said.

"Get the fuck off of me, man."

"Hey, it's yo' world, brutha," Marx said in a heavy jive accent. "I'm just livin' in it."

"What the hell are you doing?" Iraan hissed after closing the office door behind him.

"This guy Terry. You said—"

"I know what I said." Iraan brought the chair from behind the desk so he sat face to face with Jon. "Where'd you put the pictures?" Jon nodded to the drawer.

Iraan shuffled through the stack. "I said it was a theory. That's all. A theory that turned out to be a dead end."

"You ever see anything like that?" Jon asked.

"Pretty fucked up, huh?"

"I mean, I've read about it in books...but that...that's off the charts."

"What the hell did you hire the guy for in the first place?"

"You told me—"

"I know what I told you." Iraan lowered his voice. "And I'd appreciate it if you didn't tell Marx and Burmudez how you got the idea. You copy?"

"Yeah, but look at that. Doesn't that mean he did? I mean, why else would—"

"Shut up for a second so I can think. What have you told these guys so far?"

"Nothing."

Marx walked into the office without knocking. "How about this, Detective? Terry was bowling at East Side Lanes the other night. One of the folks on the mortician's bowling team just told us that Terry said some dude hassled him in the bowling alley parking lot after the game." Marx smiled. "Guess what his description is?"

At ten o'clock that night, Jon was still in Detective Marx's office. They'd come to check on him every hour, but they hadn't asked him any more questions. All they'd given him to eat was a cold bean burrito along with a warm Hi-C juice box to wash it down. No one had told him that he couldn't leave, but Jon suspected that they would have if he tried to exit. Finally, Iraan opened the door and told him it was over.

"What is?" Jon asked.

"They know how you got Terry's name. So forget the Fifth and tell them the whole story. You'll be clean and out of here in another hour."

"What about you?"

"Maybe you should have thought about that before-hand." Iraan turned to leave. "I don't suppose you visited any strip clubs in Juarez last night?"

Jon looked at him.

"Great," Iraan said, leaving Jon alone again in the office. "Just fucking great."

Jon was nodding off in the detective's reclining chair when an older man in wrinkled khakis and a polyester dress shirt sat down across the desk from him. He regarded Jon for a full ten seconds before speaking.

"Do you want this chair?" Jon asked finally.

"I'm sorry about your brother," the older man said.

"Am I under arrest?"

The man rocked in the chair before speaking. "No."

"Then I can leave?"

"Sure."

Jon started to get up.

"Have a seat, son."

Jon sat back down.

"You're mixed up in a nasty situation here," the man said. "You're aware of that, right? You heard about the Mexican girl getting all shot up in Juarez last night?"

"May I ask who you are?"

"I'm the boss."

"Of what?"

The man chuckled as he extracted a soft pack of Merit cigarettes from his shirt pocket. He pulled the plastic chair over so he could crack the window behind the desk.

Jon swiveled in his chair. "You're the chief of police?"

The man shot a plume of smoke out the window. "Close."

"Wonderful job you're doing."

He laughed. "I guess you got your legs back underneath you now, Counselor. Marx said the little slide show from the mortuary made you a bit queasy."

Jon didn't reply.

"You like this cowboys-and-indians stuff? Got the old adrenaline pumping? It gets a lot worse than that garbage at the funeral home," the man said. He nodded his head. "That was pretty tame compared to some other things I've seen. How'd you like to have that done to you, though? Have your dingus cut off and stuffed in your mouth while you're still alive?" The chief took a big drag off his cigarette. "Mr. Lennox, you're in way over your head."

"People keep telling me that. And you know what I keep telling them?"

The chief shook his head.

"That they can—"

"Stop right there." The cop flicked his cigarette out the window and crossed his legs. "Just tell me why."

"Doesn't this latest episode prove it?"

"I don't ascribe to Sheffield's or his late partner Shannon's theory about Lazaro using Terry to get rid of cartel bodies, if that's what you're alluding to. It's too much work for these lazy bastards."

"Why?"

"Son, that dog don't hunt."

"Why?"

"Because it don't." The man lit another cigarette and didn't bother trying to blow the smoke out the window this time. "Now, we could go back and piece together how you, the private eye, the mortician and the girl getting shot over in Juarez last night all fit together, but it don't seem worth the time and effort to build that case. And I wish I could order you to leave town, but you're a lawyer and you know I can't. So if you feel better being down here, be my guest. But the way you're going around poking at this hornet's nest isn't doing anybody any favors. Just ask Terry and that girl. So why don't you just enjoy the city? Take a nice trip over to New Mexico. Play some golf." He blew a vapor trail of smoke across the desk into Jon's face. "But leave the police work to the police."

The cop and Jon stared at each other for a few seconds.

"Do we understand each other?" he asked.

Jon nodded.

"Good. Because if we don't, I can promise you your ass is gonna be in a serious goddamn sling." The man got up and patted Jon's shoulder. "You look like shit, Counselor." He left the door open.

Jon waited for a moment before walking out of the station into the night. He was crossing the parking lot when he noticed Iraan's Trans-Am. Jon went across the street to a Good Times convenience store to buy himself a Diet Dr Pepper and a bag of pretzels. He sat on a bus stop bench opposite the police station and waited. A half-hour later, Iraan emerged with a large gym bag. Jon met him at his car.

"What happened?" Jon asked.

Iraan set his bag on the hood.

"Did they fire you?"

Iraan snorted.

"Jesus, Iraan, I'm sorry."

"I should have driven you back to Denver myself," Iraan said. "Letting you stay down here was pure self-sabotage." Iraan unlocked his car door. "Get in. I'll drive you home."

They didn't talk on their way back to the motel. When they pulled into the parking lot, Jon asked Iraan if he wanted to come up. He said no. As Jon was heading toward the stairs, he heard Iraan get out of the car.

"Hold on a second," Iraan called. "There's something on your door."

Iraan told Jon to wait on the lower level. He moved quietly up the stairs and along the wall until he got to Jon's room. He reached over and pulled off a piece of paper.

"What is it?" Jon asked.

Iraan dropped the note over the railing. It was written on a phone-company work order.

Call me.

"Let's talk about Mexican strip clubs," Iraan said.

— ·—

"All this means is somebody wanted Terry whacked," Iraan said. It was a little past one in the morning, and they were sitting at a corner table at a Village Inn on Mesa. Traffic was thin, but the red-light camera at the intersection would occasionally flash its strobe to catch a driver making an illegal right turn or trying to beat the signal. Something about the quick, bright flashes made Jon wince, and he finally took a seat on the other side of the table so he didn't have to see them.

The two waitresses on duty sat at the counter sharing a Sudoku puzzle. He and Iraan were the only customers.

"Don't you think it's a hell of a coincidence that I follow Terry the night before last, and then the next day he gets killed?" Jon asked.

"I don't understand the way your mind works," Iraan said, cutting into a patty melt. "Some dudes just tried to *shoot* you. You know how many folks got capped last night?"

"I know about one," Jon said, looking into his glass of water.

"Well, go on," Iraan said, chewing.

"Okay, so they've got him, but they can't let him go. They find out I'm down here, like your boss said—"

"Ex-boss."

"Right. Like he said, I'm down here poking the hornet's nest, and I get around to Terry. They figure that if I keep after Terry, he'll cop to something. Maybe they just want Terry dead anyway and need an excuse."

Iraan pointed his fork at Jon. "These guys don't need an excuse. I mean, shit, that chick's boyfriend set up an ambush outside the building she *works in*, man. These dudes don't give a fuck." Iraan chewed for a moment. "But the fact that they came across to do Terry is out of the ordinary. Even with three thousand homeboys getting hit in J-town last year, we only caught three on this side that seemed to have any direct connect to the cartels. That, along with the bloodbath at El Bobby last night, tells me something's up. But you're missing the key point here."

"Which is what?"

"That if they know you know about Terry, they know about you. What's to stop them from knocking you the same way?"

"My brother's got something. I mean, what's the whole deal with getting stopped twice in Mexico by these guys playing cops and getting let off each time?"

Iraan took a swallow of iced tea. "You know, the one possibility here you ain't been trying to think about from the get-go is that your bro was hooked into this shit. I don't know why you won't acknowledge that possibility."

"Do you want to hear about last night?" Jon asked.

"It was all right there in the newspaper."

Jon looked at him.

"Now you see what I'm talking about."

Jon took the Bowden-Everitt brochure out of his pocket and laid it on the table. He tapped the picture of Stan Everitt. "You ever see this guy before?"

— ✦ —

"Not like TV, huh?" Iraan said.

"I still don't even really know what happened."

"You got shot at and then you had to drag a body all over Juarez, that's what. That shit's gonna stay with you for a minute." Iraan was working on a piece of apple pie with two inches of old whipped cream sitting on the top. "I'm impressed you jumped out of the car for that girl. Shit, I don't think I'd have done that. You go through it in your head all the time about being in that position, and you wonder if you end up running *to* or *from* the fight. Most of the fools who say they would jump right in that shit ain't never even been close enough to find out."

"What about that big shootout you told me about with your partner? When you went in to save Paulino?"

"Dude, I was in the truck the whole time. My partner and Manny took off to save Paulino's ass. After all the dust settled, I don't think anyone noticed I was still sitting right there in the Jeep. Like I said, it takes a strange motherfucker to go running into a firefight."

Iraan sized Jon up for a moment. "Just goes to show."

"Show what?"

"You even a mystery to yourself."

Iraan took another look at the picture of Everitt on the brochure. "You sure this was the dude?"

"Positive," Jon said. "When he stepped out of the truck, this other guy, Cisneros, was taking a piss and the guy turned his head away, looked right at me."

"Okay," Iraan said. "Your brother's boss Everitt is hanging out with Cisneros. They've got some deal in the works, and that gets Lazaro going because these NAFTA guys are supposed to stay out of the game. So Lazaro puts the hit out on Everitt to show the rest of the *yanquis* that they'd better keep their noses clean. Some of Lazaro's scouts see your brother down there all by his lonesome, figure they'll snatch him. Or maybe it was just whiteboy day and they grabbed the first head they saw that looked NAFTA. But you can't tell me they kept your brother alive after that. It was your boy Lazaro who said it's better to kill six innocent men than to have one guilty man go free." Iraan chewed an ice cube. "Or maybe they're just giving your dumb ass a chance to split."

"But why?"

Iraan slapped his hands down on the table, making the silverware jump. "Dude, why you always fuckin' with me? I don't know why! Nobody knows why! Just leave it, all right?"

The waitress cautiously approached with a pitcher of iced tea. She topped Iraan off and dropped the check before retreating to the other side of the coffee shop.

"I can't leave until I'm sure," Jon said.

"I know this is your brother we're talking about, but c'mon, man...this is just like some kind of personal problem you got going. I mean, I got a good professional reason and I'm walking away."

"But if we—"

Iraan rattled the ice in his glass. "I'll agree that the idea that your bro's company was mixed up in this makes some sense—especially in light of last night's events. But all you can do at this point is keep hoping that they get whatever they want from your brother and let him go.

You're just compromising the situation. What the hell do you want out of this anyway? You want to cap Lazaro? Get some revenge?"

"I just want to talk to the man. That's it. If we can get—"

"You keep saying 'we.' There is no 'we' on this deal. I'm out, man. Sayofuckingnara. I'm a citizen."

Jon folded the Bowden-Everitt brochure into a tight square. Iraan took a look at the check for the meal and pushed it over to Jon. "Appreciate the dinner."

"Thanks for all your help," Jon muttered.

"Shit, man, if there was something I thought I could do, then, yeah, I'd pitch in. But there's no way to get at him. With all the heat over there, I'll bet dude is down in Cabo waiting tables like they say he does." Iraan slid off his chair and started for the door. "You want a ride?"

"I'll walk."

Iraan was pulling out of his spot when Jon tapped the roof of the Trans-Am. Iraan lowered the window.

Jon leaned in. "What if I could get Lazaro on our side of the border?"

"You gonna ask him to come across for coffee?"

Jon could still hear Iraan laughing as he turned left out of the parking lot and took off down Mesa.

CHAPTER EIGHTEEN

"I'm at the airport."

"Which airport?" Jon asked.

"Which one do you think? Come pick me up."

"I don't have a car."

Cheryl sighed. "Okay, I'll take a cab."

Jon pulled the pillow over his face.

"Jon? Where are you?" Cheryl was still on the line.

"Didn't your private detective give you all the details?" he asked.

"That was *not* my idea. I'm getting in the cab right now. Do any of these guys speak English?"

Jon stepped into the shower but didn't turn on the water. He got out and leaned over the sink to assess his four-day stubble and the dark circles under his eyes in the mirror. He pulled on the lime-colored Mexico shorts and a white T-shirt, not bothering to comb his hair. He went out to the walkway and knocked on Jimmy's door.

"What?!"

It was ten in the morning, and it didn't look like Jimmy had made it to bed the night before. He was wearing his surf shorts and a Jägermeister shirt. He had a smoking soldering iron in hand. Jon explained that his wife was on the way.

"You better get dressed," Jimmy said, giving Jon the once-over.

"No, I think I'll go with this."

"I get it," Jimmy smiled. "You want to give her the *waka-waka-waka*." He cuffed himself on the side of the head and bugged his eyes.

"Sort of."

Jimmy yanked the soldering-iron cord from the outlet. "You want a drink? They love it when you stink of booze."

Jon declined as Jimmy fixed himself a Crown and Coke. They went to the walkway railing and waited for the cab.

"Divorce?" Jimmy asked, hustling his balls.

"Looks like it."

"Pre-nup?"

"Nope."

"Cheers." Jimmy polished off his drink.

The cab arrived fifteen minutes later. Jon and Jimmy watched as Cheryl slid out of the maroon Border Taxi and surveyed her surroundings. She didn't pay the driver until she looked up and spotted Jon.

"Good God," Jimmy said. "She's fucking hot."

"Yeah," Jon said.

Cheryl was wearing white slacks with a matching blazer, and when she got up to the landing, she started to give Jon a hug.

"Jesus," she said, pulling away. "You smell."

Jimmy introduced himself as Major Gates.

"You're in the military?" Cheryl asked, taking a look at his outfit.

"Disabled vet," Jimmy reported. "But ready and willing to serve. You want a drink?"

Cheryl glanced at her Cartier. "It's a little early for me." She turned to Jon. "We need to talk."

"Sure, step inside."

They made their way into Jon's apartment. Jimmy followed.

"Does, uh, Major Gates have to be here?" Cheryl asked.

"Okay," Jon said. "Jimmy, I'll catch up with you later."

"You've got five minutes to explain yourself," Cheryl said as soon as Jimmy closed the door.

"There's nothing to explain." Jon said. "You can have it."

"Fuck you, Jon." Cheryl looked around for a place to sit. "You've been living here?"

"What's with the surprise visit?"

"Dr. Ghausi suggested it," Cheryl said, taking a careful seat on the edge of the bed. "He thought I might be able to talk some sense into you if I caught you off guard. Ghausi's living in your folks' guest cottage now."

"You're kidding."

"Totally serious. You and your mom both appear to be using this thing for your own purposes." Cheryl reclined on the bed. "You look terrible, Jon."

"It's been a long couple of days."

There was a knock at the door.

"Come in!" Jon called.

Sway opened the portal and took in the scene.

"Wonderful timing," Cheryl said, shaking her head.

"I hate to interrupt..." Sway searched for a word, "... this. But you might want to check out your neighbor."

Jon and Cheryl went next door, where Jimmy was lying on the floor, unconscious next to his stun gun. Jon knelt down and slapped him lightly until Jimmy came around.

"It didn't melt this time," Jimmy said, blinking a couple times.

Cheryl threw up her hands and went back to Jon's apartment and slammed the door. Sway helped Jon pull Jimmy to his feet. He shook his head a few times. "My mouth tastes like pennies," Jimmy said.

"You're a maniac," Sway said.

"Roger that. Where's your wife?"

"I think I'd better give her time to cool out."

Sway's eyes were bloodshot from crying. "Do these dreams ever stop?" she asked Jimmy as she unraveled another length of toilet paper to blot her tears.

"They come less frequently," he said. "The head-shrinker at the VA told me something like how dreams are the same as when the physical body sweats; they help process the bad memories. That's what he said, anyway. He also said I was probably gay."

Sway blew her nose. "All I had to do is get out of there when I saw what was going on, and instead I froze. And then I'm thinking about how bad I should feel about Qui-Qui, but I feel worse for myself, for having to go through that whole thing."

Jimmy opened the fridge and peered inside. "Yeah. Well. What the fuck? What are you gonna do?"

Sway lifted her feet so Jimmy could sit down. "If I had any balls," he continued, "I'd be out there telling these guys to run to Canada, warning them about the clusterfuck they're walking into. But all they care about is getting their war on."

"You can't?" Sway asked.

"I'd be a goldbricker if I did. These are supposed to be my brothers, but I'm just sitting here, letting it happen. Covering my ass with this 'Warrior Code' bullshit."

"Would it do any good?" Sway asked. "To tell them the truth?"

"Probably not."

"Why don't you go home?"

"Home?" Jimmy asked.

"Maybe it wouldn't be so hard if you got away from all this."

"All this," Jimmy said, gesturing around the cluttered room, "is the only thing keeping me from going nuts. I went back to Pennsylvania after I got out of the hospital, and it was even worse. At least I know where I am when I wake up here."

Jon knocked the back of his head against the wall. "She could've let me know she was coming. I could have saved her the trip."

Jimmy pointed a crooked finger at Jon. "If you weren't such a pussy, you would've told her you wanted a divorce a long time ago."

"Yeah," Sway said. "You shouldn't be treating her like this."

"Look who's talking!" Jon said.

The three of them sat in silence for a few minutes.

The air conditioner whooshed to life and Jon hauled himself off the saggy couch. Jimmy and Sway watched him walk out the door. Back in his room, Cheryl was lying facedown on the bed.

"Cheryl, I'm gonna be straight with you."

"Spare me," she said. "I've heard every goddamn thing you three have been saying for the past hour. The walls are like cardboard in this dump."

"Then you understand why I'm down here."

"I knew it when you left, you jerk. You were just waiting for an excuse to blow up your life, and this was the first thing that came along that you could justify. I'll admit things haven't been what we pretended they were, but really...what do you want?" She rolled onto her side. "Is it that bad?"

Jon didn't answer.

"I guess it is." Cheryl sighed and swung her legs over the edge of the bed.

"Where are you going?" Jon asked.

"I'm going to Palm Desert." Cheryl went to the mirror and stared fixing her hair. "This is sexual abandonment, you know?" She looked at Jon's reflection. "You are sleeping with that girl, aren't you?"

"It only takes one look, huh?"

Cheryl nodded.

"What about Jack Swanson?"

"I have an attorney who can get around that. Besides, I only did it to get your attention."

"You don't want to do this the nice way?"

"I don't even know what the 'nice way' is anymore.

By the way, how the hell have you been paying for this luxurious lifestyle? I canceled your credit cards."

"I had some money set aside."

"I'll have to let my lawyer know about that."

"It's not that kind of money." Jon looked up at his wife. "Did you ever feel like if you could just figure one thing out, then maybe everything else would fall into place?"

"You're talking about your brother?"

"Yes."

Cheryl touched up her lipstick. "Do you expect anyone besides those idiots next door to buy that?"

"No," Jon said, getting up. "I guess not."

        ➤ ━

"She's not so bad," Jimmy said after they'd dropped Cheryl off at the airport.

"You want to come on up to Denver for the preliminary hearing?" Jon asked. "See what she has to say about you to the judge?"

"I guess you hanging out at the Vag probably won't look so good, huh?"

"No, it won't. She's going to get the whole ball of wax."

"Some guy told me that being completely screwed is sort of liberating."

"He was lying."

Sway leaned forward between the cramped seats of Jimmy's Mustang. "What your wife said about you using your brother as an excuse? Is that true? I'm only asking because I want to know if you're serious about it now."

"I'm going to figure out what the hell happened, if that's what you're asking," Jon said. "I've got to come out with at least that."

"Good," Sway said, "because I'm going to find Lalo and fuck him up."

"You two are both going to end up getting shot," Jimmy said.

A cell phone chimed in Sway's purse. She pulled it out and looked at the caller ID. "Okay," she said. "Here's where we start."

CHAPTER NINETEEN

Sway had been too tired to tell the police any lies at the hospital, and although they hadn't been happy about the way she'd sneaked the body across the border and threatened her with a multitude of obstruction-of-justice charges, once they'd checked her story out, they started to understand her actions. The next day, she'd been going through Qui-Qui's backpack and had come across her cousin's BlackBerry. There were ten text messages and five voicemail messages waiting, nine of them from someplace called the Super Seven in El Paso. The name didn't register with Sway, so she did a reverse search on the number and came up with a convenience store downtown. Since she didn't have Qui-Qui's code to check the messages, she waited for another call from the Super Seven, which she got later that day. It was Lalo.

As Jon had noted that night in Juarez, Sway and her cousin sounded very much alike, so when Sway picked up, Lalo launched right into a rant about how she shouldn't have been interfering in his business and how she might have gotten killed in the process. After he'd given Sway/ Qui-Qui hell for following him to El Bobby, he started feeling around to see how much she knew about his little girlfriend at the Joker. Sway let him have it on that account and then promptly hung up. He'd called back a few more times, but she hadn't answered. Qui-Qui's funeral was later that day, and she half expected Lalo to show. But Lalo wasn't looking for a death notice, and the day after the memorial, he called several more times from the downtown El Paso number.

"You're saying Lalo is hiding out on this side of the border?" Jon asked after Sway relayed her story.

"There's one way to find out," Sway said. "325 North Kansas. The Super Seven market."

"You guys are going to get yourselves shot," Jimmy repeated.

"You're not going to come?" Sway asked.

"Hell, no," Jimmy said. "Two wars were enough for me."

━━▶ ◀━━

As they made their way downtown in one of the phone company's compact field pickups, Jon tried to convince Sway not to jump Lalo right when she saw him. That wouldn't get them any closer to Lazaro. Patience was the key, he explained.

"Listen to you," Sway said as she parked two blocks down the street from the Super Seven. "You never listened when I told you to be patient. You just went around messing things up for everybody. Now you want me to *cálmate?*"

"Can you go in there and see what's up without blowing the whole deal?"

"If Lalo really wants to talk to Qui-Qui, then I guess he'll talk to her cousin. But, damn, I'm promising you that I'm going to kick that little son of a bitch's ass before it's over."

"I'll help you," Jon said.

Sway stared at him. "No, you won't."

An electronic chime beeped when Sway walked through the door of the mini-mart, and the chubby white guy behind the counter put down the paper he'd been reading. He pushed his thick-framed glasses up on his nose.

"Can I help you?" he asked.

Sway looked around the store. The shelves along the two aisles were sparsely stocked with sundries, but the coolers on the wall were full of beer. A large Plexiglas lottery display sat next to the register along with a rack of skin magazines and international pre-paid calling cards. Sway turned to face the man, and his eyes dropped straight to her chest. He flushed.

"I'm looking for Lalo," she said, hunching her shoulders instinctively to hide her breasts from the man's gaze.

"Lalo what?"

"Lalo," she repeated.

"I don't know what you're talking about," the clerk said.

Sway stepped up to the counter, "Is your number 241-9612?"

"Shit," the clerk said, sitting back heavily on his stool. "I knew it was too good to last."

"Pardon me?"

"I ain't gonna pay for the whole damn year," the clerk said. "It's your guys' fault nobody ever sent me a bill."

"Come again?"

"Oh, Jesus, lady. Stop playing. I know the score. You're from the phone company." The clerk pointed at her shirt, which had the SBC logo stitched onto the pocket. "Look, I'll start paying for the damn phone, but like I said, I ain't paying any back fees, because you guys forgot to send me the bill. I even called one time, and I got put on hold for an hour."

"Well," Sway said after a moment, "just because you didn't get the bill doesn't mean we didn't send one. If you're using the service, you're obligated—by law—to pay for it."

"I knew it was too good to last," the clerk repeated.

"How many phones do you have on the premises?" Sway asked.

"This one here and one in the office."

"I'll need to check the lines to make sure they're working properly."

"Are you gonna try and screw me for the back charges or what?"

"Sir, this is part of a routine audit." Sway grabbed a grape Popsicle from the ice cream cooler. She stripped the wrapper and took a bite off the top. "But between you and me, I think you're in the clear for the old bills. We've got some real fuckups in accounting. This kind of thing happens more than you'd think. How much for the *palo*?"

"Lady, you get all this sorted out without me having to pay nothing, and the Popsicle is free."

Sway asked if she could see the phone in the office. The clerk led her into a dark storeroom that smelled of copy toner and dishwater. The man stood at the door as Sway picked up the receiver and called Jon's cell phone.

"Hey, Jeff," she said when Jon picked up, "this is Navarro from the 9612. What's this signal looking like from your side?"

"Uh, Sway?" Jon said as he sat in the truck down the block.

"Five by five? Great. I'll run this line and then scoot over to D station."

"Is this code or something?"

Sway winked at the clerk again. "No, don't bother. I'll talk to that idiot Marny in billing when I get back to the office. Bye."

"Hey," the clerk said. "I really appreciate this. I mean, I made a few long-distance calls."

"Don't sweat it," Sway said, turning her Popsicle sideways to get at the bottom bit. "But you're going to start getting a bill as of next month."

"I knew it was too good to last."

Sway handed him her Popsicle stick. "Good shit never does."

"Lalo's not in there," Sway reported when she got back to the vehicle.

"So why is this number showing up on the caller ID?"

"I'm going to have to get the other truck tomorrow and look at the AP and the crossbox. But if I had to guess, I'd bet Lazaro and his guys are routing their calls through this poor jerk's drop and then paying his bill so he never sees the calls."

"In English, please?"

"The drop is the actual line from the crossbox. It's right over there." She pointed to a large greenish-gray utility box at the end of the block. "I'll come over tomorrow in the big truck and take a look. I'll bet there's some sort of relay in there. Pretty clever."

"Maybe when you go in there, you might add a little something to listen in with."

Sway smiled. "That's highly illegal. Besides, where do you think I can find an electronic ear? I work for the phone company, not the CIA."

"Let's pick up a rack of beers on the way home," Jon said.

"You drink now?"

"Jimmy does."

— • —

"That's a federal offense," Jimmy said as he ripped open the twelve-pack of Beck's and fished one out. "Imported," he said after taking a swig. "Nice."

"The question is, can you do it?" Jon asked.

"Well…I'd need some equipment. How far would the signal have to travel?"

"We don't want to set up right there," Sway said. "So let's say a half-mile—mile, tops. I have an aunt who lives pretty close to the store."

Jimmy drained his beer and blinked.

"Purely as an exercise…"

"There you go," Jon said.

"I think I can set something up to grab the signal and transmit it that distance. I'll need equipment. We still don't know what we're looking at, right?"

"I haven't been inside the AP yet," Sway said. "You want to take a look first?"

"If it's coming through a regular phone line, I don't think it'll be too much trouble." Jimmy opened another beer by slapping the cap against the side of the kitchenette counter. The counter had been used so many times in this fashion that it looked like a Doberman had been gnawing on it. "My concern is that they've got some kind of trip built in that'll let them know we've hacked it."

"Do we need to go to the base now?" Jon asked.

"What base?" Jimmy asked.

"Fort Bliss."

"For what?"

"You said you need equipment for this job."

"Yeah, but it ain't coming from Bliss. You think I can just waltz in there and help myself to field radios and relays?"

"Then where are we supposed to get the stuff?"

"There's a Home Depot and Walmart on Mesa."

— • —

Later that afternoon, Sway and Jimmy dressed in SBC uniforms and took a truck to the phone box by the Super Seven to take a look at the setup relaying the phone calls from Juarez. Jimmy spent the rest of the evening building a bug that they'd place the following day. Jon's job was to ration Jimmy's beers so that he didn't get too drunk to finish the project. Jimmy had gutted two cheap walkie-talkies and a cassette recorder, which he then started to reassemble into one unit.

"If I didn't know what I was looking for, I wouldn't

have even seen it," Sway said. "No technician would've unless they were there to disconnect the line."

"It's nice stuff," Jimmy said as he soldered a circuit board. He was wearing safety glasses and a banker's visor with two mini-flashlights taped to the sides. "The whole relay's about the size of a box of Tic Tacs." Jimmy looked around for his beer. Jon had his count at eight, so he got another for him from the fridge.

"What about the clerk in the store?" Jon asked.

"I had Jimmy go in and take a look beforehand. It was a different dude working. But I checked the records at the office, and somebody's been paying the Super Seven bill online every month since last summer. They signed up for paperless, so no actual bills ever got sent out. Big bills, though. Like six hundred bucks a month. Ninety percent of the calls go right back into Mexico."

"Christ, if this thing works, we could really be on to something."

"How's that?" Sway asked.

"I mean, the cops would do a lot for that kind of information."

"The cops aren't gonna find out about this, because this is illegal. Some of us still have to work, you know?"

"All I'm saying…" Jon said, leaning over Jimmy's shoulder. "If it works…"

"What do you mean 'if'?" Jimmy asked, taking another swallow of beer.

CHAPTER TWENTY

Sway and Jimmy installed their tap the following day and set up the receiver—a Frankenstein boombox Jimmy had slapped together to pick off the Super Seven telephone signal—at Sway's aunt's house. The aunt was more than happy to let them convert a spare bedroom into a listening post. They intercepted their first phone conversation a couple of minutes after turning the power on. It was Lalo calling his buddy Esteban to talk motorcycles, a fairly banal conversation that Sway loosely translated for Jimmy and Jon. The only interesting part was when Lalo's buddy asked him about Qui-Qui, and if she was still giving him the cold shoulder.

"Qui-Qui who?" Lalo asked. "I already forgot about that one."

"*No mamas, güey*, you're in love with her. You shouldn't have been screwing around with that *fresa*."

Lalo sighed. "I can't do anything about it now. She won't answer the phone. She'll come back, though. Who wants to live like a peasant on the other side when they can live like a queen with me?"

The two men bid each other goodbye, and Sway punched the wall so hard she put a dent in the drywall.

"Son of a bitch!" she said, rubbing her knuckles.

Jimmy yawned. "Great," he said. "It works. Now, do we have to sit around here listening to these fools talk about their girlfriends and motorcycles, or can we go to Erin's?"

Sway's aunt appeared in the doorway wearing a floor-length black skirt and a T-shirt bearing a rhinestone image of Jesus on the cross. She asked who was hitting her walls.

"I'm sorry, *tía*," Sway said. "*Le oí decir algo malo* about Qui-Qui."

Sway's aunt crossed herself, tracing the crucifix portrayed on her shirt. "God will never forgive him for taking our little angel. So many lost too soon because of those *malcriados narcos*."

Sway asked her aunt if she had anything planned for that afternoon. Her aunt shrugged. What is there for an old lady to do? she asked. Would she be interested in monitoring the tap while they were away? Jimmy showed her how to start recording if there was any mention of a kidnapped American, Lazaro's whereabouts, or anything else that sounded interesting.

"Don't worry," Sway's aunt said, settling into an easy chair with a *telenovela* magazine. "I've seen all the movies. I know what to do."

▸ ◂

Iraan took a break from packing up his apartment when Jon arrived later that afternoon. He'd cleared off the bookshelves and was starting to dismantle the entertainment center. His white cat crouched in the corner flicking its tail, dismayed by the disruption of its home. Jon told Iraan about his phone tap on the Super Seven. Iraan sat down on the floor and mopped his brow with a bandanna.

"All of this just so you can put the question to the man face to face?"

"You said before that you know some cops who'd trade their badges for a good look at this guy."

"I might be one of them if I still had a badge to trade. It was official yesterday."

"They really went through with it?"

"Put it down as dereliction of duty and not meeting my monthly parking-ticket quota."

"I'm sorry."

"The union offered to take them to arbitration, but I said fuck it. They're a bunch of chickenshits. I should've gotten out a long time ago."

"Where are you going?"

"Houston. They've got a decent interior-design school up there. I put in my application for the fall. Figure I might audit some classes until the next semester begins."

"Interior design?"

"Don't sweat a brother for expanding his horizons."

"I still find it hard to believe that you don't care that I've got a tap on the guy who took out your partner."

"The Super Seven, huh?"

"Yeah."

"The Mexicans wouldn't let us do that kind of thing because of jurisdiction. They handed over some tapes of phone calls every once in a while as sign of goodwill so we'd keep pouring the anti-drug dough in, but it was mostly bullshit. I heard the guys at EPIC had their NSA guys 'accidentally' sic one of their satellites on a target so as to track a couple BlackBerries, but they never got anything to work off of. The calls kept disappearing. This transfer thing you're on to might explain that. I mean, who the hell would think of tapping a land line anymore? You know that shit's illegal, right?"

"What's the deal with everyone down here having BlackBerries instead of iPhones?"

"One of the *jefes* got it into his head that since BlackBerry is a Canadian company, the DEA can't tap into their network. These fuckers don't always think straight, but I gotta give them credit for trying to think."

"So do you have the name of anyone over at EPIC who might be interested?" Jon asked.

"In what? Busting you for a federal offense?"

"In using anything we get to try and nail Lazaro."

Iraan laughed. "You're kidding, right? Besides, you turn that over to the dudes at EPIC, and then it's their show and you're out on your ass. Or in jail. What good is it to you?"

"Hell, Iraan. I don't know what it's good for. But it's *something*, okay?"

Iraan extended his hand so Jon could help him to his feet. "Yeah, it's something, all right. But now you're at the heart of the problem. It's not like we don't have enough 411 on these guys."

"How much longer will you be in town?" Jon asked.

"I get the U-Haul this weekend."

"Well, if I don't see you before you leave, good luck with the interior decorating and everything."

"Interior *design*," Iraan corrected as he shook Jon's hand.

Jon spent the next two days with Sway's aunt, monitoring the phone tap. The old lady had to stick around translating the conversations because the people talked too fast for Jon to follow. It appeared that the line in and out of the Super Seven was Lalo's private connection, as he was the only one making calls through the transfer. The way it worked was that people trying to get through to Lazaro would call Lalo on his BlackBerry, and Lalo would in turn use the Super Seven landline to relay the message to another intermediary who would use his own device to relay the message once again. But instead of waiting around for incoming directives, Lalo spent most of his time calling Esteban. Their main topic of conversation was not drugs or kidnapping, but the upcoming MotoGP motorcycle racing season. Esteban was, with his boss's endorsement and cash, trying to put together a Superbike team, and he wanted to fly over to Le Mans for the Grand Prix Alice de France in order to make contacts. The problem was that Lazaro—whom the guys referred to only as "he" or "him"—kept coming up with drills for Esteban to run in Juarez. These jobs were never specific enough for Sway's aunt or Jon to interpret. "Something" had to be done with one guy; another "job" was pending in "the other place;" they needed to meet "the thing" over at "the guy's house." It was all quite vague.

"Just a bunch of *chulos*," Sway's aunt said after another conversation. "They've got all the money and no God. No wonder so many people have gotten killed. Listen to this little guy cry because he can't play with his motorcycles. No, he has to go off and shoot someone in the head. This is what happens when young people don't go to church. Consuelo told me you're Catholic."

"Absolutely," Jon said.

On the third day of monitoring, Esteban was really beside himself when Lalo called. It seemed that the boss had finally extinguished any hope of him going to France for the big bike race and instead was going to make him attend a meeting.

"Two years in a row!" Esteban exclaimed. "He's gone crazy! And this time I've got to go as the wharf. I hate the *pinche* wharf."

"*Cuidado, güey,*" Lalo warned.

"I know, I know. But, really?"

"What about me?" Lalo asked. "What's he got for me this year?"

"The bones."

"You got fucked, *güey*. The wharf is too hot and ugly. You come back stinking with all that crap on you. Besides, it's not even the same show. How can he put the bones and the wharf together? You should tell him you want something else."

"He's already pissed about the bikes," Esteban said. "I'm not pushing it."

"Hey, I've got to be the bones. People can see my face, *güey*. At least you get to go in a real disguise. I suppose the boss gets the captain again."

"Of course. He always gets the captain. It's the easiest and the best."

"What about the ears?" Lalo asked.

"Hell if I know. All I know is that I look like crap in blue."

"Is he really serious about going? Even with all this heat?"

"You know it's his favorite thing these days. I tried to tell him it was too dangerous with all the guns in town, but he says we're going. I could be over in France, chasing all kinds of hot *panocha* at the Grand Prix, and instead I've got to run around with the wharf. It's not fair. Who gives a damn about this *yanqui* shit anyway? I told him it's bad for his image. People are talking about how he's gone insane."

"When?" Lalo asked.

"He wants to do it the third day. Saturday. That's when the big guys come in."

"We'd better dig those things up, then."

The two men rang off, and Jon reviewed his notes.

"Did that make any sense to you?" Jon asked Sway's aunt. "Bones, the wharf, the captain, the ears, the American big guys?"

"Sounds like they're going to dig up some bodies and take them to the ocean and dump them," Sway's aunt said. "Maybe that's what they do every year. One big shipment of corpses." She shuddered. "There was something in the paper the other day about a ranch down in Tamaulipas where there was supposed to be a whole lot of dead bodies. A mass-grave thing. Over in Tijuana a man confessed to dissolving 300 bodies in vats of acid. It's a sickness of the Devil."

Sway showed up after she finished work, and she and Jon went to a Mexican restaurant that doubled as a car wash for a late lunch. They sat at the empty counter and

Jon told her about the call regarding the bodies and how they were going to dispose of them.

"Hold on," Sway said, taking a pull off her iced tea. "You sure they were talking about actual bodies?"

"Bones, ears, that sounds like bodies to me."

"And they were going to dump them off the wharf? The closest wharf is in the Gulf of California. You think anyone's going to drive a load of dead bodies fifteen hours to the Gulf?"

"'Who gives a damn about this American stuff anyway?' Jon read. He dropped his notebook onto the countertop. "That's what Esteban said."

Sway finished her tea and swiveled back and forth on her stool, looking out the window at the men lackadaisically washing cars. "There's something there," she said. "Give me them again."

"What?"

"Those words."

"Why?"

"*Por favor*," Sway called to the counterman. *"¿Me traes un nuevo vaso de té helada?"*

"It makes no fucking sense," Jon said, picking up his papers. *"Bones, ears, the captain, the wharf, American—"*

Sway started laughing so hard that she slipped off her stool. The cooks looked over to see what was going on as Sway scrambled back into her seat and slammed her palm down on the counter.

"*Star Trek*!" she said.

"What?"

"The *Star Trek* convention! He's a *pinche* Trekkie!"

"I don't understand…"

"Give me that pen." Sway started writing on her paper placemat. "Bones equals Bones McCoy, the doctor in the blue uniform. Wharf is actually W-o-r-f, the Wookiee-type character on *Next Generation*. The captain is Captain Kirk. Of course Lazaro would go as Kirk. Ears. That's got to be Spock. And the convention starts this weekend. I saw it in the paper. It's one of the biggest in the country. Gene Roddenberry was born here."

"Who's Gene Roddenberry?"

"The guy who created the show, dumbass. I can't fucking believe it. Lazaro is going to stick his neck out so he can go to the *Trek* convention. It's so stupid that it's not even fucking stupid anymore."

"Are you sure about this?" Jon asked.

Sway grabbed an El Paso entertainment guide from a rack by the door. She flipped to an article about the convention. "Lalo said they're going Saturday. Third day of the convention. Shatner, Nimoy, George Takei—that's Sulu—and the hot chick from *Next Generation* are all going to be there. Bingo."

Jon covered his face with his hands.

In addition to the continued monitoring of the Super Seven phone tap, Sway answered a call from Lalo on Qui-Qui's phone, and pretending to make up, gleaned a little more information about his trip across the border with his boss. Lazaro was indeed making all of them dress up as various *Star Trek* characters. They'd be in El Paso for about three hours, just long enough for Lazaro to crib autographs and then for Lalo to meet Qui-Qui and try to win her back over a couple of *micheladas*.

"What cracker came up with the names for the black people on these shows?" Iraan asked. "Uhura and Geordi La Forge?"

"No one says you have to go as a black character," Jimmy said.

"I'm going as Uhura," Sway said. "It's not like there are any Mexicans on the *Enterprise*, either. At least you've got two to choose from."

"Worf doesn't count," Iraan said. "Just because it's a brother under all that makeup doesn't mean it's a black character. That's like saying in *Star Wars* that Chewbacca was a black dude."

"Wasn't he?" Jimmy asked.

"Fuck if I know what he was supposed to be."

"Go as whoever you want," Sway said. "Be Sulu or something."

"I only get to pick from the ethnic types?"

"Be Chekov," Jimmy suggested.

"Russians don't count as white," Iraan said.

"Do you mind if we get back to the point?" Jon said. "I don't see how this is supposed to come off. Shouldn't we clue the cops in somewhere? In case shit gets squirrelly?"

Iraan threw up his hands. "If that's what you want to do, I might as well go home and keep loading my U-Haul. The cops—Feds, DEA—any of those mooks get wind of this, and it goes right up. It'd be like fifteen hungry dogs trying to get at one hamburger. They'd blow it wide open before Lazaro even hit the border. That is, of course, if this isn't sponsored by them in the first place."

"Then could we please stop arguing about what characters we're going to dress up as and start thinking about what we're going to do?"

"All I'm saying is that Geordi la—"

"I know what you're saying, but let's get back to the plan." Jon looked at the diagram of the convention center on Jimmy's coffee table. "Do we hit them inside or in the parking lot?"

"Hit them?" Iraan asked. "I thought you just wanted to talk to the dude and maybe give him a good zap."

"I'm definitely going to fry a piece of Lalo's *culo*," Sway said, not looking up from the map.

"We'll use the phasers if we have to, but the objective here is to parlay."

"Inside," Jimmy said. "You can get them into a tighter spot in the building. The parking structure is underground. No way to get in and out quickly."

"How's the accuracy on these things?" Iraan asked, picking up a phaser. "Are we gonna have to be right up on them or can we fire from cover?"

"It's going to have to be smelling distance," Jimmy said.

Iraan regarded the blueprint. "Okay, so say we get them in a hallway or the bathroom or something. We're still only going to be able to cover Lazaro, Lalo and two other guys—assuming your equipment works like it's supposed to. That leaves the other bodyguards who are going to be using real bullets. This could turn into a bloodbath if they start shooting the place up. We've got to get them away from the rest of the nerds."

"Right. That's the whole key to this, getting those

two alone. We know Lalo. What about the boss? Aside from the fact that he'll be dressed up as Kirk, we don't even know what he looks like."

"You guys are still talking about this like you're gonna do it," Jon said.

Jimmy ignored Jon. "The only way you're gonna ID the boss is by finding Lalo, and this depends on him calling before he comes across. If he doesn't call, you're going to be sorting through a lot of Bones and Kirks. He's gonna be nervous as hell with his boss on the wrong side of the border. He might not call." Jimmy looked at Sway. "I understand you wanting to fuck up the little man—"

"Fuck yes, you do," Sway said.

Jimmy continued, "But this is a hell of a lot of work for Jon-Boy just to ask the creep a couple of questions and then count coup."

"Count what?" Sway asked.

"It's how the Plains Indians used to get their war on," Jimmy explained. "They'd demonstrate their bravery not by killing a dude, but by riding up close and whacking him with a stick."

"Then they ran like hell," Iraan added.

Jimmy shook his head. "You don't see many Plains Indians around these days."

"Wait a minute," Sway said. "I want to hurt Lalo more than just whacking him with a stick."

"Trust me," Jimmy said. "He takes a shot with this, he'll be thinking about it for a while."

"So everything goes perfect," Iraan said. "Lalo calls when they're on their way to the convention center, we ID them and then somehow lure them into a corner, get

Lalo and the man away from the bodyguards without getting ventilated. Jon gets his Hallmark moment with the *jefe*, Sway gets to alter the little man's blood chemistry. How do we bust out of there before everyone else gets wise?"

"I've got that covered," Sway said. "I can get our van right next to an exit on the plaza. We've just got to pick the spot ahead of time. We can be out of there before they know what happened."

"It'll never work," Jimmy said. "Too many variables. You'll have the element of surprise, but phasers don't trump live ammo."

"Live ammo?" Jon asked.

"Believe me," Iraan said, "I ain't going in there with just Jimbo's rinky-dink ray gun. If this goes bad, I want to be able to do more than just hurt somebody's feelings."

The four of them sat around the table in silence for a couple of moments.

"You realize this isn't going to work," Jon said finally.

"No doubt," Iraan said. "Real life isn't like that Denzel movie."

"*Man on Fire*?" Jimmy asked.

"Denzel goes in and wastes fifty *chilangos* by himself. I don't care if the dude was Special Forces. That shit don't fly."

"But if he was Special Forces…" Sway said.

Jimmy looked up. "I can go down the hall and find you five Special Forces guys right now who couldn't heat an MRE without a field manual."

"You ever shoot anyone?" Iraan asked Jimmy.

"Does launching a missile count?"

Jon took a seat on the sofa. "I could probably just walk up to Lazaro if I was alone."

"Fuck that," Sway said. "I'm coming."

"Me, too," Iraan added, "if for nothing else than to see the look on Lazaro's face."

The three of them turned to Jimmy. He put his head down on the table.

CHAPTER TWENTY—ONE

Jimmy started drinking after only a couple hours of sleep. Jon tried to dissuade him from joining them, saying that it was too dangerous and that he didn't have any stake in it, but Jimmy just went back to preparing the equipment. Three of the phasers were ready and sitting on the table next to an open box of short CO_2 cartridges. Jimmy had modified his Super Soaker stun gun to fit the same charge into a smaller package, essentially a police-type taser that looked like a *Star Trek* ray gun. Jon was already dressed in his Spock outfit—sans ears; he'd put those on when he got to the convention—and Sway was next door trying on her Uhura mini-skirt. Jimmy had done himself up like Scottie, and Iraan had bit the bullet and dressed as Geordi La Forge.

"How many have you had this morning?" Jon asked.

"What? Beers? Just three."

Jon shook a half-empty bottle of Crown.

"I work better when I've got a few pops in my system."

"This isn't a few. You need to slow down."

Sway walked into the apartment in her outfit, scowling. "This is some serious white-people shit."

Iraan leaned over the table to examine Jimmy's work. "How those coming along?"

"Don't worry about it," Jimmy said.

"It's not going to explode in my hand or anything?"

"Fuck you."

"Tell me now, cracker. 'Cause if it's gonna go defective, I'll stick with the roscoe." Iraan patted the Glock he had under his red *Next Generation* tunic. "I know this ain't gonna blow up on me."

"Relax."

Jon picked one of the phasers off the table and tested its weight. It was surprisingly heavy. He tried to tuck it into his belt but it wouldn't stay there.

"Should I try the range again?" he asked Jimmy.

"No. It's all charged up. It's good for two blasts at ten feet. Just flick the back switch there and aim low."

"It electrocuted you last time," Iraan pointed out.

"I was using springs to throw the darts," Jimmy said. "These ones have got CO_2 cartridges. When the first dart hits, it cuts the wire and primes the second."

"You got the van ready?" Iraan asked Sway.

"You want me to get uniforms so we can change?"

"Will you guys cool out before one of you fries your nuts?" Jimmy said, taking the phaser from Jon. "Operational Rule Number Three: Don't mess around with the equipment after you're locked and loaded. I told you the phasers were ready, so just sit down and let me finish this last one, okay? Iraan, you should know this fucking drill."

"Hey, it wasn't me that got blown up parked at a stop sign."

Jimmy dropped the soldering iron.

"Boys," Sway warned.

Jon stood up. "Are you guys going to be okay by yourselves for a minute while I go next door?"

"Gotta take a pre-game piss?" Iraan asked.

"Yeah."

"Make it quick," Sway said. "Lalo's supposed to call any time."

Jon went to his room and paced the floor, listening to Jimmy and Iraan sniping at each other. After a couple of minutes he was finally able to loosen his bladder. He was zipping up when he heard a crash at Jimmy's place. At first he thought Jimmy and Iraan had finally started fighting each other, but then the room filled with new voices.

"DEA! Get your face into the floor!"

"I'm a disabled veteran!" Jimmy yelled.

"Get the fuck down!"

There were sounds of closet doors being thrown open and a rush of footfalls through the apartment.

"Clear!" another voice yelled.

"Get the fucking gun off my neck," Iraan said. "I'm on the job."

"You used to be, shitbird," another voice answered. "You're a citizen now, Sheffield. Check next door for the fourth."

Jon hopped into the tiny shower stall and yanked the mildewed curtain closed as his front door banged open. Someone knocked a few things around and kicked the bathroom door open before leaving.

"Nothing next door but a bad smell," the voice reported.

"Where's Lennox, Sheffield?"

"Lennox who?" Iraan said.

"The prom's over. Where is he?"

"Prom? Man, they didn't let brothers go to prom where I come from."

"He left already," Sway said. "Ten minutes ago."

"Don't you guys do any stakeout ahead of time?" Iraan asked. "Or do you just start busting down doors and violating people's rights?"

"Shut up, Sheffield. Your ass is in a lot of trouble."

"Hey, man, I'm just going to the *Trek* convention. Since when is it illegal for a brother to dress up and have some fun?"

"Don't go all 'brother' on me, fuckface."

"I don't think I saw the episode where Geordi was packing a nine," one of the intruders said. "You got a conceal-carry permit for this?"

"Aw, man," Iraan said. "This is silly. How 'bout you clowns show us some badges? I saw those DEA hats for sale at the Albertsons."

"I told you I'm a disabled vet, asshole. Get off my back."

Jon heard a walkie-talkie chirp. "This is Otter Four. Lennox is en route to the convention center. See if you can intercept him. Over."

The voice on the other end of the walkie-talkie called for a vehicle make.

"What's he driving?"

"A taxi," Iraan said. "Have you guys done *any* surveillance? You gonna give us some Miranda, or are we just supposed to keep acting like this is happening?"

"Put a lid on it."

"It goes like this," Iraan continued. "'You have the right to remain silent. You have—'"

Jon heard a thud.

"You gotta stomp higher to get my kidney." Iraan wheezed.

"Why are you putting me in handcuffs?" Sway asked. "What did I do?"

"How about an illegal wiretap to start with, lady?"

"All right, let's get them out of here."

"What's the charge, man?" Iraan protested. "We ain't done a goddamn thing and you still ain't shown us any badges."

"How about interfering with a federal investigation, for starters?"

"Oh, now I know y'all are joking," Iraan said. "Is it April Fool's already?"

"Shut the fuck up and get on your feet!"

"I cannot stand due to my injuries sustained in combat," Jimmy said.

"He's stinking drunk," one of the voices said.

"Help the major to his feet and get that girl's cell phone. Let's clear out of here before Gates's Army buddies come back and start making a scene. It's a good goddamn thing we got here before you idiots tried to pull this off."

The agents walked Sway, Jimmy and Iraan out of the apartment.

"So you know he's in town?" Iraan asked from the walkway.

"Who's that?" the agent asked.

"C'mon, man," Iraan said. "Fuck the dumb shit."

"It's all under control. You'd better start worrying about yourself."

Jon stayed in the shower and listened to the sounds of

car doors slamming and then the vehicles pulling out of the parking lot. He crawled across the floor and peeked around the blinds. Iraan's Trans-Am, Jimmy's Mustang and Sway's phone van were still parked in the lot. He waited five minutes before going next door. The apartment door was ajar. Jon grabbed two phasers and the keys to Sway's van.

CHAPTER TWENTY–TWO

Jon pulled up to an access gate at the side of the convention center in the phone company van and explained that he was responding to a call. He'd changed into a pair of SBC coveralls to cover up his blue Spock outfit and wore an SBC baseball hat low on his forehead. The yellow-jacketed security guard opened the gate and let him drive around to the back of the building. The plaza in front of the hall was swamped with Trekkies making their way to the doors, and he drove slowly to avoid them. Almost all of the conventioneers were in costume. There were plenty of uniformed police around the building, but they didn't seem to be looking for anyone specifically. Jon parked close to a side door and set out cones. Two cops standing in the shade of a nearby awning didn't give him a second look. Jon retrieved a toolbox from the back of the truck and banged on the side door until an Event Staff worker opened up. He gave him a line about responding to a call, and the man let him pass. Jon asked where the main switchboard was and the guard shrugged. Jon said he'd find it on his own.

The bowels of the convention center were deserted. Jon tried doors until he found one that opened onto a cement-walled locker room. Jon stripped off the overalls and went to the least cracked bathroom mirror to adjust his Spock ears and plaster his hair down over his forehead.

He still didn't have a place to stick the two phasers, and finally decided to only carry one of them. He examined the two guns, trying to figure out which one had been worked on before Jimmy had gotten too drunk. He selected the one that had less solder visible and made his way up to the main convention floor.

Jon kept his eyes open for a Mexican Captain Kirk with an entourage amid the display booths and enthusiasts. Conventioneers flashed him the Vulcan hand sign. He spotted a pair of men in windbreakers heading his way and turned in to a booth that had Klingon battle axes for sale. Jon examined the weapons until the men passed. He continued on through the convention until he reached a roped-off area where a couple hundred chairs had been set up in front of a dais. A notice board said that the *Trek* cast would be appearing in an hour for a talk followed by an autograph session. A few diehards had already staked out seats in the front rows. He saw several men dressed as Kirk, but they were either alone or white. From what he'd heard during Lalo's calls, Lazaro's crew would be at least seven deep. Jon had to keep adjusting his right Vulcan ear so that it didn't fall off. He made another circuit of the hall.

He spotted them on his second pass.

He recognized Lalo first. The little boxer was dressed in baggy black pants and an oversized blue medical tunic. He looked like a sulky kid not getting his way at the pajama party. The man dressed as Kirk was about 5'9" and must've weighed close to 200 pounds. Despite his girth, his uniform was immaculately tailored, and he even had a blonde wig to emulate Shatner's hair, despite the fact that his black mustache didn't match. He looked to be in his late forties. Another older Mexican was dressed as Spock, and then there were four other men done up as Worf from *Next Generation.* Jon strolled around them, pretending to read a convention booklet he'd picked off an information table. He caught a strong whiff of cheap cologne as the group passed. When he turned to follow their progress, he noticed two Caucasians in sport jackets walking a few paces behind the group. Jon slid into the pedestrian traffic to follow them. Lazaro browsed at many of the booths, chatting in fairly good English with the people stationed at them. He bought a few figurines and a large model of the *Enterprise,* which he handed to the Worfs to carry. The men in the blazers walked past the group and doubled back. Lazaro led his guys to a hospitality stand and ordered a round of beers, which seemed to cheer the crew up.

Jon could feel his ear about to come off and headed for a bathroom. Two men dressed as Sulu and Scottie compared outfits by the sinks, and they gave Jon the Vulcan sign as he walked to the last basin to splash cold water on his face. He had dark sweat patches under his arms and down his back. He tried to fasten his ear more tightly.

"Those Spock ears are a bitch," the man dressed as Scottie observed. "I gave up on 'em." Two men in blue jeans and windbreakers entered. They went to the urinals and unzipped.

"Are you sure about this?" one of them asked.

"Yep," the other replied. "We don't make a move unless they do. Short of that, we do exactly what we're doing right now."

"Which is?"

"Stand around holding our peckers."

"Bullshit," the first guy said.

"Yep," the other man said. "Total, one hundred percent, USDA federal government-approved bullshit."

"And this came from…?"

"From the mouth of The Man. We do nothing unless they make a move, and then we back them up."

"What about the other guy?"

"Some citizen with a beef. Showed up in a taxi dressed like Spock. They grabbed him right out front."

One of the men zipped up and came to the wash basins. "Are you dressed up as Spock?" he asked Jon while soaping his hands.

Jon held his hands under the running water without saying anything.

"You don't know what fucking Spock looks like?" his partner asked as he joined them at the sinks.

"I don't have clue one about this sci-fi shit," his partner replied.

"It's what they call 'pop culture,' you idiot. Anyway, like I said, Ritchie's guys grabbed the dude out front five minutes ago and took him to the office to stew until all this nonsense is over."

"Hope he doesn't call for a lawyer."

The men left the bathroom laughing.

Jon got his ear so that it felt like it was going to stay and eased back into the convention. He noted a bank of pay phones, a fire alarm and the emergency exit he'd entered through a few feet from the bathroom entrance. He paused for a moment, looking at the exit. Then he circled to the bar and saw that Lazaro and his crew were onto another round.

"Ladies and gentlemen," a voice said over the PA. "*Enterprise* crew, Klingons and Romulans. We're going to start the program with the cast in five minutes. All hands report to battle stations!"

The crowd flowed toward the roped-off seating area. Lazaro tipped back the rest of his beer before directing some of his guys to hold seats by the stage. Then he and Lalo and one of the Worfs broke off from the others, heading against the crowd for the bathroom. Jon went back to the pay phones and acted like he was placing a call. The men in windbreakers from the bathroom stood fifty feet back, watching Lazaro head into the lavatory. The lights in the convention hall came down a couple notches. Jon set his phaser on the ledge of the phone booth and wiped his sweaty palms on his trousers. He picked up the gun and slipped into the bathroom.

Lazaro was deliberately washing his hands while Lalo and the Worf covered the door. The Worf reacted first, groping under his tunic for his piece. Jon leveled the phaser and pulled the trigger. The gun chugged a CO_2 blast and a small dart jumped from the muzzle. The projectile struck the Worf in the hip and he went down in a jittery heap making an *ah-ah-ah-ah* sound. As promised, the gun clipped the wire on its own.

"¡*Puta madre!*" Lalo exclaimed. "*Es él pinche hermano.*"

Jon turned the phaser on Lalo, which stopped him from going for his gun.

Lazaro wadded a couple of bathroom towels and tossed them casually on the floor. He smiled at Jon.

"My Vulcan friend," he said. "You are making a mistake."

"Answer one question: Where's my brother?"

A bead of sweat dripped off Jon's brow into his eye. As he went to brush it out, Lalo yanked his pistol free. Lazaro tried to stop his man, but Jon went ahead and pulled the phaser trigger. The CO2 burped, but the dart didn't deploy from the muzzle. It felt like an animal with sharp, pointy teeth had taken hold of Jon's arm. He tried to force his hand to release the weapon, but his fingers stayed wrapped around the butt.

"Phaser malfunction," Lazaro said. He nodded to Lalo.

Lalo covered the space between them in two steps and rocketed an uppercut into Jon's jaw, crumpling him to the piss-stained floor.

CHAPTER TWENTY–THREE

The throbbing of his jaw led Jon out of unconsciousness. He lifted his head from the pillow to see a room done completely in white—white sheets, white walls and ceiling, white tile on the floor. The shades had been closed, but he could see sunlight outlining them. He blinked a couple of times and tentatively worked his mouth. Still lying on top of the covers in pajamas, he looked to either side of the bed but saw no nightstand or clock. Taking another survey of the room, he picked out the only non-white thing: the polished brass door handle. He swung his legs off the side of the bed, his blood feeling thick as syrup. Jon shuffled across the cool tiles to the door, which opened with a soft click onto a white hallway. He held the door frame for a moment to get his legs under him before starting down the corridor toward the sunlight. The glass door at the end of the hall slid open on silent casters. Jon shielded his eyes from the glare with the flat of his hand as he walked into the heat. When his eyes adjusted to the brightness, he saw a mouthwash-blue pool. At the far end, he could make out a figure floating on top of the water. Jon took a couple swallows to get his throat clear.

"Hello?" he croaked.

The man continued to float effortlessly, the brilliant blue water rippling around his form.

"Excuse me?"

The man raised himself onto his elbow and looked over his shoulder. He saw Jon and smiled. Then he stood up and walked across the water to the edge and stepped out onto the white stonework surrounding it.

It took my brother a moment to recognize me.

"It's about time," I said.

I got to him just as his legs started to buckle, and was able to ease his dead weight onto the deck.

—•—

In order to convince Jon that we weren't both dead, I showed him the end of the pool I'd been sunbathing in when he'd come out of the house. Lazaro had made that end three inches deep, so that you could lie down in it and tan yourself to a crisp, half-and-half style. It did also lend that added aspect of making one look like they could walk on water, which appealed to Chuy. I hadn't actually met *el jefe,* as this joint was one of his many residences in Juarez. The compound was surrounded by fifteen-foot-high hedges and a reinforced concrete wall topped with broken-bottle shards. Several armed guards patrolled the perimeter, and the front gate was constructed in the latest *narco* style: The weathered wooden exterior disguised thick steel underneath. The insides of the steel skin were filled with water so that if anyone tried to batter it open, the heat from the impact wouldn't spread and weaken the door. As Iraan had said, these guys might not think straight, but at least they thought.

My only outside company for the past weeks had been Lalo and Esteban—who stopped by occasionally to talk Superbikes or threaten me with imminent death. The staff consisted of teenage Mexican girls. These four girls, all of them Inca-looking *mestizas* from southern Mexico, cooked my food and cleaned up after me.

Clara, one of the girls, delivered a platter of fresh watermelon and cantaloupe to the white canopy my brother and I sat under. Jon still had a huge purple bruise on his jaw from when Lalo had KO'd him at the convention, which is why we were eating the fruit instead of the *enchiladas verdes* I usually had for lunch. The guys had brought Jon to the house the previous day, severely concussed and under the influence of a strong sedative they'd shot him up with to keep him unconscious while they transported him across the border. Esteban wasn't in especially good shape, either. He'd been the Worf who had taken the first phaser blast. He was still experiencing numbness in his extremities and claimed he could feel his kidneys failing. Those two had jetted off to get lunch on the outside.

"That's it?" Jon asked. "You've just been sitting up here?"

There was no point in stalling. "Look, man, I got into some trouble."

Jon started to speak, but I cut him off.

"It's not what you think," I said.

The only sound in the courtyard was the soft gurgle of the pool filter.

"I thought you got kidnapped," Jon said.

"Well, I did. Sort of."

"Sort of?"

"It's a long story."

"Apparently, we have time."

"Understand that I wasn't doing anything illegal."

Jon stared at me.

"Let me show you something."

"No, tell me. I'm sick of moving my feet."

"If I could bring it to you, I would."

Clara brought out an ice bag, and Jon held it to his jaw. I started for the house. Jon reluctantly followed.

I led Jon into the other wing of the house and we took white marble stairs to the basement. We went through another white door into what the boys called "ESPN." Thirteen-inch plasma monitors covered one whole wall, twenty of them in total. One fifty-inch monitor anchored the center. A control panel dominated the middle of the room, similar to the ones used to broadcast sporting events. Three white leather swivel chairs had been set up behind the board. Jon sat down in one of them as I took up my spot in the middle. The panel in front of me was the master board that all the feeds came into.

"Recognize any of those places?" I asked, flicking the small HD monitors to life.

Jon leaned forward.

"The boys say he's got these setups in all his houses. Let's see if we can find your home away from home." I started toggling switches until I got the security cameras from the Vagabond up on the monitors. There was a camera at the end of the walkway on each floor, as well as another covering the parking lot.

"Okay," I said, "there's your Army buddy's Mustang."

"Jimmy," Jon said.

"The major, right?"

"That's Jimmy."

"Well, it's only noon, so I guess he's still asleep."

"How did you get the—"

"Just wait." I toggled the switch to bring up the intersection on Mesa half a block from the motel.

Jon moaned at the images of the Wells Fargo ATM that flashed up on the board.

"It's pretty simple, really. All Lazaro has done is tap into the city's traffic-cam network and a few independent systems. There are thousands of them in El Paso and Juarez. It took me time to figure them out, but once I got it down I could pretty much keep tabs on you. I've got all the places you went on this program."

Jon still looked dumbfounded.

"Okay, so we start at the Vagabond." I switched the top left monitor to the security camera at Jon's motel. "So say you leave here. Then I go to either of the lights down the way on Mesa." I flipped monitors two and three to the stoplight cameras. "I see where you're going. Then we go down to the 7-Eleven, or over to the police station, etcetera. Once I figure out which direction you're heading, I try to keep up with you by switching cameras. It's not easy to get them all lined up, but what the hell else do I have to do up here? And if I screw up, I've got your BlackBerry signal." I flicked on a screen with a digital street map of El Paso. "The GPS chip in there showed me how you were moving on the grid."

"Fuck you," Jon said.

"Believe it, man. It's Big Brother out there, and all Lazaro has done is spend a shitload of cash to harness it. The city of Chicago has a system exactly like this, but they've got microphones set up to provide sound, too. I'd say Lazaro's got more at stake than Chi-town, though. I mean, the guy is putting $200 million through here every week. He uses this to track his shipments and watch his competition. It's—"

"No, Chris," Jon interrupted. "I mean, 'Fuck you.'"

"Consider me fucked, brother."

We let that settle for a second.

"What I can't believe is that you've been watching me this whole time."

"Somebody had to keep tabs on you," I said.

Jon stared at the black-and-white traffic monitors for a few minutes, his eyes trying to follow cars from screen to screen.

"How long was I out?" he asked finally.

"You've been back there in that room for a day and a half. After Lalo knocked you out in the bathroom, they shot you up with tranquilizers. Here, look at this." I slid a DVD into the console and played back the scene I had cued up from the convention center cameras. There was Jon by the phones, and then the shot switched to the bathroom. Jon hitting Esteban with the phaser, and then the phaser short-circuiting in his hand, and then Lalo stepping up to paste him with that uppercut. I reversed to show the punch again.

"Okay," Jon said, reaching over to eject the disk. "I get it."

"I took one of those without going down."

"Good for you. How'd they get me out of there with all the cops watching?"

"Here, let me show you." I started to push the tray back into the machine, but Jon stopped me.

"Just tell me," he said.

"Those guys shadowing Lazaro were DEA. They were obviously on the lookout for you so they could stop you from doing anything like what we just watched. Here, look at that punch one more time in slow motion." Jon grabbed the disk and Frisbee'd it to the other end of the room.

"Anyway, the DEA guys came into the bathroom right after you got knocked out, and once they realized who you were, they helped Chuy get you the hell out of there."

Jon turned to me, gape-mouthed. It looked like it hurt him to open his mouth that wide.

"Well, it seems that Chuy's been feeding the DEA a bit of information…"

"So they let Lazaro just cart me off?"

"Apparently the feds have decided that between El Animal's Zetas, the Sinaloa boys and Lazaro, Lazaro's the lesser of three evils."

"How the hell could they make a deal with Lazaro? He icepicked one of their guys to death—"

"…And we paid bin Laden to fight the Soviets. Look, I guess they decided to let bygones be bygones."

Jon moved the ice bag to the other side of his face. "I thought they didn't even know what he looked like."

"He sure as hell doesn't look like Captain Kirk."

"So Lazaro flipped? Just to get to the *Trek* convention?"

"Well, I think it's more involved than that. Chuy probably figured that joining up with the feds was a good way to get El Animal out of the picture. As far as I can tell, he grabbed me as a sort of goodwill gesture to the DEA. Thought I could give them some dirt on what Everitt and Cisneros were up to. In return, he got a free pass to see Shatner. You fucked that up, by the way."

Jon shook his head. "This is Disneyland."

"*En español,*" I added.

"And them? Sway, Jimmy and Iraan?" he asked.

"The DEA took the three of them someplace and ran them through the wringer until they were sure Lazaro was back in Mexico. *Luego se fueron.*" I put my hand on his shoulder. "Don't think about it too much. It'll just give you a headache. Look, man, you found me. I'm actually kind of blown away."

"Couldn't you have just given me a phone call?" Jon hung his head over the back of the chair. "Now what?"

I turned off the monitors. "Well, that's the part that's still kind of up in the air."

"Up in the air?"

"It's not what you think."

— —

Lazaro's pad was so serene that it was easy to forget you were still on the wrong side of the border. The way he'd done everything up in white and then surrounded the perimeter with those high hedges and bougainvillea made it so you could barely hear the muted hum of traffic beyond the walls. Sometimes the wind would blow that unique old-sponge J-town stench of sewage and burning tires into the compound, but mostly it felt like the Four Seasons. I had one of the maids find Jon a pair of swim trunks, and we sat out by the pool. Jon hadn't said much since we'd been in the surveillance room. I rang for a bucket of Pacíficos and started drinking. Jon's ice bag had mostly melted, but he kept the cold pouch to his jaw.

"Everitt was the one who approached me about the whole thing," I explained. "At first he just wanted me to get my Century Pass, so I figured he was going to have me start picking up the slack in Juarez. Most of the guys in the office had pretty much had it with Mexico by that point."

"I thought they were all former Army. Bowden made them sound pretty tough."

"Yeah, well, maybe they knew better than to get their asses shot off. But I think it was mostly because Everitt didn't want to use them. As a matter of fact, I don't think Bowden was really involved, either. He may have cashed the checks, but I'll bet he was playing ignorant, just like me."

"That wouldn't be too hard."

"Anyway, it got to the point where I was pretty much working directly for Everitt. It wasn't anything too exciting. Just B.O.V.s, making sure the factories had all the stuff on-line they were saying they had. It was actually a pain in the ass, having to go across every day. But it was kind of surreal, you know? Commuting into a warzone for work? But I figured Everitt had something for me, so I kept doing it. The fast pass made it okay. You hardly ever had to stop for a search or anything. They call it *quemando las placas.* Burning the license plates. You cross enough times and Customs gets it into their system that you're cool."

"So they started having you load up your Tahoe with coke," my brother said.

I laughed. "I may be dumb, but I ain't stupid. They move a hell of a lot more weight than I could fit into my truck."

"Then what was it?"

"So I do those broker runs for a couple months and then Everitt asks me if I want to make some more commissions. My first thought was the same as yours: He wants me to start smuggling dope. He tells me not to worry, it's strictly business. What he needs from me is to be the on-call white guy in Juarez all week. We've got a whole office of Mexican brokers in Juarez already, but they're just Facebooking chicks all day.

"But all the bad news about J-town is getting around the States—the Americans who come down to look at space want the reassurance that a white man isn't taking that stuff seriously. So I start going over first thing in the morning and wait for these Americans to show up. But nothing's happening. I'm just sitting there in my office with all these slouchy-ass-chair Mexican brokers, surfing the Internet, waiting for the phone to ring. Let me tell you about a Mexican real estate guy at a desk. It's like they're fucking lowriding. And I'm like trying to sit up straight to establish bwana status, and these dudes are just sinking below their desktops like crocodiles. I think they were actually selling soap or some shit."

"Back to the point, please." I was feeling the beers a little bit.

"Where was I?"

"Your cover."

"Right. So, even though I'm not doing a damn thing, I'm getting an extra three grand a month 'commission' on my paycheck."

"You didn't think that was unusual?"

"Of course I did. I thought maybe they were loading my truck up with coke bricks while I was talking shit with the receptionists. So I parked where I could watch the Tahoe from my desk. Nothing ever happened. I did two months like that, and, honestly, I was starting to wish they would ask me to do something crooked because I was bored out of my mind."

I shook the little silver bell, and Clara the maid trotted over to sink two more Pacíficos into the ice bucket.

"So, finally, one day my phone rings and it's Everitt. He wants me to swing by this office park and pick something up. I figure this is it, right? So I drive on over, and this Mexican guy loads a filing cabinet in the back of the Tahoe and tells me to take it back to the El Paso office. Well, I'm not completely lame. I pull over a couple blocks away from the office park and check the thing out. Nothing but this black, two-drawer metal filing cabinet. I look for anything in the sides, on the bottom. Nothing. I figure it's just a stupid drill, and I head home. The only funny thing is that the guy who helps me load the truck tells me to take the Free Bridge. This is the main one going into downtown. Now, that's kind of strange, because I've got the DCL pass and it doesn't really matter which bridge I take, but what the hell? It's a ten-minute wait, as usual, and then the Customs guy takes a look in the back and waves me right through."

"A dry run," Jon said.

"You could say that. But here's the thing. The calls start coming in more regular, right? It's always Everitt, but usually a different phone number. And each time I think Carlos—that's the guy at the office park—is going to finally give me a real package. Never happens. It's always something completely random."

"Like a birdcage," Jon said from under his ice bag.

That surprised me. "Yeah. Like a birdcage. How'd you know about that?"

"There were four of them in the storage shed. Your landlord threw all your stuff into it."

"Where'd you send all that?"

"I didn't send it anywhere."

"Why the hell not?"

"Where was I supposed to send it?" Jon asked.

"There was some good stuff in there!"

"Get on with the damn story."

"I'm talking like at least $5,000 worth of shit! I mean like an hour on eBay five grand. You just left it?"

"What the fuck did you want me to do with it? It's in a storage space. Your landlord probably took all the choice stuff before it went to the locker."

I drained my beer. "Well, that's kind of it."

"How can that be 'it'? We're sitting here by the king-pin of Juarez's pool."

"Okay, I knew I was doing *something* with all these random loads. The best I can think of is that they had a couple Customs guys on the take and each time I came across it was a signal. Birdcage means something, filing cabinet is another thing. The times were always random and I usually went over a different bridge. What they probably did was have the shipment—or whatever it was—come along right after I got to the bridge and tipped off the agent. They never told me, and I didn't really want to know. So this goes on for a few months and my checks are still coming in, right? I can't figure out anything illegal that I'm doing until one day I get the call to go over and take pictures of a warehouse, which is what I'd been doing before all this other weirdness started. I figure it's business back to usual. Next thing I know, four guys are kicking the shit out of me."

"Lazaro's guys?"

"And some white guy, who I'm assuming was DEA. Now, *that's* a guy I'd like to get my hands on. Dude was very liberal with his pepper spray. Anyway, they knew all about the phone calls and the phony tip-off loads I'd been running. They knew Everitt and El Animal were old running buddies from their military days. But it took them a while to realize I didn't have anything for them besides an office park, a phone call and a guy named Carlos who had a lot of birdcages to give away."

Jon shook his head.

"At any rate, at the very least they figured I could give them a good lead on Everitt and Cisneros. And here's the greatest part: They thought *you* were in the game."

Jon lowered the ice bag. "What?"

"Well, they kept me going because they were trying to use me as a chip to get Everitt. At the start, they figured I couldn't be as dumb as I was coming off. But a week went by and I was telling them the same story. My usefulness had about come to its end. Then all of the the sudden you showed up and started fucking around. I was trying to tell them up and down that you had absolutely nothing to do with any of it, but you were at too many of the right places. They were especially interested in what you were doing with that cop Sheffield. How'd you hook up with him?"

"Random bureaucratic incompetence."

"Well, he's apparently been on their radar for a long time. If there was anyone in El Paso who was going to make a move against Lazaro, it was him. Then there's that U.S. Army major you were rolling around with."

Jon looked incredulous. "You can't tell me these guys thought Jimmy had anything to do with anything?"

"Look at it from their point of view: Within a couple days of you getting to town, you were hooked up with a narcotics detective and an Army officer with top-secret clearance. Even the fact that you were using a BlackBerry like all these other guys instead of an iPhone seemed to mean something to them. It certainly looked like there was some method to your madness. And when you led them right to Everitt and Cisneros the other night at El Bobby, they figured you were the missing piece. They get you, they get Everitt. Basically, you were so stupid that you looked really, really smart."

Jon considered all that for a moment. "How do you know all this?"

"Man, they had me tied to a chair for three days. Then they had me up here trying to keep track of you on those monitors. It's not that hard to put all those pieces together."

"How much longer were you going to let me twist in the wind?"

"It's not like I had much choice."

"What about Sway and Jimmy and Iraan?" Jon asked. "What are they supposed to think?"

"They're supposed to think you're dead. And shit, for all I know, Esteban and Lalo are on their way over here right now to end us both. It's not like I'm exactly in control of the situation here. I keep waiting for that DEA guy to show up again so I can assert my citizen's rights, but it looks like we've been hung out to dry. Shit, for all I know, *you're* Lazaro and all of this is some kind of sick setup."

"What are you talking about?"

"I'm just saying it seems a hell of a lot more likely that you're running this whole program than that you came down here find *me*." I let out a laugh that sounded cracked even to my own ears. "All this other stuff I can kind of put together—Lazaro, the DEA, Everitt and Cisneros—but you laying it on the line to rescue me is beyond my realm of imagination."

Jon wandered over to the bar on the other side of the pool and refilled his ice bag. I'd gone through a six-pack, and I guess the beers were making me a little more emotional than usual, because I started to cry as I looked at my brother across the shimmering pool. I tried to stop the waterworks before Jon got back, but the tears kept slipping out the corners of my eyes and running down my cheeks. Jon saw I was crying, but he didn't speak as we sat there for a few minutes. I put a towel over my head to hood my face.

"I mean, really, what do you care?"

Jon didn't say anything.

"I'm sitting there in that video room, watching you stumble around screwing things up, and it was almost like you actually wanted to find me. Like you might maybe give a fuck for once in your life." I rubbed my eyes with the towel. "And now you're up here, all bent out of shape about some losers you've known for a week and a half. It's like you're sorry I'm not really dead."

Jon started to say something, but I cut him short. "You know what I was most happy about when I realized I wasn't dead? That I'd get a chance to see if anyone cared. Think about that. And for a minute, I thought you did. Apparently, I was wrong." At this point I really started sobbing, and no matter how hard I willed myself to stop, I couldn't. I was mostly embarrassed, but there was some other part that felt absolutely relieved, like pressure had been building up behind this dam inside me and the water was stacked up all the way back to Denver. And then the whole thing just broke. I was crying so hard that I didn't realize Jon had pulled me out of my chair and wrapped me in his arms, and for a few minutes I just let myself hang there. Jon didn't let go, and pretty soon it was hard to tell who was supporting whom.

CHAPTER TWENTY–FOUR

My brother wanted a lot of heads. First of all, he thought we should really set up Everitt, figure out a way to hand my old boss over to Lazaro and the DEA so they could make him pay for all the trouble he'd put us through. I had to remind Jon that I'd sort of gotten myself into the fix to start with by agreeing to play signalman, but that was all *ex nihilo* to him.

Priority Number Two for Jon was to drown Lalo and Esteban in the pool. He used the word "justice" a lot, which is pretty funny considering he previously worked for a corporate law firm and the only justice he ever pursued was of the monetary-compensation variety. We sat out there on the veranda in our fluffy white robes, my brother alternately filling in the blanks for me about his time along the border and then hatching schemes to get his payback. It was a good thing that Lalo and Esteban's English was as bad as my brother's Spanish, because they'd been hanging around the mansion waiting to find out what to do with us, and I don't think Jon's ravings would've helped our cause.

"Just because we missed that Everitt guy the first time doesn't mean he's not a dead man," Lalo said. "And the only reason you two faggots are still alive is because the boss has lost his mind."

"Tell them I want my phone back." After getting even with Everitt and all the Mexican parties involved, Jon's next priority was getting in touch with his El Paso associates to let them know he was okay.

"This isn't a phone call situation," I explained. "I think you need to take a moment to consider how unlikely it is that we're even having this conversation."

Jon paced the pool deck. "Okay, forget Everitt and my phone. What the hell are we still doing here?" He turned to Esteban. "When can we leave? *¿Cuándo poder salir?*"

Esteban shrugged. "You are suppose to be dead."

Lalo ran a finger across his throat. "*Muerto. ¿Me entiendes?*"

"Can't you talk some sense into these guys?" he said in exasperation. "And I don't understand why you're so buddy-buddy. You've still got scars from where they knocked you around."

I touched the lumps on my face from the beating they'd handed me that first day. There were parts of my face that didn't seem like they'd ever regain their original shape, even though the pain wasn't so terrible anymore. To tell the truth, I hadn't given our future much thought. Despite Lalo's continued threats to kill us, I'd been enjoying the days, watching my brother get all bent out of shape. And it wasn't like we were living hard by the pool, which, combined with my two weeks of captivity, had dulled the logical fear that our lives were in the hands of a drug lord who liked to dress up as Captain Kirk. I asked the boys what our options were.

Lalo spat into a planter and reported that Lazaro had talked to them that morning. We had one choice.

"*Dos*," Esteban corrected.

"You can kill yourselves," Lalo said. "We're supposed to let you take poison so it won't be too bad."

I glanced at Jon. He didn't appear to have understood what Lalo had said. "What's the other option?" I asked.

It took Lalo a couple of minutes to explain the proposition. He was clearly pissed that this route was available, and said that before the boss lost his marbles and started making nice with the DEA, such an offer would have never been imagined. Jon leaned forward, trying to follow the conversation. I drained my Pacífico and rang the bell for another. When Lalo was finished laying out Lazaro's plan for us, he threw his lawn chair aside and stormed into the hacienda. Esteban looked up from cleaning his nails to give me a look, which I took to mean that this was the best—and only—deal we were going to get.

"What did he say?" my brother asked.

"Well, we can commit suicide…"

The reality of that hit Jon pretty hard. "They're serious?"

"If Lalo had his choice, we'd already be toast. And it wouldn't be as easy as taking cyanide."

"So what's the other option? I heard something about Cabo San Lucas."

Clara brought me another cold beer. I thanked her and she gave a half smile before she padded back into the house in her bare feet. I squeezed the fresh lime into the neck of my beer bottle. It was one of those tiny Mexican limes that don't offer much juice, but, really, when you're in the position my brother and I were in, you couldn't get caught up complaining about the fruit. Once all the static with El Animal and Everitt blew over, there was a decent chance we might actually get back to the States in one piece. Although it behooved the parties involved to have us disappear for a little while, it didn't have to be forever.

I looked at Jon and couldn't stop the smile from creeping across my face. Maybe the new, sort-of-compassionate Jon could handle the proposition. It would certainly be interesting to watch him try, because this was the kind of task he was especially ill-suited for.

"Get on with it," Jon said.

I set my beer down on the pool deck. "How do you feel about waiting tables in Cabo for a couple months?"

CHAPTER TWENTY–FIVE

Leave it to a *pinche narco* to give a man a $100 bill after the banks closed on a Tuesday. Arturo fingered the money in his pants pocket and wished his tuxedo shirt was as crisp as the bill. He walked past the lobby windows of the Wells Fargo building and saw his distorted reflection. He looked like an *extraterrestre* with all the blinking neon bracelets and light sticks dangling from his shoulder bag. The truth was that he'd only put on his Polaroid Man outfit and grabbed a dozen skinny roses to make his wife think he was coming across. As soon as he was out of sight of the apartment window, he'd turned down the side street and headed for El Buho to drink a few beers. The *narco* in the *maricón* motorcycle jacket had tapped him on the shoulder and told him what he'd have to do for the $100 before he'd been able to take a sip of Tecate.

A taxi was parked outside the Camino Real hotel, but the odds of the driver having change for the $100 were pretty slim. That is, if the *chingón* would let him into the cab in the first place. Arturo stood under the bus shelter outside the central library and waited for the 15 Mesa while his lights continued to blink all around him like a swarm of fireflies.

He could, of course, just head right back over the bridge and forget the whole thing. But you never knew when the *narcos* were watching, and as soon as you thought you'd pulled one over on them, you'd find yourself in the trunk of a car with your hands duct-taped behind your back. It was better to go along with the plan and have it over with. There'd be plenty of time for drinks afterward, and he wouldn't have to worry about the *narcos* tracking him down for not finishing the job.

Arturo was the only passenger heading up Mesa. He pulled the stop cord when he spotted the 7-Eleven at the corner of Brentwood. The *narco* had told him the store would have what he'd need to complete the assignment.

The cashier sighed when he set the bottle and the $100 bill next to the register. She ran a light-brown marker across the face to make sure it wasn't fake before she counted out change. Arturo slipped the four $20s, the $10 and the $5 into his sock, keeping the $1s and coins loose.

There were only a few customers inside the Hope and Anchor bar when he pushed through the door, and naturally they all averted their eyes when they saw it was the Polaroid Man. People thought he would go away if they didn't make eye contact, but it didn't matter to Arturo. He was used to people ignoring him. On a weekday night you couldn't count on anyone being drunk enough to buy, so you had to get right up on them. They'd usually give two dollars for a rose or fifty cents for a pack of *chicle* just to get rid of the old man.

He spotted the trio he was looking for right away. Not that you could've missed them. Very few *negros* came to this part of Mesa, let alone with a pretty girl and a strange-looking gringo. Arturo walked straight over to their table and made eye contact with the woman. Women were usually nicer to the Polaroid Man.

The woman smiled in that way they all did, saying *pobrecito* with their eyes, like you might be their grandfather or something. Arturo held out a rose, and, considering the money in his sock, he thought about just giving it to her. No doubt she was very pretty, but there was something sad about her, too. Even though he hadn't looked at the men yet, he could tell that they were also depressed. The three of them were acting like someone had just run over their dog.

"*No, gracias, señor,*" the woman said.

"*¿Una foto?*" Arturo pointed to the camera hanging from his neck.

"Not tonight, man," the black one said.

"*¿Una foto para tu amigo?*"

"I ain't buying this guy anything," the black man said, nodding to the beat-up-looking gringo.

The gringo finished his whiskey in one long pull. "You're breaking my heart, brother. I can't believe you don't want a picture of me to take to Houston and put up in your locker."

"Man, I don't need a picture to remember what *your* sorry ass looks like."

Arturo raised the camera and pressed the button. The old flash made a weak popping sound, and the print wheezed into his hand, still milky and undeveloped. It was a dirty trick, to take the picture and pretend you didn't understand enough English to realize they didn't want it. Sometimes they refused to pay, but usually they gave you a few dollars, which was important, because the Polaroid film was becoming hard to find. In a couple of years, there wouldn't be any more left. Everyone used the *pinche* digital cameras now. Arturo waved the print to speed the fixing of the image.

"I'm not paying for that," the black one said.

"Oh, come on." The gringo reached for his wallet. "The old dude probably hasn't had anything to drink tonight. *¿Cuánto?*"

"*Lo siento, señor, pero esta foto es para su amigo.*" Arturo checked to make sure the picture had come out all right. The exposure was dark, but you could still see the faces. The *narco* had made a point about that.

"Say what?" the gringo asked.

"He says the picture is for our friend," the woman translated. "*No lo entiendo. ¿Qué amigo?*"

Arturo tucked the picture into his pocket. "*Su amigo en Juarez.*"

The black man shook his head. "This old dude is crazy. Jimmy, give him five bucks."

"No way! I thought I was getting a picture."

"You guys are impossible," the woman muttered.

Arturo found the best rose in his bunch and handed it to the woman. "*Esto es un regalo de mí,*" he said. "*Y esto es un regalo de tu amigo. Tu amigo que hoy está en buen estado de salud.*" He reached into his bag for the liter of Diet Dr Pepper and set it on the table like the *narco* had instructed him to do.

Arturo executed a bow—*muy formal*—and headed quickly for the exit. He glanced over his shoulder to make sure the men weren't trying to chase him, but they were just staring at the bottle of soda. The woman picked it up like it was some kind of relic.

Arturo couldn't figure out what soda, a report of good health and a Polaroid of three gringos had to do with anything, but it didn't matter anymore. He'd made $97.44 in one hour on a Tuesday night. Sometimes the *narcos* weren't all bad.

The Polaroid Man crossed Mesa and headed back to the border.

El Paso Exec Arrested in Drug Sweep

ASSOCIATED PRESS

El Paso, TX -- Prominent El Paso real estate executive Stanley Everitt was arrested Friday after a series of coordinated raids by the DEA and Mexican anti-drug forces on both sides of the border aimed at slowing drug traffic through the region.

Everitt, a partner in the firm Bowden-Everitt, has been accused of operating a drug smuggling network in conjunction with Jorge "El Animal" Cisneros, a former Mexican Army general who is now the reputed leader of Juarez's Zeta cartel. Although several Mexican nationals were arrested in the raids, Cisneros remains at large.

According to the DEA affidavit, Everitt allegedly provided warehouses and transportation on both sides of the border for the Zeta gang's large shipments of cocaine and heroin.

"This is a huge blow to the Juarez cartels and a major victory in the war on drugs," DEA spokesperson Chad Rojas told reporters.

A spokesperson for Bowden-Everitt had no comment on the arrest.

Bowden-Everitt was the employer of Chris Lennox, an El Paso-based real estate broker who, along with his brother, Jon, vanished from the Juarez - El Paso area last month. They are believed to be cartel victims.

The DEA's Rojas said that the disappearance of the Lennox brothers was not related to their current investigation.

ACKNOWLEDGEMENTS

First and foremost, this book would not be possible without the love and support of my brother Chris. It was difficult to write a book about siblings who don't like each other because that has been the furthest thing from my own experience. It was also my brother who opened the doors to El Paso and Juarez for me so I could research this book. Chris moved to EPT 14 years ago, and the people of that city have welcomed and embraced him completely. Although it might seem far-fetched that three strangers would bond together to help an outsider like Sway, Jimmy and Iraan do for Jon in this book, you'll have to trust me when I say that El Paso is the one town where that idea isn't a stretch.

With that in mind, here's my rapper's list of all the good folks in EPT and Juarez who have been instrumental in the writing of this novel: Jennifer "Sneaky Sis" Giese, Jonathan, Keith and Becky Myers, Eric and Laura "Larry" Borrego, Chad and Sara McCleskey, Arthur and Atheal Flores, Phil and Tessie Hernandez, Bernadette Gonzales, Lee Roy and Jessica Montion, Dave Roukey, Matt and Robin Niland, "Milly" Jacobs Landry, Kurt and Robin Gross, James and Dionne Billstone, Laura "'Lil Strelz" Bagley, Rebecca Rojas, Kristy "K-Dog" Quintana, Kathy Quintana, JB and Sassie Colquitt, Anthony "Rocky Horror" Flores, Clint and Becky Lee, BJ Donnelly, James Silliman, Greg and Nicole Ehrhart,

Julio Pablos, Isham and Olivia Randolph, Charlie "Chuck D" and Laura "Cleopatra Jones" Intebi, Monica and Keith Mahar, Asher and Jody Feinberg, "Young" Cole and Laura Gearhart, Kevin and Kelly Hayes, Molly and Boo Hiett, Annabelle Estrada, Tony Nash, MF Galbiati, Jay and Chrissy Kleberg, Jennifer and Todd "Money Putt" Segall, Shae "The Hard Way" Searls, Jerome "Raining Tickets" Elenez, The Hope & Anchor, the 7-11 on the Corner of Brentwood and Mesa, the UTEP Library, El Paso CC, Coronado CC, Aceitunas, G3, Hemingway's, Tim Hardaway, The Kentucky Club.

I also give my profound thanks to the following people who have supported me during the writing of this book: Niecy, Jo Giese and Edward Warren, Wendy and Irvin Barnhart, Lynn Rhodes, Whitney and Everett Torres, Maria Antonia Perez, Gladys "Babe" Giese, Betty Perez, Eduvijes Perez, Ana and Pancho Josephson, Jane Le, Sarah Pitts Bjorklund, The Yu Family (Alan, Big Tony, Mei and Harry), and Diane Harrigan. Thank you all for everything.